Frances Fyfield has spent much of her professional life
practising as a criminal lawyer. She is also a regular broad-

of the series
and in Deal.

COLD TO THE TOUCH

FRANCES FYFIELD

SPHERE

First published in Great Britain in 2009 by Sphere
This paperback edition published in 2010 by Sphere

A CIP catalogue record for this book
is available from the British Library.

ISBN 978-0-7515-3928-8

Typeset in Plantin by M Rules
Printed and bound in Great Britain by
Clays Ltd, St Ives plc

Papers used by Sphere are natural renewable and
recyclable products sourced from well-managed forests and certified
in accordance with the rules of the Forest Stewardship Council.

Mixed Sources
Product group from well-managed
forests and other controlled sources
www.fsc.org   Cert no. SGS-COC-004081
© 1996 Forest Stewardship Council

Sphere
An imprint of
Little, Brown Book Group
100 Victoria Embankment
London EC4Y 0DY

An Hachette UK Company
www.hachette.co.uk

www.littlebrown.co.uk

To Barbie Boxall
with love

ACKNOWLEDGEMENTS

Thanks to Elizabeth and Brett Luckhurst.

PROLOGUE

Scene One

Smithfield, London in the darkest hours before dawn on a winter's night.

She was drunk, inebriated, intoxicated, pissed, something like that, no doubt about it. Plus a little something else which made these bright lights extra bright, and the colours of the vast wrought-iron gates very strange. Such great big gates, made to repel and attract multitudes, each thirty feet high and standing open, decorated with huge motifs of Tudor roses and curlicues painted turquoise, pink and purple without a single sharp angle. These gates rose to a point half the height of the domed glass ceiling inside. She noticed a single seagull wheeling above the building, its plaintive mewling audible above the hum of noise, and the profile of its wings caught in the glow of light which came through the roof and that stopped her. How strange to be able to hear *that* above everything else and to be able to see it so clearly.

She looked at her own hands. Hardly a tremor. She was not so drunk after all; she could even tell the time. Drawn by the golden glow of light and life, she walked towards Grand Avenue, pausing to touch the iron of the gates and look at the old clock hanging from the ceiling and then retreating to the other side of the road to finish her cup of tea first. The tea was strong and bitter, looking like rusty water in a white beaker, but it would be a shame to leave any of it. She lit another cigarette and watched a limousine with darkened windows stop further down the road, the vehicle contrasting nicely with the white vans that proliferated otherwise. Someone got out of the driver's side and went into the light of Grand Avenue. It could not be him, because he never drove himself, but still her heart beat faster. Not him; he could no longer drive. He would walk the short distance or be driven in a taxi and a taxi would take him back.

The white vans were more at home with the white light, and men in white coats and matching hard hats standing outside the gates, smoking as if each drag was the last, chatting quietly, too, as if the conversation was the purpose of living. *How's business then? Bad? Good? Middling?* Men lied all the time, especially about business. There was not a woman in sight, except for the girl behind the counter in the caff, although there were bound to be women inside because shopping for meat was not the sole prerogative of men even if the buying and selling of it wholesale was.

Sitting around for an hour had made her numb. She knew the temperature would be cool in there even though it gave the impression of heat. Dressed as she was, she was burning up because Le Club Solstice had been as hot as hell. What a laughable contrast there was in this scenery of brick walls, darkness, light, pink and purple Tudor roses, men in white coats against a nightlife of frantic dancing in another kind of meat market on the opposite side of a road.

The Cock Tavern inside the precincts of Grand Avenue was the place where those who traded in meat or dismembered it could buy their alcohol any time and no one would think twice about a lone woman buying either vodka or breakfast. He could be there but she didn't think so, not his scene. He would be selecting and buying. The tea and the fresh air had done the trick; she was halfway sober and still angry, touched her bare arms where the skin felt warm, clutched her bag to her side and set off. She was a cook, she would tell them: she had every right to be here in the interests of her own science, and didn't they know her? She had been there before on the arm of a meat-buying man with money, influence, all that shit. A good-looking man, if you liked them with fine, cruel faces.

Beyond the gates inside Grand Avenue she encountered a sea of light and quiet industry. She walked as far as the clock. From here, two further avenues led off left and right, stretching into brightly lit infinity in rows of shopfronts full of flesh. She knew where he would pause, where he had been proud to show it to her once if only from the outside, and she squinted at the numbers on the various stalls she passed, looking for fifty-five. Only the best for him.

Fifty-five was unmanned, not a sign of a man in white coat or hat. They were beginning to pack away the front of the stalls at five-thirty in the morning, business winding down, most of the deliveries out already gone, deliveries in finished by two, plenty of people backstage finishing orders. Last time she had come here, it had been as a guest not encouraged to go backstage, told it was dangerous, none of her business. How men loved their little mysteries.

She slipped between the counter of stall fifty-five through an aisle that led out the back, to where the lorries docked at their outlet doors well above the ground, like planes at an airport docking at a port to allow the passengers off. She had seen from the outside how a man would step off the raised platform of an ice-cold truck, unload one chilly carcass at a time off the rail in there, heft it over his shoulder and lift it, complete with hook, onto the slowly moving conveyor rail suspended from the ceiling which carried it down the dark corridor into the lit workrooms at the back of the stalls. He might pat it goodbye and watch it move off before going back for the next and the next and the next. Each carcass was propelled on its hook down the long metallic corridor leading to the storeroom, the incoming stock moving in a line parallel to a row of empty hooks travelling back. Inside, the carcasses were corralled in serried ranks hanging from the ceiling at a convenient height for dismembering. The smell was clean and cold. Ranks of dressed carcasses of beef, each headless and footless, hung inside out, presenting their spines for inspection. Smithfield no longer smelt of blood. Slaughtering was done far away.

The cold in the storeroom repelled her and she shrank back against the corridor wall that led out to the lorry port, and then turned inwards again, because the corridor too was full of carcasses waiting entry to the store, queuing up for the privilege. She was dizzied by the presence of raw meat and bone; she was a trespasser and she wanted out, maybe she could go that way, to the open door at the back, and jump to the ground, or find the last lorry, get out somehow, or hide. She had lost all sense of her purpose for being here; she had strayed into the wrong place. There was a sudden vision of the abattoir she had visited as a child alongside her dead father and she reminded herself that all this too was dead and beyond feeling, as he was.

Then, as she skulked in the corner, one of the white-coated men came into the room, whistling. He selected the last beast in the front row, sized it with his eye, stood back and surveyed it. The top of his white hat was level with the middle of the carcass's spine and he attacked it effortlessly and precisely. The knife he used was a curved machete. First, he used the point to prise away the heart, which he flicked out and flung to one side, then he hacked away a section of rump, then sirloin, each joint tossed aside with an accurate aim into a selection of plastic bins she had failed to notice. The beast on the hook did not move until he swung it round and with casual ease excised a section of the neck, weighed it in his hand and then discarded it. He had all the finesse of a samurai swordsman and some of the ceremony. His fast-wielded weapon had deadly precision and the carcass did not protest. The tip of the blade began to chisel delicately between the ribs and it was then she stopped holding her breath and started to scream. Put it back, she was screaming, put it back together. Look behind you, look behind you, leave it alone.

Someone came down the corridor from behind her. He put a hand on her shoulder and said something. Not a Smithfield man with a shirt, collar and tie, a delivery man, who was grinning at her, anxiously, motioning her to come. A nice face and big brown eyes. *Pretty girl get out*, he said in a thick accent she could not decipher. *You want me to lose my job?* Then he was elbowed aside and told to bugger off, and men in white coats descended, gentlemen all, surprisingly courteous with a trespasser, all of them seeming old. No one said you silly cow – not apposite in the circumstances, one said later. They arrived from all corners, picked her up bodily and carried her out, still screaming but not resisting, finally only muttering, past curious faces right to the end of Grand Avenue and then into the street. You can't come in here without a pass and certainly not without a hat and overall. What did you think you were doing, girlie? Drugs, is it? Been to the club, have you? Some sort of protest?

I'm a cook, I wanted to see.

Whatever, someone said, stick to the kitchen. We can either call the police or you can leg it. Only you're getting in the way of business. Just go, OK? Don't come back. You could have slipped on a knife, could have got locked in, could have lost us our jobs. No one gets in the way of business.

Halfway up Fleet Street she realised it was already on the edge of dawn and that all those white-coated, well-padded men with their shirts and ties had been relatively gentle in their own way. They could have been worse and she could have been better. The gentlemen butchers of Smithfield, distant cousins of their savage forebears. She thought of how the executioner with the machete could have hung her up and sheared off her feet and her hands without drawing breath. She was cold again, feeling for the talisman of her mobile phone, walking quickly and halfway steadily uphill against the sound of traffic. Not many pedestrians yet, but traffic. A taxi slowed, yellow light glowing invitingly in the half-dark, but she ignored it and walked on because she knew there was not enough money in her bag to take it as far as she wanted to go, which was all the way home. Home was too far away, so she went on walking, wishing it would stay half dark, wondering if there was blood on her clothes like the rusty marks on the white overalls of the men. But it was not like the abattoir – the blood in the market was dry.

Now she was in a side street, walking faster, humiliated and beginning to get angry, feeling for her mobile phone, but it was too early to phone, even for her. You bastard, why did you lift me up to drop me down, and then she was beginning to hum whatever tune it was that the white-coat man with the fucking machete had been whistling which had somehow transposed itself into a hymn. *All things bright and beautiful/ All creatures great and small*. No, not that. God loves you, babe. Pictures from history, stray snippets of information rising up without invitation to distract her from the awful present. How it was that St Bartholomew, he of the church at Smithfield, was flayed to death, and how, once, men sold unwanted wives in the cattle market along with the animals they had driven thither. Poor sheep, poor cows, driven by cruel drovers with collies and cur dogs. The history of the place was in her dead father's old books and she was remembering being told that the market was also a place of slaughter, the streets around running with blood, littered with offal and how hers were far luckier times to be alive. She had a sudden sensation of a hook piercing her shoulder and hoisting her to gallows height in an ice-cold room. She remembered instead the nice eyes and guttural voice of the first man and was ashamed that she might have risked someone losing their job.

And then, ahead of her, was a familiar figure, walking the same route slightly quicker. A glint of plentiful hair and a swinging cloak which looked as light as feathers, dancing along, entirely at home with the early hours, as if setting out or coming back made no difference to her speed, moving along as if every destination and assignation deserved the same enthusiasm, as eager to get there as she was to go away. Dear Sarah might have speeded up when someone shouted her name: it might have made her break into a run, but this time she recognised the voice, slowed down and stopped and turned, slowly and wearily, showing a face that seemed so much older and wiser than her own.

'Jessica? Not now, love, please. You silly thing. What have you done now?' The voice suggested affection and exasperation. 'Got enough money to get home? Here.'

There was a twenty-pound note in her hand, and a scarf wrapped round her neck and the other woman was walking away, no hugs, no kiss, no comfort but a clear message. Sort out your own mess; no one else can, the footsteps away telling her that.

What did she mean by 'home'?

Slumped into a doorway, Jessie dreamed of walking down over the cliffs to the village, towards someone who loved her as she wished to be loved, whoever that was, dreamed of making someone happy. Her shoulder hurt and her bare legs were as white as lard. What kind of fool was she to pursue a man into the depths of Smithfield Market? What would she have said? Hello? Please love me like you said you would, you promised.

Then the footsteps came back, wearily.

'Come on, Jess. We'll find some breakfast. Come home and tell me about it.'

'I wish I could be like you, Sarah.'

'No, you don't. Come home and tell me.'

'Come home with you? Oh, please. Can I?'

Jessica, Jessie, Jess, Jezebel, she had been called all these, perked up quickly, smoothed her hair. It was a knack – she had an ability to move from misery to joy within a second; she ran from one to another on a constant collision course like a child learning to walk.

'Home to your flat? Oh, thank you, I love your flat.'

'I wish I did. It doesn't feel like home any more.'

They were walking briskly in the right direction with Sarah striding and Jessica almost skipping along beside her in the cold.

'But it's so nice, your place. So central, so easy.'

'Borrow it any time you like. I've never felt quite right with it since I had a fire. A long time ago, but I can still smell the smoke.'

Scene Two

'I can't smell anything but coffee,' Jessica said, sitting in the kitchen, sniffing appreciatively. 'Coffee and perfume. Those are the smells that belong with you. You're so kind, Sarah, so kind to let me in.'

She hugged Sarah from behind, impulsively and briefly, meaning it. She was almost irritatingly humbling in her appreciation of a warm room, of a single gesture, of anyone listening. Sarah had never known someone who so delighted in the details of everything, was so anxious to please and so keen to repay being noticed and accepted. There would be flowers later: Jessica was capable of blowing a week's wages on flowers and thank-you gifts, even for a cup of coffee and toast. When Jessica Hurly said she would do anything for you, she really meant it and probably would, so Sarah was careful not to ask. Jessica would have gone to jail for a friend: she would have punched the bully boys at school: she never forgot a good deed and was incapable of ignoring the most fraudulent beggar even if it meant there was not enough money to get home. A kind fool. Jessica had a consistently passionate if misguided desire to make things right for people and in that pursuit was sublimely incapable of looking after herself. Sarah was older, looked at her with older eyes. Jessica was a loved acquaintance, to be treated with caution, because whatever her admirable qualities, judgement always fell prey to spontaneity, reserve gave way to anger, with glorious

10

and sometimes disastrous results. She lived in the moment.

'I'm not being kind and the company's nice,' Sarah said, briskly but softly. 'Now tell me what the hell you were doing getting into Smithfield meat market at five in the morning. Why?'

Jessica warmed her hands on the china coffee mug, tracing the pattern of flowers and leaves with her long blue-varnished fingernails. She waited half a minute, moved her hands to touch the mobile phone hanging on a leather cord round her neck.

'I was being absolutely stupid. I went out and got a bit drunk and I was angry and sad, stupid. I had this overpowering desire to see him, you see, and I thought he might be there, buying the meat for Das Kalb, like he does, so it seemed worth a try. He goes there at night, so I did too, in case . . .'

'Who?'

Jessica hesitated, forcing herself to smile, although big fat tears rolled down her cheeks, bearing the last of her mascara in their wake. She looked better without her armoury of aggressive make-up, the absence of which failed to disguise a strong but piquant face with huge eyes and a wide mouth, all offset by long black hair that Jess twisted into a knot only when she worked around food. She was a beautiful girl, far too uncertain of herself and her own temperament to have developed her own style. Clothes, shoes, fingernails, hair, lipstick, all clashed in colour into a gorgeous cacophony of experiment. She would make a stylist ache. She was an individual beauty still in the making.

'I went to find the Love of My Life,' Jessica said, dramatically. 'The one and only. He told me to stay away from him, but I can't.'

'There's no such thing as the love of one's life,' Sarah said,

11

crisply. 'Or at least not until you've lived a little longer than you have.'

'It was him who said it,' Jessica said. 'It was him who said he'd love me for ever and ever.'

'And you believed him?'

Silence fell. City silence, full of the weight of traffic and machinery. The air-conditioning unit in the well of the old block of flats sprang into life with a muted breath and the world outside was a distant invisible roar. Sarah thought that advice at this point was impertinent and redundant: distraction was better, perhaps. Let Jessica return to the subject, or weep or laugh, as she wanted.

'Yes, I believed him. I still do, but he doesn't know what he wants, or what's good for him. I wanted to take him home,' Jessica said. 'I wanted to take him home with me, so I could go, too. Maybe make it up with my mother. If I took home the love of my life, it would all be all right, wouldn't it? Everything would be all right.'

'You can't make a man love you,' Sarah said.

'Can't you? I think you can. What you *can't* do is give up on something precious. You've got to try and keep on trying, however much you cock up.'

Another silence. Jessica looked up with a dazzling smile. 'Don't worry about me, Sarah love. I'll think about something else and talk about something else, try it another way. I can't let him lose me again, that's all. Still, I was stupid.'

She jumped up and prowled round the kitchen. A shot of caffeine had Jessica back to normal, high-spirited, angry, sad, communicative in bursts, hyperactive and ever-helpful.

'Sarah, I can't bear the idea of you not being happy in a place like this. I thought you had the perfect life. God, do you remember that dinner party when we first met? Awful. You got me out of there before that poor man killed me. First time I came here. I was *awful*. Sorry.'

'One of the more entertaining evenings I can ever remember,' Sarah said. 'Only we didn't get much to eat.'

Then they were grinning, then giggling loudly and uncontrollably: two women who knew what it was like to make fools of themselves. A couple of anarchists in the church of ego worship.

'You poured soup over a man's head,' Sarah said. 'I've always meant to ask you, just what was the final provocation to waste all that food after you'd gone to the trouble of cooking it?'

'Don't know. I was sorry for it afterwards. It wasn't that he kept changing his mind about what he wanted, it was because he was a *bully*, and he made his wife cry in the kitchen and he wanted his guests to be miserable and envious. The food would have been wasted anyway. I said sorry to her. I sent flowers.'

'My God, you're magnificent when you're angry,' Sarah said in a breathy, adulatory voice.

'Am I? Good. Maybe anger does it. I'll try it out more.'

'Oh, no, don't.'

Jessica was standing centre stage, first messing up her hair until it was a wild mass hanging halfway over her face, planting one hand with her customised blue-painted nails onto one generous, thrusting hip, shaking her other fist at an enemy, crossing her eyes, making herself into a parody of fury and laughing at herself. Prancing and stabbing like a demented prima donna and still giggling.

'Like this?'

'Terrifying,' Sarah said, laughing with her. 'Not for wimps.'

Jessica sat down and ran her fingers through her hair, pulling it back into place.

'It's worse when it's genuine. It's what you do when you really are a wimp. My mother said I should have been an actress, hysterical roles only. She was probably right. I don't know how to stop it.'

'Maybe you should go back and see your mum. Take a break. Maybe you should write it all down and think about it. Where does she live?'

The sombre mood came back. Jessica stared into the middle distance, fixing her eyes at a colourful plate hung on the wall.

'She lives in a lovely place, the loveliest place in the world. Home. I can't go back, though. Not yet, not until I've proved myself. Why does everything take such a long time? I need to go back with him and maybe then they'd see the sense of me. Can't go back until I'm a good daughter and make things right for all I did wrong. All that fucking anger for nothing. I'd love to go home, but I can't.'

She turned her huge troubled eyes on Sarah, smiled slowly.

'Change of subject, OK? I hate people who talk about themselves all the time. So, Miss Fortune, if you don't feel easy here, where would you like to live?'

Distraction. Sarah spoke slowly, willing to distract and be distracted, allowing herself to dream. Thinking of how much she would like to be a million miles from here, somewhere where the smell of fire was only woodsmoke. Her home had been sabotaged and her ease with it never recovered, but the dream had predated the damage by years and years.

'A cottage in a village close by the sea. With honeysuckle round the door and places to walk. Cliffs and sea and feeling safe. Without any noise except weather. I've dreamed of it all my life. I've always loved the sea. Always thought that when I'd got enough money I'd give it a go.'

'Really?'

'Yes, really. I was taken to the sea for the first time when I was five, longed for it ever since.'

'I don't believe it! Yes, I do. When can you go? I can do something for you, Sarah, really I can. What time is it?'

Jessica leapt to her feet, was up and pacing round, striding out of the kitchen with her mobile held close to her ear, speaking staccato, softly for her, persuading, getting them to call back, trying another number, talking, texting, mainly talking, walking away down the long corridor of Sarah's apartment, her voice fading away and coming back. *You're sure? Fine. Yes.*

She detoured to the bathroom: Sarah could just about hear her, still talking, Jessica who could do three things at once before collapsing into grief. Then she strode back into the kitchen with clean hands, scrubbed face and a look of triumph.

'You can go next week,' she said. 'Honest, you can. You can do what you like, Sarah. We can make things happen. Try it. It'll work if you believe it. My mother owns it: you don't have to meet her, all done through an agent, but it would be nice if you did. Maybe you could tell her I'm not as bad as I'm painted. Maybe you could tell her . . . Oh, nothing.' She snorted into a handkerchief. 'Maybe not. Just go and try the dream, why not? If you want to go, it's there, it's perfect for you. Not a bad little cottage. The agent says yes. Just go and pay, it's empty.'

'Don't you speak to your mother?'

Jessica shook her head violently.

'No. I write to her sometimes. She doesn't write back. She's ashamed of me and ashamed of being a widow.'

'It's a good idea, writing letters. Makes you focus. Better than e-mail.'

'Yeah, right.'

Then her face crumpled. 'Why doesn't he love me? Why? When did he stop? What did I do? All I did was find him. He loves me.'

Toxic grief.

Scene Three

Six a.m. and darkness still going on. What to do with this silly big bitch before anyone saw? Drag her down to the road; make it look like an accident. Well, it was an accident, surely, if only an accident waiting to happen to an animal of such suicidal daftness that she could be described as a creature who had been asking to be killed from the moment of birth. Her hairy hide was full of buckshot, enough to kill smaller game, but not her although she was mortally wounded, snarling and snapping, defying rescue or pity with her blood-shot eyes, her coat soaking wet from where she had dragged herself down the hillside through the damp grass, flanks heaving, unable to move much further; but it might take her a while to die even if she could still bite and he thought he should let her bite his hand and die defiant.

He studied her for a moment, admiring her for snarling rather than whimpering. Then he walked round her, sensing her struggling to move her head to follow him with her desperate eyes. He put his boot on her head, gently, leant over, judged the angle and stabbed her in the neck with his hunting knife, twice, to be sure of it. When she was finally still, he lifted the hind legs and began to drag her towards the road through the gap in the hedge. She was surprisingly light for all her size as if most of her bulk was in her hair. The road surface was warmer to lie on than wet grass. All sorts of animals migrated there for early-morning warmth, offering themselves for roadkill. He laid her out across the carriage-way. There, good girl, nothing hurts any more, the first car will hit you and explain it all. Hope it's a posh one and you do it damage. Good girl.

He was halfway over the fields with his air rifle and knife before a white van sped round the corner and slewed to a halt with the wheels inches from the body.

Someone had nicknamed that bitch 'Jess'.

Not a good start to the day.

The man halfway over the fields thought he would so much rather fish than hunt. Fish blood was cleaner, some-how, although it was just as red.

CHAPTER ONE

The backbone of the village consisted of one long narrow
street, twisting and turning downhill towards the sea and at
first it looked as if that was all there was. A lane of different-
shaped, differently styled houses either on the road or
standing back politely behind competitive front gardens.
Turnings off or turnings on led away from the main thor-
oughfare. The gradient down to the coast was gradual until
the last turn, where the road wrenched round to a short
steep hill, with a glimpse of the sea through the trees from
a car window before the route went inland again. Flat coast
became cliffs in a mammoth upheaval reflected in the con-
tours of the road itself since one side was lower than the
other. The street was entirely devoid of any views except
the next bend. Even the sea was a hidden feature to any but
those with the houses boasting an outlook in the higher
reaches of the turnings off and on. A place for privacy, with
the last conspicuous signpost announcing its presence
at least a mile away on the main road. Turn right for

Pennyvale and nowhere else, because at Pennyvale the road ran out.

That was the secret of the place, Sarah thought, looking down at it from halfway up the cliff path. You could never see the whole of it from any given point. From here she could see tantalising glimpses and part of the twisty street. It had no obvious centre, no flat communal place, and although it had veins and arteries leading somewhere and a single lane, marked unsuitable for heavy traffic, leading to the next town, it had developed and eclipsed in a random way that left no throbbing geographical heart, apart from the three shops. You would see even less in summer than in winter from up here, because of the trees. For a place so close to the sea it was impossibly verdant, much more at home with the green hinterland, turning its back on the waves as if it did not need them. Those who lived here ate more meat than fish.

On the coastal path, on her now traditional morning walk that took a different route each time, Sarah was thinking of village concerns and wondering how much the geography of the place affected the attitudes of the inhabitants or how much choice it left them. The location was smug and snug because apart from the two rows of houses right next to the shore and the ribbon of dwellings leading away south they were safely uphill from the sea and sheltered in the lee of the cliffs. They could grow almost anything in their gardens and they were not isolated as long as their cars functioned and they could get away. It would have been different without at least one car per household; then they would have treasured their village hall, the street would be thronged and the church more than useful ornament. They would have been far more open to inspection if they had not been able to close their doors, order in their own entertainment and drive away from home. The parking of cars, the disposal of cars, the manoeu-vring of cars in a main road built for nothing more than horses seemed to be the greatest source of conflict. From her vantage point up here Sarah could see two shiny motor cars in a stand-off, refusing to give way to each other. Doors slammed; there were distant voices. The slow progress of the rubbish-collection lorry three mornings a week caused mayhem, goods deliveries in large white vans were trouble-some and anyone moving house could block the artery for a whole day. Moving house seemed to happen often; it was either a local hobby or an obsession and as the place was oth-erwise perfect in a picture-book kind of way Sarah wondered why. She had no intention of moving away herself yet – she had scarcely arrived – but she had been there long enough to notice that houses changed ownership frequently, or maybe that was only now in the springtime of the year.

Going to church on the Sunday before last had been one of many novelties. Sarah could not remember when she had last been to church apart from the occasion of a wedding where the marriage had not lasted a year despite the cere-monial blessing. It had seemed like a good idea to go to church here in order to prove a certain willingness to inte-grate – although she only wanted integration on her own terms. Sunday service had proved to be an invigorating expe-rience because of the eccentricity and uncertainty of the vicar. Any vigour and colour in the chilly Victorian church of St Bartholomew was provided solely by the vicar's robes and his evident enjoyment of them; he was clearly a priest who made a sartorial effort on duty. He conducted a merci-fully short morning service with a deal of panache and waving of arms, addressing his remarks and his readings to the small children who were encouraged to monopolise the front row and lead the ragged singing. Andrew Sullivan had a fine voice and an almost comical enthusiasm for conducting this orchestra and their unruly overexcitement had been a pleasure to see. Don't worry about the words, he whispered to them; just make a noise. They did: a big shrill echoey din.

It was somewhere to park them for an hour on a Sunday morning, she thought with a cynicism which could have been unfair, while noting that the rest of those present were old. The vicar was at ease with the children, camping up the proceedings like a pantomime dame for their benefit, but otherwise seemed painfully shy with the rest of his small congregation as he exhorted them to return to the vicarage for a cup of coffee if they wished. It was such a humble, half-hearted invitation that Sarah wondered if he really meant it or if he was merely being diffident to save himself the humiliation of refusals. She herself had got as far as the open front door of the vicarage, turned into the hideous hallway, and then turned back abruptly after she had peeked into the receiving room at the front of the house. There was something pathetic in seeing a man on the youthful cusp of middle age fiddling anxiously with teacups in a gloomy room occupied by a sole visitor who was criticising the way he ran the service. *Can we have proper hymns?* and him saying, No, Mrs Hurly: if there are children we simply have tunes. Sarah had backtracked without being observed, regretted it later. An opportunity lost, but she had been seized with shyness and the elegant woman visitor had reeked of irritable loneliness and it was not the right time. Yes, she wanted to meet the woman, but preferably alongside others in a less depressing room and as for the vicar, she thought he was a kind, well-meaning soul whose best would never be good enough, even when he smiled, which he might not have done sufficiently often. That was a shame, because it transformed him. Perhaps he was like herself, not belonging – as if anyone truly belonged here.

The squat church at the turn of the hill was not going to introduce her to anyone else she wanted to know, except him, perhaps, and that was because of a particularly delicious moment during the service when he had lost his place in the Bible because of the pages sticking together in the middle of his reading a crucial piece about Charity. *He was not charity is nothing but a tinkling cymbal . . .* and then the vicar's whispered *Oh BUGGER* had reverberated around the church as loud as a bell, leaving the children giggling and their elders pretending not to have heard.

Sarah was sitting with her back against the signpost that directed walkers towards the cliffs, admiring what she could observe of this secretive idyll and ignoring the spectacular sea view straight ahead. Perhaps it was wasted on her simply because, like the rest of them on a Friday morning, she was far more interested in the bustle of humanity than she was in the inspiration afforded by landscapes or seascapes devoid of people. She had never understood Wordsworth, nor anyone to whom Nature was a primary source of solace; it could be secondary, but primary, no: a backdrop to humanity, that was all, a vivid reminder of how small one was and how arrogant was the attempt to control the uncontrollable. Flowers were pretty, and green was green and the sea was the most perfect view of all but it still did not compare with a crowd of interesting faces. There was nothing motherly about Nature. She took a last glimpse to see if she could identify the rooftop of her own tiny house, at least a hundred yards uphill on one of the veins that led away from the artery of the main street. Just. It had a red-tiled roof, but then so did most of the rest. Then she turned her face towards the sea and opened the post.

Sarah had been in her new, old house for less than a month and still came out of doors every morning to open the post. She had secured a six-month rental on this particular house through an introduction hurriedly made through her friend Jessica Hurly. Jessica's mother owned the house: there was a rental vacancy and it had all happened very fast. She had been handed the keys by Mrs Hurly's agent, and had yet to meet her landlady, although she knew her by sight because Mrs Hurly had been the discontented woman in the vicarage living room, haranguing the poor vicar about the service. She was a woman who complained a lot, the sign of an empty life. *Approach with caution, and only as a stranger*, Jessica had said. *She's a very unhappy woman. I've given her plenty of cause. I'm trying to make it right in my own way, but I can't, yet. Mummy stopped laughing a long time ago, but she used to laugh.*

Jessica had not elaborated, clammed up, said it would wait and Sarah could find out only if she wanted, never mind. There was plenty enough time to creep up on Mrs Hurly in a sideways motion, at the hairdresser's, perhaps, or better still, encourage Mrs Hurly to approach her. It was clear from conversations in the butcher's and from that single sighting in the vicarage that Mrs Hurly required deference, at least. Too much else to do.

Sarah thought of Jessica increasingly often, wondering what her friend had let her in for, because it was only Jessica's love of the place that had led her here, via the route of the fulfilment of her own dreams of living in a cottage with honeysuckle and roses round the door. A place that did not smell of an old, malicious fire and made her feel free to breathe.

Almost none of the post was addressed to her, which made it all the more interesting. The mysterious previous occupant had failed to have his mail redirected and had left no forwarding address. She would have been happy to oblige and forward it all for as long as it took, but since she was denied such an opportunity to be helpful she regarded his post as hers to open and examine by right. He had practically invited her to do it.

Sarah was thinking that the role of a postman was not quite what it had been, with far fewer privileges than in the old days. Once upon a time the postman would know details about every household for as long as he remembered what he delivered. He would know who was away and who was at home, the state of their finances, the identity of their correspondents. He would deliver all the bills and all the birthday cards, invitations, cheques, parcels, et cetera, and would therefore be able to guess, if he chose, who had sent them and what was inside. It was a job she would have liked herself. Electronic communication surely took half the fun out of it, made people's habits less open to a postman or anyone else. Still, there was plenty left to chew on in Mr J. Dunn's post.

It was chilly on the cliff path, would probably be awful in winter. Sarah's plan to own a dog was under review when she considered the obligation of walking it in all weathers and also because Mr J. Dunn had definitely kept a dog. There had been copious evidence of that in the house he had vacated. The house Sarah had rented stank of dog and desperation and she had visualised a tired old man living there until her examination of the post revealed someone far

younger. Not a large dog, the butcher told her. Poor thing, it
went mad in there, never got enough exercise, he drove away
and left it all day: you could hear it barking. She guessed Mr
Dunn had not been popular. I wouldn't know, the butcher
said, never knew him to talk to, he shopped here, a bit for
bones and I would see him drag that dog out occasionally,
not often enough, even though he loved it to death.
Neglected dogs like that can get vicious. Then they get feral
and no one can catch them, not even Jeremy.

She had met Jeremy, the butcher's assistant, once. Jeremy
was plain, surly and vulnerable, the type she warmed to at
once. He was another sort of male creature who touched her
soul, like the hapless vicar, although the vicar was blessed
with infinitely superior looks. The butcher's shop was the
real heart of the village. Sarah had seen his white van creeping downhill from the fields beyond, disappearing into the
trees and out again. Since the recent demise of the Post
Office/Newsagent, the butcher and the next-door hairdresser
were the pivotal information points, surely, but the butcher
most of all.

She read J. Dunn's letters with interest, resisting the temptation to let them fly away in the breeze. The first was a
notice of a medical appointment; the second a communication informing J. Dunn that he was on a debtors' register for
non-payment of something and the third was a handwritten
envelope containing nothing and addressed to J. DUNN
DECEASED. The postman had still delivered it.

Ah, my dears, Sarah said to herself. It's as well that I need
you more than you need me. I do not wish to be needed.
Wanted? Interested? That was another matter. I have a slight
unofficial mission to begin to reconcile Jessica with her obvi-
ously estranged mother whom she has not seen since she

left, and although she has not specifically asked me to do that I have a feeling that it's what she wants me to do. She wants me to find out things she cannot tell anyone, and yet she can't demand it. Otherwise I have no moral obligations to do anything other than to BE. Thus there is only one family I want to know about and that's Jessica's lot. No, I lie: I want to know about them all, but they are slow to tell me. One moves slowly here and there is plenty of time, especially when you have made a vow only to look at your e-mail once a week and rely on verbal communication. I'm doing fine, fat and lazy. Sarah's dear, anarchic friend Mike, who had carried her here, reluctantly, in a borrowed white van had said she would never last the hectic pace. *You'll go mad, doll.* She missed him most of all, more than any of the other lovers; missed his reckless and nicely opportunistic way of life as well as his knowledge of an alternative world, but she was determined to prove him wrong. *Call any time, doll. I'm always there for you.* She had not called. He was one of the reasons she had wanted to leave, because she was at risk of needing him. It was confusing to need someone you could never quite trust.

It was nine-thirty when Sarah saw the single police car, visible through the winter trees, stopping in the vicinity of the shops she could not see. There was a tingle of excitement from seeing such an urban thing as a police car. Maybe someone had come to find Mr J. Dunn and his dog. She turned her back on the village and faced the sea. This, after all, was what she thought she had come to find. The rest could wait.

PC Chapman opened the door of the butcher's shop and found him alone, save for the omnipresence of dead meat. His eyes went straight to the back wall.

27

'What a beast!'

'Yeah, big fella, once.'

'Big all over.'

'Heavy, for sure.'

'Never seen anything like it.'

'Haven't you ever been for a walk, then, and seen a cow in a field?'

'Scarcely.'

The butcher nodded. 'That figures. Blokes like you drive round in cars and only get out when you've run someone over. Or when someone else has, right?' He shook his head, mournfully, taking any slight sting out of his words by smiling and pointing. 'I tell you what, son, do you think you could move that car of yours before we have a riot round here? Only it's rush hour. Pull it in next to the van, for God's sake. We're not due a lynching for at least another month.'

The policeman nodded and went out and moved the car so that it stood next to the butcher's van on the narrow apron outside the shop. Parking it next to the van somehow diminished his own vehicle and made it look domestic. In the time that took, Mr Sam Brady flung a pile of meaty off-cuts into the mincer, knowing that all he had to do if he did not feel sociable when the bloke came back was turn the damn thing on and drown him out with the noise. The visitor was only a copper from town and he hadn't made an appointment. Nothing urgent, anyway, otherwise there would surely be two of them. The policeman came back, stood and stared at the rear wall of the shop where the two quarters of beef hung on the rail, waiting attention. His eyes had glazed over in lustful admiration. Definitely a meat eater, then, because he was looking at the hind quarters of a well-hung carcass as if he wanted to stroke it, like a hungry man looking at a pole dancer, jangling the coins in his pocket.

The beef quarters were enormous. Sam could see the cop gauging the heaviness of each as they hung suspended from those useful S-shaped hooks on the steel rail, the hook piercing the buttock of the thing, taking the weight at the top and letting it hang, tapering through the leg bones to a blunt end. No hooves. A well-hung piece of beef was beautifully coloured, from the off-white of the fat to the ruddy brown and dark red of the meat, the colours harmonious and easy on the eye. Could have made wall paint for fancy houses, nice old colours from this kind of palette. The meat tones were the same as the complexion of Sam's face and hands, ruddy brown to white to the rusty red of his nose. God bless that nose of yours, his wife told him: you can smell what's rotten from fifty metres, and so he could, just as he could smell trouble and knew that there was none, just at the moment. As long as the copper hadn't come about Jeremy. Sam showed his age, calling a policeman a copper.

The shop smelled sweet, as it always did. Cleanliness was next to godliness; the lack of it was ruin. At the back of the shop was a kitchen area, including sink, kettle, oven, the other chopping board, dry stores, and the sacred cathedral of the chiller. The policeman cleared his throat and shook his head, still lost in admiration.

'You don't get this where I live. All local meat, is it?'

Sam winked. 'I like people to think so. This one isn't. Local as in Argentina via London. Cheaper.'

Sam took a knife from the rack and laid it next to the board. Then he picked up the axe.

'Anything I can do you for?'

Thwack, thwack, thwack.

Three chickens on the board were suddenly halved. Sam threw them on a tray. The policeman pointed. Pointing was rude.

'That big-fella beef. Shouldn't it be in the fridge?'

'You mean the chiller? No. It's been in the chiller for three weeks. One degree above freezing. Took it out this morning. Want a feel? Solid as rock. Got to warm up a bit before I take it apart. 'Swhy I'm messing around with chickens and sausage. Lots to do today, got to get ready for the weekend rush. Not much custom yet, plenty of work. What did you want?'

The policeman laughed. He wasn't as young as he looked. 'All of it,' he said. 'Rump, sirloin, stewing steak. As long as it's beef.'

'You can't afford it.'

They both admired the magnificent hindquarters hooked to the rail. They were easy with each other, but not quite. Sam relaxed. It wasn't about Jeremy. The policeman spread his hands in mock surrender.

'I'll settle for a kilo of the Cumberland sausage and ask you to answer a question. The sausages because you're a proper butcher, and the question because some old biddy uphill said you know everything. I'll pay cash for the meat, and do you know how I find someone called J. Dunn? Only it's a warren round here, and someone said he lived in one place, and someone said another, so I don't know where I am.'

'And we're all supposed to be interrelated and know where everyone lives, are we? Well, we aren't and we don't. Even I don't live here, although I was born here. What's he done?'

'Look, I just deliver the brown envelope, telling him to go to court. Even if I knew, I wouldn't be able to tell you.'

The butcher grinned without any meeting of eyes.

'Parking, I'll bet. The only fines round here are for parking or the TV licence. Or maybe it's about that dog of his. He was ever a careless young man. He used to come in for bones.'

Sam was not going to say anything else. He reached into the display counter and impaled a row of sausages darker in colour then their more pallid counterparts on adjoining trays. The colour of them reminded him of brown mottled carpet, and he could smell the herbs. Next to the Cumberland were other trays of diced beef, minced lamb, red rump steak and a large fillet of beef that looked as old as shoe leather. The window display was empty, waiting to be filled. Jeremy would do the bulk of the sausages tomorrow or Wednesday. The kilo was lifted in a single fat thread and fell plumply onto a sheet of greaseproof paper plucked by the butcher with his other hand. The whole place smelled so wholesome and the policeman shuffled his feet, feeling the sawdust underfoot. Sweet-smelling and bloodless, as if the blood had been absorbed and already digested. PC Chapman shopped in supermarkets, grazing amongst the pre-packed joints to find anything that might suit a carnivorous appetite created by his old mother's stocks and stews. He liked the clean raw smell, hadn't been in an old-fashioned butcher's shop in years and could not remember the ones of his childhood smelling like this. He sniffed: apples from the basket in the corner; lemons from the bowl on the counter; rosemary in bunches ready to use with the lamb. He did not know what all the smells were, only that he liked them as well as the sight of the sawdust on the floor and he was still looking round, sniffing like a bloodhound and unaware of looking ridiculous when the wrapped sausages were dumped on the counter in front of him. Never knew this place existed and, come to think of it, most people in the nearest town didn't know either. No call to come to Pennyvale on a daily or weekly basis, no police station, no community cop, no law enforcer other than the traffic warden, no need. Just peace and quiet and good meat. He felt envious and ignorant and also superior.

'So, do you know where this J. Dunn lives, then?' he asked, fishing in his pockets for money.

Sam shook his head, took down a knife from the rack behind him and began to sharpen it. Such a thin blade it had, out of all proportion to the handle, as if it had shrunk from being an axe and transformed itself into a dissecting tool, capable of cutting the most delicate of slices. Chapman glanced at the wall behind the counter. There was an arsenal of knives.

'Nope, and I never did, not really. I know he's a daft lad and he was renting from Mrs Hurly, up Benham Lane, behind the church, but I never knew the name of the house. Never delivered there, see? He only came in for bones for the bloody dog, see? I might know customers, but I don't know everybody. That'll be five pounds ninety-five. We take cards.'

Not cheap – blatant overcharging. Chapman sorted out the exact money, counting it carefully. Sam put it in the till and wiped his hands on the front of his apron. He was far cleaner than a doctor, although his white overall bore signs of the last carcass he had embraced en route from the chiller at the back to the rail at the front.

'Only I reckon you're out of luck, anyway. Wherever he lived, he moved, months ago. I heard he got a job driving lorries or vans, up north or somewhere. There's a woman lives there now. She rents the place, like he did, but she hasn't got a dog. I mean, that poor bloody dog. Wasn't its fault it bit people. Any road, he's gone, that's for sure. Probably took the bloody dog and went. Doubt if he was paid up on anything, either. Might be a few more summonses and that. I reckon he was one of them refugees – from divorce, I mean, quite a few of those hiding out round here. Usually a lot older than that, though.'

Sam's gaze towards the wall was guileless. He was restless, gazing at the hindquarters with longing, and PC Chapman was immediately suspicious, until he thought he realised the reason for the butcher's preoccupation. The man wanted to start work on that hunk of meat, itching to make the first cut. Chapman thought he would think twice about making a complaint in this shop, what with Brady's high complexion and all those knives.

'Don't you lot ever do joined-up thinking? I mean, does right hand know what left hand's doing? Dunn kept his mad dog until the order came through that it had to be destroyed. One of your blokes came out to fetch it with a special van and everything, only he was too late as well. Don't you talk to each other?'

'There seems,' PC Chapman said, resorting to police-speak and backing away, 'to have been a breakdown in communications.'

After the police car had pulled away, Sam hoisted the first hindquarter off the hook and over his shoulder and then let it drop on the block. He liked cutting meat in the open shop with everyone seeing what he was doing, not only because it was skilful and he was proud of it but because it helped his reputation as a totally professional above-board kind of man. What you saw was what you got when it came to both butcher and meat. But dammit, it was still too soon to have at this hulk. It had only been out of the chiller for two hours, still solid as a rock, and he could not make an impression in the fat with the full force of his thumbs. It remained impervious to touch and inflexible and suddenly he did not want to touch it at all. He almost wanted the copper to come back. Where were customers when you needed them for distraction, for a joke, for a time-wasting chat about politics or the weather or golf or fishing? Where was Jeremy with his freshly killed rabbits and funny eyes like a sheep's, and where was that shy new foreign bloke delivering all the way from Smithfield at whatever hour of the day or night suited him? Trustworthy, got the orders right, but not much of a joker, not like the old one. Sam was feeling shaky. He checked the front door: there was no one in sight. Then he went backstage to the chiller.

The machinery rattled loudly as he pulled open the heavyweight door to a small room. One big walk-in super-cold refrigerator, pantry size. Half full or half empty, whichever way you looked at it. No Health and Safety inspections due for a good while yet. Two headless pigs hung up by the feet in halves, neatly split down the spine. The wholesale stuff on the shelves at the side, duck breasts, chickens in boxes, smaller joints of lamb to the left, strings of sausages hanging in a curtain. Sam pushed his way through those to the back, just to check if it was still there, drying out nicely.

There she was, in her own corner, quite apart from the rest.

J. Dunn's dog, vacuum-packed. One medium-sized, insufficiently desiccated, shrink-wrapped sanitised dead bitch, awaiting collection and decent burial.

Now, was anyone ever going to believe that a man like him could be so sentimental about roadkill?

He shut the door on the chilling room and sighed. Not much custom yet and not much help, either. He would have all the time to chat to Mrs Hurly when she came in.

Poor old bitch.

Chapter Two

Dear S,

I'm leaving you this e-mail in the hope you won't read it. (You said you were going to leave the laptop under the bed.) I'll probably delete it, anyway. Not good to send e-mails when you don't even know what day of the week it is. I'm doing what you suggested, writing things down in order to think them through, never was much good at writing, though. Too slow, but it's very late and there's nothing else to do until it gets light.

I went back to DK, nicely, in the afternoon. It's no use, I can't keep away. I can't help the fact that I smile when I know I'm going to see him and I can't get out of the habit of storing up things to tell him. I bought him flowers, he loves flowers and what's wrong with bringing a man flowers? I know the effect they have on me, they turn me into putty.

You should see him, Sarah. What a figure! If you saw him you'd see what I mean.

I wasn't drunk. I just wanted to give him my gift, say I was sorry for whatever I did wrong the last time, tell him I'd

*talked about him to a friend (you) who made me see sense.
Told me that you can't make a person love you, you can only
make him respect you, so could he respect my feelings for
him? Could we be friends?*

*Then he went ballistic, because I'd talked about him to
someone else. It maddened him, how dare I discuss him?
Whatever there had been between us was a secret and I was a
silly tart, a blabbermouth and he was ashamed of me. He
shoved the flowers back into my face and pushed me out. Get
this woman out, he said. There was the man there and he got
the man to shove me, couldn't bear to touch me himself. Get
her out of here, he said: she can't afford to pay. The man was
laughing.*

I went, but I was crying so much I could scarcely see the way.

*I think I want the anger back. I know it's destructive, but
it's better than feeling like this. That's why Mummy's angry
all the time, because it beats the shit out of feeling so sad and
humiliated that you can't move.*

*Besides, I think anger's the only thing he does respect. I
think it's the only thing that'll make him see sense.*

*I shan't send this, Sarah. It isn't fair on you. I don't want
to bother you with words – or with me, for that matter. I
want you to be happy discovering a lovely new life, a
HOME. Do it for me.*

Why can't we all be happy?

*I feel better now, but I'll go back. Quiet as a diplomatic
mouse.*

DELETE.

Don't get angry with God, get even with everyone else.

*Great wits are sure to madness near allied . . . and thin parti-
tions do their bounds divide.*

He was trying to whistle. The Reverend Andrew Sullivan, vicar of the parish, had a headache, made worse by the bleak sun of this spring morning, and it was not a condition alleviated by prayer. The headache was due to alcohol and the resentment he felt towards his own fatigue had no shame attached. The wine had been excellent and he was in a state of grief because there was no more of that kind left to follow. Andrew Sullivan needed more than the forgiveness of God: he needed oxygen, and he pulled his dark glasses over his eyes and headed uphill for the fields. The brightness of the sea would be too much today, tempting him to walk straight over the cliff and plunge into it. The glorious memory of first-class wine might turn him into Icarus.

He had one whole hour to liberate his soul before meeting a small group of pre-school children in church. After that, he had to be ready. They deserved better; they were the high point of his week.

The path to the church led uphill from the bottom of the main road, just where the road itself curved sharply. It was difficult for a car to negotiate, let alone a wheelchair. The church was the last seaside outpost of the village, apart from the two rows of houses stretching out below on the flat land adjoining the shingle beach, the alternative village, part of it but divorced from it, with its own seaside pub and separate life. No one ever came to church from those two rows of largely second homes, but they attended the butcher assiduously, on Saturdays. Andrew thought that the butcher had a better chance of saving souls than he had, although he might also propel his customers towards heaven or hell by encouraging them to eat so much cholesterol-rich meat. Andrew walked uphill briskly away from the sea. He preferred it at a distance.

Kiddies' club at eleven on Fridays. In a better mood now, he thought that the under-fives were an absolute joy, making him feel as broody as a mother hen. All he ever did with them was tell them stories. Leaving that aside, there were too many children in this village as well as too many dogs.

Clear of the trees that backed onto the churchyard, facing the expanse of the meadow, he paused in irritation. There was someone on the path ahead of him – that bloody woman, ambling along as if she had all the time in the world, which she probably had, dreaming about the countryside as if she had newly discovered it while this was *his* walk, *his* place during weekday mornings at least, his very own path. The trouble with being a vicar, even in his non-vicar-like dress of jeans, walking boots and shades, was that he was still the vicar. Which meant he could not ignore people: he would have to say hello when he drew level, and people, in their turn, would expect his whole attention. They could be rude and demanding, while he could not. It was as if they paid his wages.

Still, he was curious about her, even if irritated this morning. She was new to the village, like plenty of others, but with the difference that she walked all over the place, apparently aimlessly and without the usual alibi of walking the dog, the husband, the child. She had no other props, like a sketchbook or a map, and was entirely unselfconscious. He had spotted her at the back of the church once. She had not stayed to shake hands.

'Good morning!'

Oh Lord, he was as bad as anyone else, putting on the bonhomie as if he had been sent from a casting agency to play the vicar in a pantomime, conforming so easily to the clichés he despised. Hearty, gay vicar, forever interested in all the forms of humanity that the village could afford, even the Widow Hurly who owned so much and acted as if she owned it all.

'Good morning,' Sarah said. 'Lovely day.' Then she gave him a wave, as if ushering him past her, out of the way, clearly not expecting him to stop and without any wish to make his acquaintance. Perversely, that irritated him too, so he fell into step beside her. It was an awkward step, forcing him to abandon the narrow path that was only wide enough for single file and stumble along beside her on the field. He looked at her feet, approving of her hiking boots, although not of the full skirt which billowed round her calves.

'A perfectly lovely day, I agree,' he said, willing himself to believe it. 'About time we had a day like this. Good for the soul, don't you think?'

She stopped abruptly. He stopped, too.

'Look, vicar, you don't have to interrupt your walk, you know. You don't have to talk to me just because I'm here. And you'll need to walk faster than I do.'

She was shooing him on, he realised, giving him the chance to stride ahead and her to watch his backside. Staying or moving were equally embarrassing options. She smiled at him and he found himself laughing. She was rather beautiful when she smiled.

'I'd like to walk a way with you, if you don't mind,' he said, surprising himself not only by saying it but by meaning it. They walked on, harmoniously.

'Is there a code for those who walk out by themselves?' she asked. 'Perhaps there should be. You know, a certain kind of nod or wink that indicates you're not going to stop. Perhaps a way of carrying a walking stick or wearing a hood. So, if you're carrying a stick you put it over your shoulder to indicate you don't even want to say hello, let alone pass the time of day. Or you'd know, by the same code, not to talk to anyone who put their hood up as soon as they saw you.'

'I hate wearing any kind of hat,' Andrew said. 'Even in the rain. Makes me feel as if I'm in blinkers and I can't see properly. You're right, though a code without words, like traffic lights, might dictate a certain walking uniform to be worn on all occasions and I'm not sure about that.'

'Nor me,' she said. 'Fancy having to dress up before going for a walk and remembering the hood and the stick. And does one have to exchange names with someone you meet on a walk, like today? I always thought not, as long as you remember the name of the dog.'

Apart from the boots, she was clearly not dressed for walking, or perhaps, on reflection, she was, striding out in that full skirt on a windless day like this. The soft wool jacket would absorb water like a sponge and looked as if it would be more at home indoors and the scarf was frankly frivolous. She looked as if she had come out in the nearest clothes to hand, fresh from bed. She would blow away like thistledown on the cliffs.

'No names, no pack drill,' he agreed. 'Although that gives you an advantage over me, because you know I'm the vicar and I don't know who you are.'

'All right, I've seen you in a dog collar but that doesn't mean I know who you are. It means you're inhibited by having an identity while I'm not. I can say what I like.'

'And I can't?'

'No, you can't. You can't say fuck off out of my way, because you *are* the vicar.'

Sarah shoved her hands in the pockets of her skirt and grinned across at him. The path turned north across the field and became broader underfoot so that they could walk more easily, side by side. Andrew found he was enjoying himself. The further he was away from the church the better he felt.

'You're dead right, of course,' he said. 'I can never say exactly what I want as long as I'm talking to anyone who lives in the vicinity. I have to do vicar-speak, and express interest and concern, in case anyone detects my deep-rooted frivolity. In the same way, most people have reservations when they speak to me. They always have to include the fact that they don't believe in God but think He's by and large a very good thing.'

'We will not mention God, the devil and all his works,' Sarah said solemnly.

'The best conversations happen between strangers on trains, don't you think?' Andrew said. 'Until one finds out what the other does, and then all sorts of prejudices and I-don't-like-people-like-you come into it. Better to be ignorant, uninhibited strangers?'

'Why not? Suits me. I could forget you were a priest and make up a whole new identity for you on a clean slate. You could be the freak who goes for a walk without a dog, the terrorist in hiding, the subversive, the serial rapist on the run, the celebrity in retreat, the reformed gangster, the embroidery specialist, that sort of thing. Any preference?'

'Not really. Pretty standard prototypes, really. They probably all live here already, anyhow.'

'But no one quite like you?'

He sighed.

'No, there's only one vicar with the burden of a blameless past.'

They had reached the top of the hill, out of the safety of the valley, facing the track over the next field. The sea was to the right, calm and sparkling, the church and village below hidden by trees and the landscape ahead nothing but another field and a copse.

'Whoever I am,' he said. 'I think I hate this place.'

Sarah shook her head. 'No, you don't, vicar. There simply isn't enough venom in your voice. Hatred's too strong. Perhaps it simply eludes you.'

She turned by the stile that led to the next field and climbed over it nimbly.

'Having a hangover doesn't help,' she added.

He ran to catch up with her as she raced ahead.

'Whoa! Slow down. What are you, a witch?'

'No more than you're a wizard, vicar, and you might try sucking a peppermint before getting close to the congregation. Or take off the dark glasses – the sun's not that bright. Shall we sit?'

She had been aiming for the bench at the top of the field, speeding up in order to sit down, which suited him fine. She looked so languid that he had not thought her capable of sprinting. He was out of breath and she was not.

'How nice of someone to put a bench here,' she said, giving him time to recover, patting the seat beside her. 'Have you read the inscription? *In memory of Harold Cley, who loved this view.* I tried to find him in the churchyard but I couldn't. Is that some big family name round here, or was he simply passing through slowly?'

Andrew was ashamed that he had never noticed the inscription on the bench, or taken much notice of the names on the gravestones either. In three years here he had never thought the history of the place went anywhere near explaining it. If there were dynasties here, other than the Hurlys, they were surely long gone.

'Do you have a particular liking for this spot, that you run towards it?'

'Of course. It's the only place to sit in half a mile, which makes it its own reward. It's a destination but, more than that, it's probably the best view of the village. An incomplete view – they all are – but this one isn't quite as infuriatingly incomplete as the others. I've tried it from all sides, still can't get a handle on it, but if I was planning a heist or an invasion I might start here. Or there.' She pointed to the other side of the valley, beyond the buildings, 'Or there.'

'*Were* you planning an invasion?'

'I don't know yet,' she said seriously, 'I'm deciding whether to invade or retreat.'

'Wish I had the choice. No, not really. There's too much to do here, but the option to retreat would be comforting.'

'That magic word, *choice*. Don't like it. Anyway, do you need it? I hear you've done magnificent things since you've been here, massive achievements with the church, doubled the congregation.'

'Who told you that? You've only been to church once. I saw you.'

The breeze blew Sarah's hair across her face. 'A woman I was sitting next to in the hairdresser next to the butcher's told me – well, she didn't tell me exactly, she was talking to someone else, shouting, really.'

'One of those grey-rinse arguments?'

'No, I think the other one was deaf. Anyway, the first one said how the vicar had done wonders by going back to traditions and concentrating on the music and, against all the odds, it made people go more. She was pretty mean about the last vicar before you, a "happy-clappy" sort of chap who had them all hugging one another and it didn't work.'

Andrew shuddered and pushed his sunglasses to the top of his head.

'He fancied himself as more of a counsellor and, oh God, they made such miserable sounds, that congregation, all five of them. Fancy getting them strumming guitars and humming when there's a perfectly good organ; he even abandoned the choir, the vandal – I've only just got it back. People like to *sing*. The last vicar believed that his ministry was all about personal engagement with lost souls, one at time. He wanted people to confide in him. Me, I only joined the church for the music, you see, although I do like the frocks.' He sighed. 'So far, so good, but getting the pews out of there and making it more of a concert hall, well, that will set the cat among the pigeons, even though the acoustics are marvellous. Sorry, I'm going on.'

'I like *going on*. Meeting place, centre for music, what other things would you do?'

Andrew waved his arms, embracing his own ideas. 'Parties, concerts, raves in church, with quality control, of course. Buddhist feasts and Hindu festivals, the Chinese New Year, all suitably accompanied. Visiting sopranos, tenors with attitude, pantomimes, theatrical extravaganzas . . .'

'A *son et lumière* in the graveyard on the summer solstice,' Sarah said. 'A formal blessing of the sea, with cannons and orchestra. Feasting and jousting to music. And, as a sideline, the vicarage restyled as a glamorous knocking shop to raise funds.'

'Yes, YES!' He clapped his hands. 'I particularly like the last. A work-creation scheme. First, they sin, then I absolve them, then they sin again. We could really do with a lot more sin, and the vicarage is *so* gloomy. I can't afford a decorator, can't afford anything. I'm over-housed and underpaid, you see.'

'I'll do it,' she said.

He stopped abruptly.

'Do what?'

'Paint the vicarage walls.'

'Why the hell should you do that?'

'Because I'm underemployed and I need something to do.'

He paused. This was a gift horse, staring him in the mouth. 'Are you running away from something?'

She considered the question.

'No. I'm running towards.'

'Is that your line of business, then? Interior design?'

'Among other things. I've made a serious study of ceilings.'

Andrew leapt to his feet, twisting his hands in excitement, the dual effect of stimulation and opportunity.

'Oh, do come back to the gloomy place for coffee . . . oh, no, I've got to say hello to the under-fives. Can we speak later?'

'Sure,' she said, standing up. 'If you promise to tell me all the gossip.'

'Delighted, I'm sure,' Andrew said. 'If only there was any.'

She stiffened her hands in her pockets and the skirt billowed around her.

'Shame on you, vicar. A creative man like you? If there isn't any gossip, you could surely invent it. That's what I'd do. I'm Sarah, by the way. 379 033.'

That's what I'd do.

He watched her stride away, further uphill and into the woods, out of sight. Then he ran downhill, vaulted the stile and only when he approached the church felt the remnants of the hangover. That sobered him. Surely it had made him delusional.

That's what I'd do. That is what I would do if I were a different kind of man with the courage of my own convictions and a bit more energy. That is what I would do if I used my time instead of thinking 'What if?' I could have painted the walls in the bloody house two years ago instead of singing myself to sleep. I would have examined the gravestones and found the ghosts with money, that's what I would have done. I could have told Mrs Hurly to stop talking to me, because I can't make her life better. Tell her that spitefulness does not take away sadness, only work does.

He turned aside into the vicarage for the key and hurried back to open the church door. The key was theatrical and ludicrous, giving an impression of gravity, while the door itself provided real security by its very appearance. Andrew approved of the arched church door, made of weather-bleached oak studded with iron, although he preferred the small door round the back that led into the vestry, even though, whenever he went in that way, he expected to find something dead on the floor. He had only found cats in search of sanctuary in here.

He propped the front door open and smelled that church smell of trapped warmth with undertones of cold as he stepped inside the foyer and through the next set of doors into the body of the church, adjusting his eyes to its dimness.

Perhaps she could paint this, too. Bring back the original bright and vulgar Victorian glory to its now-faded ornateness.

Paint it red.

Surely St Bartholomew would approve.

What on earth was she doing here? Sent from heaven?

Andrew thought of the under-fives with renewed pleasure.

Then he thought of Mrs Hurly coming to tea in the gloomy vicarage living room and sighed with resignation. That was surely not the sort of gossip Sarah would want to know.

Or perhaps she did.

CHAPTER THREE

There was nothing to compare with the joy of going home, especially if it felt like home and there was the prospect of a weekend with nothing to do but walk.

Sarah went back uphill to her own house. Not strictly her own in terms of actual ownership, but then, she had discovered that real ownership was tenuous, fragile and risky. She was here because she was wary of the home she owned and wanted to find another.

It was an advantage not to feel indebted to the landlady who had left her cottage full of J. Dunn's dog hairs. The original mess of it gave her freedom to change it as much as she liked and there were so many other compensations. Location, location, location, which meant an angled view of the sea from the attic-bedroom window if she stuck her head out and craned left and it was this tantalising glimpse that drove her out every morning, straining to go like a dog on a leash, wondering what fresh smells today? There was an energising advantage to a limited sea view and creaking stairs.

Wanting to get out every morning never meant she was unwilling to return. It was thrilling to go up to your own front door with a good feeling even though it was not quite her ideal house, only the one she could get. The village had been selected for her by chance through knowing Jessica and she was a great believer in spontaneous coincidences like that, but the house itself was hers only because it was available. She had made a visual examination of every other visible house within her size range and already knew that she would swap her cottage for one of those in the two rows right down by the beach, set apart from the rest and looking out directly to the sea, but this was good for starters. A sweet, sad house in need of rescue, thus catering to her own speciality, also with certain vital ingredients, such as a porch at the front with the promise of honeysuckle growing over it in summer, and a small south-facing yard of a garden at the back, almost empty apart from dead things in pots and a tiny border. It was the stuff of dreams all the same, the life-lottery win, the almost perfect existence promised by a six-month lease on a cottage with honeysuckle round the door and the sea at the bottom of the road, with room to nurture cabbages and flowers.

The realist in Sarah had always known that such a dream was only a kind of analogy for something else, such as being reconciled to disappointments, free of duties, responsibilities and obligations, not having to go to work and being able to pay the bills with ease. A state of not wanting anybody or anything other than what there was, like living on one side of a river without constantly craving a better place on the opposite shore. All summed up in a vision of a cottage in a village with a large expanse of water attached, about as far distant from central London traffic and a pressurised career as it could be without emigrating. Being in a place where the land ran out; the delightful end of the road. Not that she had ever been deluded by the notion of a perfect way of life; ambition and discontent and even a little bit of fear were so vital to achievement and survival, after all, but she knew the importance of dreaming. Of getting a dream, kicking it about, trying it on for size like a new skirt and then, if necessary, chucking it away and trying on something else. The cottage with roses round the door could mean a state of *not needing*, but a state of complete self-sufficiency would have to involve a complete frontal lobotomy. It was not natural. She might regard herself as profoundly irresponsible, wanted to be *divinely* irresponsible, a merely optional extra in other lives, but that was not quite possible, either. She was far too interested in humankind to remain aloof; could not quite disengage however hard she tried; responsibility followed affection and that was that.

It would be nice if you got to know my mother, Jessica had said. *But you don't have to. Just be happy. I'm not going to bugger things up for you with introductions. You don't need them.*

You'll go crazy here, Mike had said when he'd delivered her to the door in an uninsured, mysteriously obtained white van, *without something to do*. He was a case in point. He loved her, but he would do perfectly well without her and that was all she had ever wanted for him and he was right about her needing something physical to do and she had embarked on that immediately. She had redecorated every place she had ever occupied, whether she owned it or not (ownership was all in the mind, after all) and most of the bubbled walls in her cottage were already liberally covered in 'orchid white'. Paint always lived up to its promise, never disappointed, and she took immense satisfaction in the very names they gave to the stuff. Sarah had breathed on the honeysuckle branches to make it grow and the backyard was littered with trays of seeds and bulbs. She was going to stay here long enough to grow cornflowers and sweet peas at least and learn not to uproot them just to see how they were doing. That was what people did with relationships. Not a good idea to question things about their right to grow or not.

The walls were incompletely fresh; there were the few things she had brought with her standing alongside the utilitarian pine furniture left either by her landlady Mrs Celia Hurly or by J. Dunn. For the first two weeks she had been here it had rained incessantly and that had been when she had made it home. She was accustomed to big high-ceilinged rooms and found small ones so much of a doddle to paint that she looked forward to the challenge of the vicarage for further distraction. She felt detached, but she could only ever be semi-detached.

The phone rang, sounding threatening in the empty room, bringing city to village with a clarion call. Jessica; it had to be Jessica. Sarah took the phone out into the backyard and sat on an upturned pot. There were young seagulls on the roof next door, jockeying for position on a TV aerial, howling for Mummy. A March wind blew gently.

Sarah didn't like mobiles. Jessica Hurly lived by hers, could talk in a train, a bus, a taxi, in the middle of a crowd or a meal, went everywhere with the thing glued to her hand. She would hold up the checkout line, chattering and arguing while fishing for her money, completing a purchase with gestures and smiles while talking throughout, and then getting away with it by saying sorry and being gorgeous.

She liked the challenge of talking against a background, giving away where she was, and although Sarah had once detested the horribly public nature of such conversations the irritation had long since been counterbalanced by the wonderful eavesdropping opportunities. She longed for people to shout out confidences in crowds, especially Jessica whose phone was vital to her health because without it she might fall down the nearest black hole. Jessica needed another voice to make her pause; another opinion to clarify her own, an echo for her every sentiment. Jessica could play the whole scale of her emotions on a number of instruments, but only her mobile phone could prevent her from acting them out. Thankfully, one of her many saving graces was a melodious voice.

She could see Jessica stabbing the phone with her long trademark blue-varnished nails.

Sarah tried to list the most frequent phrases she used when she spoke back to Jessica, then and now, face to face or on the phone. They were mainly brief and to the point, such as *Perhaps not*; *Think again*; *I wouldn't if I were you*; and *Don't*. How Jessica had ever concentrated long enough to become a chef was a mystery: she must have taken in knowledge through the skin, acquired the instincts at her mother's knee, perhaps, in the same way that Sarah had learned a talent for painting walls in the early hours of the morning. Jessica was a cook par excellence and being an emotional prima donna went with the territory although high temperament was not always welcome in someone catering private parties for those who paid highly for the privilege of having the last word. Jessica had never quite mastered the deferential mentality required for such occasions and her career was precarious, to say the least.

Sublime food was no compensation for broken crockery and noises off and nor did Jessica's magnificent appearance always reconcile an aggrieved host to the state of his kitchen, unless she remained behind to offer something additional to the menu. As for men, she seemed to be as obsessive about their particulars as she was about culinary ingredients, but unlike her instinctive skill with the latter she never seemed to get the mix right. As mistress of many a humiliating compromise herself, Sarah was a sucker for a person who refused to do it, but her affection and admiration for Jessica was compounded by a slow-burning nagging worry because Jessica was gelignite and Jessica in a state of unrequited love was like a piece of volatile explosive with a tricky fuse.

'Guess what? He told me to fuck off,' she said without introduction.

She had resiled from this theme for a week; now she was back. Once launched, though, her recitatives on the subject were always continuous, assuming the respondent's intimate knowledge of the last episode of the long-running saga of her life, whether she had mentioned it or not. Sarah could only respond in the same way.

'Again?'

'Yes. Again. The stupid shit. I wrote you an e-mail about it, didn't send it, so don't look. I did what you said, waited at least a day, but then my blood boils again. Anyway, I'm going to sort it out with him. If he thinks he can treat me like that he'd better think twice, the shit. I thought I'd go down to that pretentious restaurant of his and vomit all over his tables. What do you think?'

You don't want to know what I think. Nothing had altered. The same obsession, the same man as before.

Shame. Sarah had thought that Jessica had stabilised, but no chance.

'Why?' Sarah said.

'What do you mean, why? He bloody well deserves it.'

'For what?'

'For saying fuck off, the shit. How dare he do that?'

'Because your dogged devotion was boring him? Because you were embarrassing him? Because you were bad for business?'

'How can I be bad for business? The last time I went there I was in that black dress. You know the one I mean? The vintage killer? And I was nice.'

She had not mentioned that. Sarah stayed quiet. There was a big dark sigh.

'Oh, right, I think I can see what you mean. Not good for business to have a row in a posh restaurant like DK when his place is full of people. Anger doesn't work, right? Shit.'

'So when were you going to stage this sad repeat performance?'

'Like now. Just when they're queuing up for lunch.'

There was the sound of traffic and footsteps behind Jessica's voice. Sarah could see her, standing on a corner next to a Tube station and part of her hoped that all the passers-by were enjoying the obstruction and the conversation as much as she would have done if she had been one of them. It gave her a sudden wave of city-homesickness. Must go back soon, before I forget what it's like. I don't want to *forget* what it's like.

'Hmm. Could we think back a little? What was it you wanted to achieve?'

'I want him to love me. I love that man so much. We're made for each other. He has to love me. We belong.'

Sarah suppressed a laugh. Love, that many-splendoured thing, to be avoided at all costs, especially with this wretched man of Jessica's who, even from brief misdescriptions, sounded like everything that Sarah herself would dislike. She imagined him as large and carnivorous, a man who might take a bet on a gifted girl like Jessica who was good enough to grant an opportunity, plus a few introductions, until he grew tired of her demands and dumped her. Such was life: Sarah knew that round of that particular carousel all too well and knew you had to jump off. He owned or managed a restaurant: that was probably part of the appeal, as in something to talk about. Sarah halfway understood the in-between bits, such as Jessica working for him or with him once, briefly, until he did not need her any more. She knew only a fraction of it: the information came out in gulps between rapid changes of subject as Jessica veered away from and then towards self-indulgence, shame for it, and sudden fits of secrecy. Despite her gratitude, Sarah could feel herself beginning to yawn. Such all-consuming passion for a lost cause of a man made her weary and glad to be beyond it.

'Well, making a scene isn't going to do it, is it?'

Echoes upon echoes. A revving car, urban voices, some-one shouting *See you, bye*, sounds of the bleep, bleep, bleep of a pedestrian crossing, then Jessica's own clickety-click heels crossing to the other side and that heavy breathing of hers which indicated hesitation.

'So you don't think it's a good idea, then?'

'No.'

Sarah looked at her watch. Early London lunch hours. Jessica's threat was probably an empty one, like so many of them were. Sarah could hear her reaching the same conclusion, as if Jessica had only just thought of how a big gesture might be ruined for lack of an audience. Jessica could vomit by a sheer act of will.

'You told me I was magnificent when I was angry,' Jessica said.

'So you are, but I doubt if it's universally appreciated,' Sarah said sharply. 'And if you love him,' she went on into the ensuing silence, 'doesn't that mean you want him happy? With or without you? Isn't this just selfishness?'

That was a long sentence in the circumstances. There was a lot more to say, such as you're a beautiful, spoiled child, and there will always be someone else, as there has been before, will be again, and all the blah, blah, blah she herself might not have believed when she was twenty-three, plus other platitudes, such as look, go to work on yourself; no man is ever going to cure those insecurities, especially if you pursue him beyond the grave. *Beyond the grave?* Where did that come from? She'd been reading too much and she shivered as she listened and stayed silent, waiting for the sound of gears turning in Jessica's mind. She was not going to sound like a wise old aunt telling Jessica to concentrate on what she was good at, like food and artless generosity, grow up.

'I always know where I can find him,' Jessica said. 'If he doesn't love me, and I'll die if he doesn't, I could almost wish he was really dead.'

'Maybe, love, but you don't want him wishing *you* dead, do you?'

Another pause for silence and the click-clack of heels before Sarah spoke again, trying to lighten the tone.

'So what's with the rest of the day? Everything else going OK? I can hear all those London noises. It's so quiet here.'

Jessica seized upon the change of subject with suspicious speed as if she had overstepped the mark, revealed too much. Giggled. Crisis over.

'Quiet? Is it really? I don't remember that, I remember all sorts of lovely noises. Anyway, I've got these prats to cook for this evening, twelve of them. Fucking stockbrokers in W12 on a tight new budget. Oh, shit, almost forgot. Must go, got things to collect. You're right, no time to be mad. Look, if you're homesick that makes two of us. I'm riddled with it, keeps me awake. I miss you. Hey, what are you doing down there, anyway? Lots of lovely walks? Has spring been springing? You don't notice it here.' Then, 'Have you met my mother yet?'

'No. Not yet. I've seen her in the distance. She looked well – and rather elegant, I thought.'

Sarah did not quite know why she was being economical with the truth: that Mrs Hurly had left a distinctly unpleasant impression when Sarah had seen her in the vicarage. Or why she didn't add in the fact that she was apprehensive and did not want to know Jessica's mother at all.

There was a sudden trill of Jessica's infectious laughter and Sarah felt her shoulders relax as if some small danger point had been passed.

'That's all right, then. As long as she's well. She *is* elegant, isn't she? I'm proud of her really and I don't blame her for not being proud of me, but I'll make her proud of me. As long as she's well. I've been writing to her a bit. God, I miss her shouting. You can always catch her in the butcher's shop. She owns that, too. She just goes in there to torment them. She can be awful, got a temper like mine, doesn't mean it. I love you, Sarah. I want to come home and show you everything.'

She would finish the call before she started crying. Sarah knew that, because there were some limits to what Jessica would do in a public street and crying was one of them.

'So why don't you just come home?'

'You know why.'

'No, I don't. You keep saying you'll tell and you never do.'

That much was true. There was plenty that Jessica wanted to say and couldn't or wouldn't. Jessica had a love–hate relationship with the place where she had grown up and it was her descriptions of this village that had lured Sarah to it. *Oh God, Sarah, if you want a picture-book village hidden between cliffs, I've got the one. My mother owns four houses there. It's the most perfect hell-hole if you like sea and greenery; greenery gives me vertigo.* There was more to her love and loathing of the place than that, but it had never been fully explained in their long, meandering, constantly-changing-tack conversations over Sarah's kitchen table. Sarah had never known if this was withholding information or simply forgetting to include it. Or wanting Sarah to find out for herself, without prejudice. Or not wanting it, or not knowing quite what she wanted. That last guess made sense. Jessica did not know what she wanted about many things.

'I can't come back. They want to kill me.'

Overdramatic again.

'Nonsense, love,' Sarah said, soothingly. 'You're far too beautiful for that.'

'I am, aren't I? Am I? So why doesn't he love me? Oh, shut up, Jess. Where are you, Sarah? I can hear seagulls, oh my God, I can hear seagulls. I adore them. I love the seagulls. They're brave and shameless. They scavenge for a living, like me.'

'Like me,' Sarah echoed.

The gulls were still crying on the roof and Sarah held out the phone so that Jessica could hear them better. They did not sound musical to her own ears, only plaintive and haunting. Then she held the phone back to her ear, listening to Jessica's footsteps, now free of the crowd and moving faster.

'I'll do it,' Jessica was saying, excitedly. 'I'll do it, I'll come home. I can do it if I know you're there. Maybe I can bring him back. No, why do I have to wait? I can sneak in under cover of darkness and sneak away before dawn. I can stay with you, can't I? Just to look. Listen to those bloody seagulls and look at the sea. Make me a really long recording of the seagulls, will you? Send it to me.'

Sarah was smiling at her excitement.

'Why do you have to come under cover of darkness?'

'I burned a lot of boats,' Jessica said airily. 'But I'll do it, I'll come back.'

'When?'

'Soon. Any day now. Why should I wait? Soon as I can. Let me hear those seagulls again.'

Sarah looked up to the roof. The gulls had flown. The phone call ended.

Sarah had forgotten to buy anything to eat and listening to Jessica reminded her of food. Left to herself, any variation on the theme of eggs and toast would do, but not when she thought of Jessica's standards. Jessica demanded fine oils and herbs and fish more exotic than any that were available here: town fish, like tuna, swordfish, scallops and wild salmon. Fish was her speciality: Jessica really didn't like meat. Sarah picked up the phone and asked for a taxi to take her to the little town three miles away down the coast. Jessica unsettled her: there was definitely something wrong with

Sarah if she wanted to see the inside of a big supermarket. Besides, she needed more paint. Classical grey for the vicarage, best not to let the vicar have the choice.

It would be dark by the time she got back, and it was even nicer coming home in the dark. Maybe she would always be an urbanite: maybe the city was locked in her. Then she thought of urban dinner parties and shuddered. On the way to the next town, in the back of a battered taxi with a taciturn driver, she thought of the first time she had met Jessica Hurly.

W11, environs of Holland Park, long after dark. Huge house, Lansdowne Road or somewhere. No supermarket food allowed. Mine host already flushed. Purpose of dinner party: to show a degree of financial prudence and showy-offishness, as well as a fat torso. Look, guys, just look at this house. See the furniture? Clock the design features? And why are we having this party? Think on. Because I've had a bloody good bonus and rather than ram it down your necks with a party in some old-hat cost-a-bomb place like the Ritz I'm having it here in my own home, and I scarcely know some of you, but you're all guys I need to know, like my dentist and possibly some whose noses I want to rub in it. I've got a wife, her over there; I've got a kid with a nanny in the upper regions of MY house and all's well with the world, thank you. There's even a fucking pedigree cat. No credit crunch here for me. So let's raise a toast to me and all the mega-deals that got me this house that no one else could afford and all this vintage champers. Shall we sit? (At MY table, with the Villeroy and Boch china. I really wanted you to see that: not dishwasher-proof, but the cook will see to that. Cheers!) Pity it's too wet for you to see the garden at the back. Designed by . . . What the hell's happened to that bitch of a cook? Had to have a word with her earlier. She isn't cheap, bit of a looker, though she said we couldn't eat the starter with spoons! Well, I mean, I need to use these very fine spoons we got as a wedding present and I thought I'd ordered soup, but she said I'd chosen foie gras with figs, silly cow, so I said change it, I want to use the spoons, surely you can knock up a soup? And I'm sure I said meat rather than fish.

Are we seated? Did you like the canopies, sorry, canapés? Looked lively, didn't they? Jolly well served, too, those tits of hers are like kittens in a basket. Who? No, she comes highly recommended by that bloke who runs DK, Das Kalb to us, that little place near Smithfield, does meltdown steak, he kills it himself. No, not cheap, either, this cook, but not nearly as much as taking all you unimportant little fuckers out to a slap-up meal there. Plus wine, of course – do you like the glasses? Ah, here she is, does it all on her own, you know. Clever girl.

Yes, I am a clever girl sometimes, Jessica said afterwards in another kind of taxi. So sharp I could cut off my own nose to spite my own face. I'll never get paid, but it was worth it. Don't you see? I knew what he was thinking. He was one of those who can only feel big by making everyone else feel small. He didn't know that it's never money that makes a man.

The clever girl came in with the cucumber soup, stood poised in the doorway that led from there to the kitchen, framed in light like an avenging angel in perpendicular heels. Nigella Lawson, eat your heart out. She teetered towards him, coquettishly and steadily bearing a huge silver salver that looked too heavy for her slender arms to lift. Chairs scraped back for men to take it from her, but lift it she did, to a great enough height from which to pour it all over his head. Blue nails, virulent green soup. It wasn't the action,

Sarah decided: it was the wholehearted cheer that followed that dealt the mortal blow to his pride.

It was cold soup, Jessica said. I wouldn't have done it with hot. I didn't want to hurt anyone. It just felt like something that had to be done. If I was like him and made people squirm for fun I'd want someone to teach me that I couldn't get away with it.

Halfway down the supermarket aisle, blinking in the artificial light and hating every minute of it, Sarah wondered if this was the kind of episode that Jessica in her current mood might well repeat this evening or another evening without the same moral justification. Whether Jessica's anger was always in response to genuine provocation and outrage, or whether it was the formless, destructive sort that came from being angry with oneself, Sarah was not sure. Now that Jessica was six months older, she hoped there would be no repetition and she loaded the trolley with an abundance of everything so that she would only have to return later rather than sooner. Then she moved on to the only part of this vast store that she did not actively dislike, which was the Do It Yourself section. Paint. Three times seven-litre cans, heavy stuff. Presumptuous of her to choose for him, but instinct told her he might like it that way and it would save time.

It was early-evening dark when she got home and lugged it all into the porch: wine, fish and paint. She had forgotten herbs, but Sam the Butcher said he could get them any time, him or Jeremy would. Jeremy, that plain lad, could collect whatever she needed from the herb beds at the back, and any time soon she would be able to collect wild garlic and fennel from the beach herself.

She was not that close to Nature. Nature could take care of itself.

The phone rang. This time it was the vicar. Call me Andrew.

'Do you really mean it? About painting the vicarage? The main room, anyway? Only I thought I'd give you a chance to change your mind. I've got masses of white paint. Do you mean it?'

'Yes, but not white.'

He laughed with relief.

'Oh, good. Not white. So sterile and godly. Marvellous – er, when did you think you could start? I mean *we*, only I'm busy all day tomorrow, then it's Sunday, and Monday's difficult with meetings and things and . . .'

He was flustered and hurried, anxious that she should not go.

'The day after, then. Start on Tuesday. I'll give myself a long weekend to limber up. It's supposed to be very cold again next week. A good time to be in.'

'Are you sure? What about the colour?'

'I thought a nice classical warm light grey,' Sarah said. 'With your white paint as undercoat. I've taken the liberty of buying some. Was that very presumptuous of me?'

There was not a murmur of protest, only a sigh of relief.

'Sarah, please presume as much as you like. I'll enjoy it.'

'And I'll look forward to it.'

She put down the phone, smiling at the prospect and cautiously pleased to have got her own way. She already knew the right colours. She had seen that graveyard of a room. Time spent redeeming it would be good for both their souls and she liked the thought of that.

Jessica flitted across her mind on the way out. Sarah could

lie in bed all weekend if she wished. There was nothing she had to do: she was a free agent and time flew sweetly when you were free. She had a hundred miles to walk and a garden to tend. She had formed a talent for irresponsible postponement and she was thoroughly enjoying it.

Chapter Four

Dear Mummy,
I want to come back, but I don't know how.

Who would I talk to? They all hate me because of what I was. Why did you ever let Daddy grow such a chip on his shoulder, and then drive him away – but no, I suppose it was Life did that. Whipped butcher's boy, wants big house, blah, blah, blah, then leaves home to die. How clichéd he was. You too, I suppose: unloved grande dame plays sourpuss. I'm sorry, I know why you do, but people could love you, you know. They did once.

I did, I do. You deserve better.

If I came back, I couldn't even cook for people. They'd think there was poison in it, so I couldn't do anything, because cooking's all I can do. Not that it made me able to keep a man, did it? Still doesn't. Love doesn't work, Mums. They always love the dog best.

He would have come back for the dog. Even Jack would come back for the dog. I know I told a lot of lies, but the bit about the vicar was true. I wish you hadn't trusted him, but then you have to trust somebody.

Hope you enjoy your view of the sea. Wonder what it's like down there – can you hear them fighting outside the pub on Saturday nights? Can you hear the gulls?

I wish you'd get e-mail, Mummy, it makes writing easier.

I hope you've stopped using the baby buggy for shopping. I know it's practical, but . . .

It's going to get better, Mums. Spring is springing.

Tell me I can come home.

Jessie.

That had been the last letter to plop through the letterbox, the third in a fortnight, and now it was Monday again after another interminable weekend and there had been none this morning otherwise she would have heard. She had begun to miss the sound; it was as if Jessie's letters had their own sound. All sounds here were distinct.

Down in the last two streets of cottages that spread from the bottom of the hill and turned their backs on everyone else, Celia Hurly contemplated the restrictions of the view from her bedroom window. The view was endless, revealing nothing but sea and sky and unutterably tedious for revealing nothing more until a crowd of menacing seagulls appeared to hover and scream, filling the space and blocking out the sky. They came so close to the glass, they made her shield her eyes and yell, but once they were gone, wheeling away as suddenly as they had appeared and leaving the clouds intact, she wanted their noise. Nothing was left but the muted sound of the sea, and the lack of noise from the letterbox downstairs.

The wooden frame of the sash window had the effect of

framing and dividing the view. From her bed, she could see the sea through the bottom half, the sky tapering into the horizon through the top and even when she snuggled further down into her bed the damned horizon would never quite coincide with the middle of the window so that sometimes she thought she was looking at it through prison bars.

Damn the seagulls and that silly fool who threw out stale bread for them most days. You could set your clock by her and yet, each time, Celia Hurly was shaken into angry surprise.

She had been sitting on the side of the bed and now she reached for her stick to wave at the last departing seagull before falling back with the effort. The horizon rose above the central bar of the window. She did not have the energy to open the window and shout at dotty Mrs Smith, because if that stupid woman did not know by now that seagulls had no need of her bread there was no point in telling her. She had been cooing and throwing bread for these scavengers all year, always choosing to do so outside someone else's house so that the crap went onto their roofs and windows, not hers. It wasn't a personal vendetta, so Celia vowed to continue to smile at her should they meet in the hairdresser's, because that was the right thing to do. And then, maybe, rub guano into her hair.

Bloody seagulls. Bloody endless sky seen through too small a window and prison bars.

The room was Spartan. The painted floorboards were rough on her feet once she left the safety of a small sheepskin rug at the bedside and moved towards the door. Everything in here was white, or off-white, depending on its age. White sheets, pillows, a yellowed bedspread and curtains best described as parchment and never closed since she hated the dark. White walls. The metal of the iron bedstead, also painted white, but chipped, was cold against her palm. She pulled on a white towel dressing gown over a cream night-dress, thinking how she had never liked white, not even for a wedding dress. It was only as a deterrent to her own worst impulses that this room was so plain and ill-designed for comfort. She kept it that way to put herself off spending too much time in it, but the strategy had failed because bed was still the best place in the world.

There were times when she thought of herself as a lizard that had lost its legs by a process of evolution and had turned into a snake. A year or three of burrowing under-ground, sliding rather than walking, had made the legs redundant until all she was fit for was hiding under a rock. Still equipped with muscles and fangs, as well as with some capacity for the lightning strike, she had perhaps taken to the undergrowth of her own mattress a little too soon. It was not as if she could not walk, but she could scarcely see the point. There was nowhere she wanted to walk towards, and nowhere from which to run.

Celia Hurly, widow of the parish, had moved several times in the same village, descending from the biggest house to the smallest, and with each move going further downhill, geo-graphically. She retained ownership of four properties, including this hovel, and she planned to go back to any one of the others sometime. Maybe. Owning three properties subject to rental arrangements was a way of keeping her options open, but the last move had been a mistake. She had thought she wanted closeness to the sea, but she didn't. She had lived at the top of the hill and now she lived at the bottom with two houses either side that were empty during the week until gumbooted families came from somewhere and played with nature and each other from late Friday until Sunday afternoons. Non-villagers came from surrounding towns and other alien places to drink in the pub three doors away and have drunken fights after closing time, which she enjoyed. Such fun, my dears. She had moved each time because she had wanted to, and now she was stuck with the view and a role as a landlady which she only relished sometimes. The late Mr Edwin Hurly, who had been as difficult to acquire as he had been to keep until he wilfully released himself from the burden of life, would have approved. He had always liked white walls and might have enjoyed the thought of his widow being reduced to this screaming boredom with her own brand of venom neutralised. Mr Edwin Hurly had been an excellent provider, common as muck and hell to live with, as bullies are. The only love of his life had been his late-born and only legitimate child and even that had not lasted. He had come to prefer animals. The first thing Celia had done when he drowned on one of the deep-sea fishing trips he took every year to give himself a challenge and get away from the place he had failed to conquer was to get rid of the dog.

Another perfect day, then. The vicar is coming to tea. I can sing yet. Did I mean sting or sing? Someone will deliver organic vegetables and someone will come in to clean, so everything is all right with the world.

I would like to know who that woman is who took Jack Dunn's house, and why she took it in such a state without making any complaint about the dog hair. I would like to know where Jack Dunn's mad dog went after it was dumped on me, as if that was going to make up for the unpaid rent, but the agent deals with that. I don't care. Jack Dunn called his wretched dog Jess. That was why I couldn't keep it.

She stood by her window and sang DO-RE-ME-FAR-SO, loudly. The view remained roughly the same and no one noticed.

At high noon, inside the white room, Celia dressed in careful shades of grey and black: she could still afford her good old clothes whatever other economies she might have to make. She descended to the front door. Ignoring the lack of letters on the mat, she took her coat and her own version of a shopping trolley and opened the door. Manoeuvring the buggy, she sidestepped the puddles in the road outside, got to the end of the track flanking the houses and pushed herself up the steep incline, keeping to the middle of the road. Cars always stopped for someone pushing a baby buggy, not knowing that this buggy was empty. Celia was on her way to enliven the dull lives of the butcher and that horrible boy. She had all her spite and anger about her today, because she was sick of feeling simply sad. The boy only came in after twelve. Mrs Hurly reckoned she was the only person alive who knew exactly who he was: she could see a resemblance to that drowned good-looking bastard, her dear late husband.

Please come home, Jessie. Please understand that I am way too proud to ask. Please just arrive.

On her laborious way uphill she rejoiced in the muscular strength of her arms and the sound of cars braking either in front of her or behind. Everyone waited for the not-so-regal progress of the black widow Hurly, not because they knew who she was but because she was there.

'Are you open yet?'

The publican of The Star turned round quickly at the sound of a voice, ready to throw away his cigarette. With some amusement he had been watching Mrs Hurly make her way out of the sea road and creep up the hill. She could go a hell of a lot faster than that if she wanted; she was hardly ancient yet, or not in comparison with so many others who lived further up the hill. The village was a good place for aged widows far older than her to break their necks. It was polarised: suffocated by old men and women, hidden adults and small children. Once the kids hit school age they went away for years, got used to finding their entertainments somewhere else; the next town at least, which was so much more sociable than this. They came home from school, took off again and finally fled, except for a few of them. This was not the best place to have a pub when the main custom came from the weekenders, the occupants of the caravan park lurking discreetly behind the cliffs and the out-of-hours drinkers. A Monday just after midday was not a good one on which to ask if he was open yet.

'I'm always open,' he started to say. Then he recognised the face. Hurried him in.

The principal butcher's boy, referred to as an assistant, came in three days out of six, never early and always looking as if he'd had a hard weekend. Look at the state of him. A study in acne scars, a stupid hungover look on that unobservant thin little weasel face was what Mrs Celia Hurly saw and Sam always had the impression that she would like to pinch him, hard, except that she wouldn't want to get close enough. What was it with her and him? He thought he knew but he could have been wrong. Not a good afternoon for Sam the butcher, but Mondays were not his favourite days. At least no policeman had come to call, as on the Friday before. Jeremy, otherwise known as The Boy, would have hidden away at the sight of a uniform, on account of a long track record in the Youth Court, ten miles away: drunk and disorderly, out of his head on beer and spliffs, no money for anything more serious. Always under suspicion because he knew so much about firearms and other lethal weapons from the time he had worked in an abattoir, which was another piece of history that singled him out. One brick short of a load, it was whispered; at any rate a man with a general air of hangdog disgrace, and an absence of charisma. Jeremy the loser, the one with the missing cathode, the lad who looked bad at the start of the day and worse at the end because by then he seemed to have put his head in a vat of lard. Whenever indecisive (often) he ran his hands through his hair – there was no stopping him. His long blond hair was his best feature and he managed to mess that up too, so he looked even more like a prematurely aged hormone-driven teenager in need of the love of a good woman. Sam doubted the existence of a woman with enough patience to mine this particular twenty-eight-year-old gem, unless they could share his penchant for killing things. Harmless enough: Jeremy only took his air rifle to rooks, nuisancy pigeons and the rabbits which proliferated on the cliffs. Plenty spare, he told Sam: they need culling, why not eat 'em? There was a steady demand for Jeremy's rabbits, as long as no one knew where they came from. Always fresh, especially in spring. Soft and splendid, as if they had never known such a thing as rigor mortis and a life beforehand.

'Good morning, Sam, how nice to see you,' Celia Hurly said. 'Blood on your hands already, I see.'

Help. This was a spiteful day. A bad anger day: he could see the signs. She must have had a bad Sunday. Celia cooed at him in the same way that Mrs Smith cooed at deaf overfed seagulls, apparently regardless of their response.

'How nice everything looks. So clean. Sam, so very clean. I marvel at you really, managing with so little help.'

'Got plenty of help, Mrs Hurly, thank you. There's always our Jeremy and you know I've got a couple of lads in the afternoon for the hosing-down and scrubbing – if they turn up, that is. Not a germ in sight.'

'I didn't like what I ate yesterday.'

'No! Really! Why was that, I wonder?'

'I don't know. I just didn't like it.'

'Well, I never. Does that mean you're a bit poorly? Was it breakfast or dinner that did it?'

'I think the meat was bad.'

Sam shrugged, smiled; nothing you could do with Mrs Hurly on a bad day except humour her and deflect her from talking about the rent. Humour her, as everyone did, because she owned so much, including the freehold of the shop he leased from her fair and square, as he had from her husband, dating back to the days when old Hurly returned to the place of his childhood and bought everything he could for next to nothing, even the abattoir in Ripley. Who did she think she was, acting like a landlady when she didn't need the money and couldn't cancel the lease anyway? He wished he understood her and then decided it was better he did not. She just needed to lord it, so let her and if she also wanted to use his shop to announce any information she wanted spreading round, that was fine, too. He knew she could rely on him for that.

'Wash your mouth out, Mrs H. It wasn't any meat you had from here, was it? Otherwise you wouldn't be back for more.'

74

'Who says I want to buy anything? Can't I just pass the time of day?'

'Any time, Mrs H, any time. You could just come in for a lemon and we'd be pleased to see you.'

A downright lie, although the old duck did have some entertainment value on a good day, but otherwise, even with all that posturing as if she ruled the roost, she was only another widow like so many of the rest, although a bit better off than most and much more elegant, however she stooped. And a good customer; marvellous how much meat she could eat and waste and you had to be patient with her, on account of that and the fact she was on her own with a daughter like that, although whose fault that was, well, anyone's guess. You don't give a girl like that delusions of grandeur and expect her to behave well. No, he could put up with Mrs Hurly, as long as she didn't start on Jerry.

Who chose that moment to come out of the back with an armful of sausage which he dumped on the stainless-steel table to the left of the counter. Jerry was the best sausage maker on the planet and he was holding fifteen feet of pure pork snake to his chest with real affection. Easing the spool of sheep intestine skin onto the nozzle of the meat tank, pressing the motor pedal with his thigh and guiding the meat mix through his hands into the tubular skin so that it emerged evenly into a snakelike penis of even circumference – well, it was all a bit phallic, made them giggle, so better done out the back. Everything was moist. The sausage snake shook out of the machine's nozzle wetly and flopped. They often joked about it and swore at the machine, Jeremy and he, but not in front of the public. Jeremy looked as if he was handling a python: he was fully focused on the job of controlling it as he began his assembly line. He twisted off half of the sausage snake and suspended it on a hook so that it hung down like a smaller snake, with both ends level: then he began the twisting process, turning the snake into links of sausages. Pinch, twist, loop the end through, pinch, twist, loop, like plaiting hair, and lo! a row of sausages hanging in glisteningly symmetrical pairs in seconds. He picked up the next half of the snake.

Sarah, watching from the door, wanted to clap.

'I hope your hands are clean, Jeremy,' Mrs Hurly said. 'They don't look it.'

His hands were purple with cold and his face was flushed, the beak of his nose redder than his mottled forehead. The trainers beneath his trousers were greyish-dull, with a much-washed look, like the flaccid synthetic material of the trousers which flopped round his ankles and the faded shirt collar which poked, crooked, above his splashed apron at his narrow neck. He kept his back to her and touched the sausage tableau lovingly. Then he moved sideways to deal with the rest. Sam moved towards him, patting him on the back in passing as if to encourage him not to turn and face the enemy.

'Clean as a whistle, Mrs H. You know that. Like everything here. And isn't he clever? I never could string sausages as quick as that, and all the same size, too. He's a natural – well done, that man.'

'He's a dirty little beast,' Mrs Hurly said.

Sam began to whistle and look busy. If in doubt, sharpen a knife and take no notice. Pray for someone else to come in at the same time as Mrs Hurly, just as he did when he had a salesman in the shop. Bettaware, Tupperware, purveyors of plastic thingies, telephone lines, any damn thing, they could take up an hour a day. He glanced over to where Sarah stood at the door. She'd heard. Nice woman, chatty but reserved, he liked her, remembered he'd promised to get her herbs. Made a change from widows, but living in that place vacated by Jack Dunn, surely she knew that she was in the presence of her own landlady? He always had time for a woman who did not quarrel with the price of fillet steak.

'Look at him,' Mrs Hurly said to no one in particular, addressing her remarks to the ceiling as if only the ceiling would hear.

'Did you ever see anything quite so ugly-wuggly?' she asked. 'Or *quite* so awfully drab? Like he's been in the washing machine on the wrong cycle and come out the same *grey*, apart from the nose and the awful complexion. I don't know why you let him in here. Can't be good for business – who'd want what he's touched? Who knows where he's been?'

'Now, now, Mrs Hurly, mind the language. What can I get you?'

'The runt of the litter,' she continued. 'The nastiest little doggy. Can't he do anything about his face? Can't you send him next door to fix his hair? Shave it off to make it cleaner? Yes, a shaved head would be better, then he couldn't pass on his nits.'

Jeremy was reaching to place the second sausage length on the hook next to the first. The rail of hooks was set at the furthest reach of his long arms. The sausage slithered and slipped onto the sawdust-covered floor. He began to stamp on the meat with his feet until the sausage skin burst and the pulp mingled with the sawdust. He wiped his trainers on the mess and slowly turned around to look at Celia Hurly. Then he plucked a large knife from the rack. He held it above his head in both hands like a dagger, advanced a few steps uncertainly. His sweater rode up to show a fraction of pale torso: there were tears on his high-coloured face. Celia Hurly stood where she was, rooted to the spot in the middle of the floor, looking at him like a rabbit caught in headlights. Jeremy took one step further, his arms shaking; Sam watched, paralysed, thinking fucking do something, and then, out of his sideways vision, that woman stepped between Jeremy's sausage-strewn trainers and Celia Hurly's gaping face, tickled Jeremy's torso with her gloved hands. Tickling, not scratching, like someone tickling a kitten's tummy.

'Hey,' she said. 'That was great what you did with those sausages. Can I have some, please?'

The knife descended, as if of its own accord, until somehow it was cradled harmlessly across his chest, with his arms folded over it. He looked down at his sticky feet, then back up into Sarah's face, level with his own. Slowly, he began to grin.

'Cost you,' he said. 'Once they've gone on the floor, they're in the bin. I'll get wages stopped. Only joking.'

'You've got lovely eyes,' Sarah said. 'What's your name?'

The sweater and shirt had fallen back into place. She pulled his jumper down over his waist and straightened his collar, neatening him up. From behind them Mrs Hurly screamed.

'Sausages,' Sam muttered. 'Talk about sausages.'

Mrs Hurly screamed again in a short, sharp bark. Sarah turned and kicked her in the ankle. Mrs Hurly stopped screaming and started shouting.

'What what what . . . That little bastard tried to kill me, you saw, you saw, coming at me with a knife, and you . . . you kicked me. You saw what he did.'

'What knife?' Sarah asked pleasantly. 'I didn't see a knife. Did *you* see a knife?'

'No,' Sam said.

Sarah was blocking Celia's path towards the counter where Jeremy had retreated. Celia tried to sidestep her; Sarah moved in tandem so that they looked like two people rehearsing a dance routine and under cover of their odd movements the knife went back on the rack and Jeremy disappeared out to the rear.

'You kicked me!' Celia screamed, trembling with rage.

'Did I? I'm so sorry, I do apologise, it was an accident. You can kick me back if you like.'

Celia's jaw dropped.

'Can I ask you something?'

'What?'

'Were did you get that coat? It's really nice. Lovely line.'

'I . . .' Mrs Hurly clamped her mouth shut and stared at Sarah in disbelief.

'Anything I can get you, Mrs H?' Sam asked. 'Only it's half-day closing.'

'On a Monday?' she hissed. 'Since when?'

'Since now, Mrs H, I can have half-day closing any day I like. There's always tomorrow.'

Celia turned away abruptly and retreated to the open door where she grabbed hold of the baby buggy that she had left outside and began to walk away uphill, looking old and weary. Sam moved quickly to shut the door behind her and turned the open/closed sign to 'closed'. Then he strode towards the back of the shop, jerking his head towards Sarah to indicate that she could follow if she wanted. She did.

'Put the fucking kettle on, Jerry,' he yelled.

She could hear the sound of someone crying.

An echo in her head. I shouldn't have done that. *I wouldn't do that if I were you. DON'T.*

Mrs Celia Hurly would have said the same things to her daughter as Sarah would herself.

What a nasty old bitch. But no one was just that: it was never that simple.

Sarah went backstage.

CHAPTER FIVE

'He wouldn't have done anything, you know,' Sam said. 'He really wouldn't, even if he wasn't stuck to the floor. But I don't know quite what I'll do if she calls the police.'

'I was there,' Sarah said. 'There was no knife.'

'Sure about that?' He put a mug of tea in front of her. They were leaning against the deep stainless-steel sinks in the tiny kitchen area at the back. It was warmer than the small anteroom that led to it, via the stores and the chiller, and still only a few steps from the front.

'Perfectly sure,' she said, drinking her tea boiling hot. 'And I promise you, people tend to believe me, especially when I'm not telling the truth.'

He could see that. She had the bright-eyed direct gaze of innocent credibility and absolute conviction; she would convince anyone. Even that copper from last Friday would believe this redhead rather than grey-haired Celia Hurly, whatever her status and volume. Sarah would inspire belief with a pitying smile and a whisper. He put Sarah at forty;

that gave her at least twenty years on Hurly. Not fair, really, but then, Hurly had started it.

'Yes, I bet they do. Why did you do it?'

There was no hesitation.

'She was being absolutely poisonous. She deserved to be slapped rather than stabbed. I wanted to stop it.'

'He'd have tripped over his feet before he got there, you know.'

Sarah nodded. 'Yes, he probably would, and I probably knew that, too. I wasn't taking much of a risk. I'm not brave.'

'You move fast.'

'Only sometimes.'

Sam gulped his tea and shifted his bottom against the sink, shook his head. 'Beats me how you know how to make our Jeremy stop in his tracks. All you have to do is say something nice and touch him. He doesn't get much of that, it works every time.'

She shrugged. 'He's a man, isn't he? Do you know how he got the scar on his forehead?'

'He says it was a meat hook, they can catch you sometimes, but I don't know. He's somebody's bastard, all right, used to work in Hurly's abattoir. The Hurlys owned a lot round here, though he sold most of it before he died.'

'And that was Mrs Hurly? Who owns my house? Charmed, I'm sure. Why on earth has she got it in for him?'

Sam was relieved not to have to tell her that she had just kicked her landlady, and that others might be hanged for less, but he wasn't going to tell her everything, only enough.

'Don't rightly know, only Jeremy and Mrs Hurly's daughter once went to the same primary school, down the road, when it was still here.'

There was the sound of energetic sweeping and whistling from the shopfront. Jeremy had passed by twice, fetching broom and bucket, silent and smiling as he squeezed past. He seemed sublimely indifferent to the inevitability of them talking about him, or maybe that too was a rare privilege. Sam leant forward and whispered, 'They were sweet on one another, like little kids can be – he must have been a pretty little lad once – and they sat together and she got nits. Jeremy was blamed, like he always is. Mrs Hurly went mental, took Jessica out of there and sent her somewhere else while Jerry got his head shaved. He stayed sweet on her, though, not the only one round here, no, no, no. Or the only one to get nits. He'll start scrubbing the block in a minute. It's very high-tech – do you want to see? Poetry in motion, our Jerry.'

'You trust him, don't you?'

Sam gulped the tea and threw the dregs into the sink.

'Depends what you mean. To keep his temper when he's goaded, maybe not. To have the key to this shop and know his meat backwards, yes. To take my daughter out swimming and boating when she was a kid, to take you out on the beach or in a boat and show you where to find herbs and get everyone home safe, yes. To get here early and open up the shop, yes. To make sausages, yes. Phone him up in the middle of the night and say I've broken my leg, or the car broke down, come and find me, yes. Enough?'

Sarah laughed, pointed to a curled photo pinned to a corkboard alongside paper invoices near the sink and the kettle. The photo showed three beaming blondes.

'Christ, that's been there for ever. Those three are mine, all grown up now, two married, grew up around Jerry and that school. He's older than he looks, Jerry. They were all kids then. Oh yes, I trust our Jerry, as much as you can ever trust anyone who's been a bit bashed about. But,' he lowered his voice, 'I'll have to be honest and say I'm ever so glad he was never sweet on any of mine. I love the silly bugger, but he isn't the dream son-in-law, even if he does know his meat. I'd better get on.'

He heaved his bulk away from the sink and looked at her approvingly. He liked the way she noticed things, eyes everywhere. He'd forgotten that photo, forgotten half the things he'd ever known. She was taking in details like a Health and Safety Inspector, with a lot more charm. She noticed him noticing her noticing, and smiled, half embarrassed to be caught out.

'Sorry,' she said, 'but I love the back end of shops. I like the dirty bits, like seeing how things work. Can I stay a bit?'

'Only if you're useful. Jerry!' he yelled. 'This lady wants to know how to clean the block. Shall you show her?'

'All right.' A happy growl from the front.

'Then she wants you to take her on the beach to find herbs, OK?'

The shout was even louder, the reply too.

'All right!'

Sam took Sarah's arm and guided her to the front of the shop.

'I know you're going to be helping out the vicar with his decor, he said so when he bought his two sausages this morning, mean bugger, you must be mad. But if he needs extra labour Jerry'll help out, nothing he can't do, as long as you don't take advantage. If you do, I'll skin you, only I've been trying to find him a champion these last ten years.'

High-tech. This is how you scrub a butcher's block, or at least the way I do.

'You really want to know?'

'Show me and I'll do it.'

'Look at it first. Big butchery day today, started early, so this block's been well used, see? And only got sponged yesterday, so it needs the scrub, get the fat and blood out. Love this block, a foot thick, dipped in the middle, solid oak. Weighs a fucking ton, when it wears down turn it over and start again, takes years for that. First a big bucket of hot water and detergent, any old kind. Scrub it all over, work in the soap, lift the fat and the grease to the surface, scrub it out of the crevices. Do that twice, big fat brush, not the hardest brush, that's later.'

They were both talking at once. Sarah started on it, sloshed the water on the block, soaking herself. Then she scrubbed randomly.

'You're using too much water and too much fucking soap, do it in sections so you know where you've been,' Jeremy said. 'No worries – where do you come from, by the way? Not round here, I've seen you out walking, I saw you on the cliffs, miles away on Sunday, only you don't really know where to go, do you? OK, that's enough, now for the hard part. Two kettles of boiling water, dissolves the soap, see? A gallon's enough, the block's only five by three, only then you've really got to get the shit out. Lots of clean sawdust on top of the water, cover it, go on, use more, pour it on.'

He showed her: she did it. First the steaming water, which brought bubbles to the surface, then a thick layer of fresh sawdust poured from a sweet-smelling sack, absorbing the water. She spilled plenty. Then he showed her how to draw quarters on the sawdust with a finger, so she would know where she was and not miss out any part of the surface.

'Now you scrub really hard, no, not the same brush, it's

dirty as well as the wrong kind of brush, see what I mean? You need a hard wire brush. Start at the corner of square one, you've got to scrub until that wet surface is so dry it's white, scrub that sawdust in and scrub it out, big brush, use your arms. Good, you've got it, less water another time, then the next quarter, then do it all again. Watch it change colour.'

Sarah scrubbed in sections as if her life depended on it, watching as the sawdust soaked up the moisture and the surface changed from dark to lime white as if it had been bleached. Jeremy chatted. Sam laughed at her clumsiness.

'Would you believe,' he said, 'that stuck-up Mrs Hurly's daughter used to like doing this when she was a kid. She liked it here. Kids do.'

Sarah paused for a minute, let that sink in along with the sawdust. It figured. Jessica Hurly liked hard work. She continued to scrub, even after Jeremy said that's enough. Then they scrubbed the legs of the table, leaving her exhilarated with the achievement. She stood back and admired.

'Can I do this every day?' she said.

'We don't do it every day.'

The sun was leering through the window, the way it would for another hour. Sarah swept the floor and sprinkled more sawdust, the natural cleanser, forgetting how cold it was in the room. Sam put on his coat to go home and unlocked the front door.

'You want a job, you got it, provided you don't want pay. Scat, the pair of you. I'm off.'

Sarah had never really explored the beach, concentrating on the heights and the fields behind where she could look down, so far preferring to avoid the sea at sea level. The single-track road to the next town ran roughly parallel to a flat expanse of shingle: scrub-covered beach for the first mile after the houses ran out. Beyond the flat expanse the beach dipped sharply, so that the point where the sea actually embraced the land was invisible except to someone who walked over the rim. Invisible but never inaudible, either murmuring or roaring at a safe distance, still scaring her down at this level with the knowledge that it could at any time either creep or roar up the banks of stone and engulf her, like the hungry beast it was. She had walked via the road to the next town, feeling exposed even there, because no one else walked and when a car hove into view she had to step back onto the bank. The road turned inland, leaving a bicycle track by the edge of the shore. Then the cliffs ran out and the beach became a broader, bleaker expanse without shelter, with a fabulous horizon but little temptation to venture over the shingle, which was hard on the feet. It had seemed unwelcoming and impenetrable, the scrubby bushes and hardy thistles forming a dense untidy litter, denying free passage anywhere away from the cycle track. She could not imagine it crowded, even in the height of summer. It was a million miles from the warm sandy beaches of holiday destinations, bleak, wild and empty in the late days of winter when she had arrived and avoided it. She told Jeremy she had been a sissy about the beach itself and was waiting for warmer weather, or at least a day without a stiff breeze coming straight off the sea, challenging anyone to come closer. She had definitely needed a guide to the beach, and now she had one, as well as a near-perfect day to broach its alien landscape.

Jessica's voice came back. *I burned my boats.* They were partway across the level stretch of half scrubland, half shingle that she had regarded as another kind of jungle, making for the sea, and she was full of the joy of discovery. Not only was this a whole new view, it was an alternative world: the scrub was not the grey stuff she had dismissed, but glorious harmonious growth in delicate shades of green and silver, tight buds of pink and the beginning of tufty yellow flowers on pale stems. There were drifts of feathery green fern close to the ground, bordering the myriad pathways which meandered forever onwards in an indirect route towards the bare shingle. It was like being in a benign maze of colour, nothing growing higher than the knees. There were shrubs blown sideways by the wind, still standing and creeping, determined upon survival albeit without elegance, nudging at thistle leaves still soft in the spring. Jeremy was telling her about the pinks and the red-hot poker flowers which would come later. You wanted herbs, he said; there'll be plenty of fennel and sage and garlic anytime soon. Best in May, though.

Once they reached the rim Sarah turned back to look at the land. The cliffs sloped away on this side of the village, flattening out but still hiding it. She realised that the most complete view of the place was from the sea itself, and even that was incomplete. Standing on the rim of the steep slope which led down to the now shockingly close waves, she felt she really was on the edge of the world and had the exhilarating sensation of having conquered something, plus the satisfying knowledge that she was going to come here again and again.

'Can you swim here, Jeremy?'

'Oh yes, but watch out for the current. Swim and fish, especially fish. More fishing than swimming. See the boats?'

Yes, she could see the boats, a small colony of them

parked on the sea side of the second shingle shelf, hidden either from the track or from anywhere except the sea itself. The colony of boats, winches and sheds was a startling reminder of humanity in the middle of nothing. Another invisible scene, solid shapes gaining focus as they walked closer. Sarah was puzzling out how they came to be there, how did they get there: how did they get from there into the water and how were they hauled back – a list of questions forming. It was clearer when they drew closer, crunching over the shingle, she awkwardly, he to the manner born, and she could see the wooden planked runway leading down to the water's edge and away from the colony into the scrubland, see the winches and the chains and gauge the disparate sizes of the five or six solid boats, each with a cabin, room enough for two perhaps and for tackle. Two of them had huge bulbous motors attached to the stern, bent back into the boat: the others did not. They lay about in various attitudes of drunkenness, mostly old and worn and hard-worked. They all looked in need of repair, crippled boats, some with charred wood, hibernating for winter and spring, needing love and money. Sarah tried to imagine taking one of these out onto the ocean and could not, even though she had seen others this side of the horizon without ever thinking from where they might have started. The colony was deserted. Again she remembered Jessica saying *I burned my boats.*

There was a purpose in everything, surely. Jeremy patted the prow of the first boat with the sort of absent-minded affection he might bestow on an old pet.

'I'm working on this one,' he said.

This one stood upright: she could just see a random mess of nets and metal drums inside it, human detritus in the wheel cabin – abandoned thermos flask, a coat and a grubby cushion – and could see it also as someone's home from home. Maybe no one took these old broken boats out to sea: maybe they just came here on warm days and sat in them until they reeked of fish.

Jeremy had been a quiet companion, grinning over his shoulder and leading the way downhill and along, responding to questions without volunteering much while she was content to be led. He did not behave as if he owed her anything, or as if there was anything odd about responding to an order to take a helpful stranger for a walk. He had been asked to show her the beach and that was what he was doing, simply taking the chance to return to a favourite place. Now he leant his long arms into the boat and stared across it.

'Nobody fishing today,' Sarah said.

He nodded at her statement of the obvious.

'Not every day. No point today, not a good day for it. Besides, these aren't seaworthy yet.'

She was grateful not to be blinded with science as to why it was not a good day for it, although she was curious to know if the boat colony represented the getting of a living from the sea or was merely for sport. It looked too businesslike to be a luxury activity; the boats were hardly streamlined for simply cruising around. The dinghies she had seen out at sea were for fun: these were workhorses.

'We had one of these once,' Jeremy said. 'Least my grandad had. He took me out when I was little. I liked it best, but then when you've got a boat you like it better than anything.'

She could see that: you would love one of these better than life, especially if it sheltered you and earned you a living.

'What do you like doing best, Jeremy?'

He thought about it.

'Sex, if I can get it.'

She threw back her head and laughed – there was no doubting his honesty now. It was probably what most truthful youths would say, perhaps only to a woman of her age who was beyond the pale.

'Never there when you want it,' she said, 'that's the problem. Or maybe too much of it when you don't.'

'That's never been my problem,' he said.

He handed her the bunch of fennel he had picked from beside the pathways, looked up to the sky.

'Otherwise I don't know what I like best, down here or . . .' He pointed back towards the cliffs. 'Depends on the day.'

Sarah decided to chance her arm.

'Did you ever have sex with Jessica Hurly? Is that why Mrs H doesn't like you?'

Now it was Jeremy's turn to laugh. He moved from the side of the boat, picked up a pebble and threw it towards the water. They were still a distance from the waves that were munching at the shore gently in unusual calm, twenty yards maybe, but she saw his stone drop into the water, felt she could hear it plop. There was nothing else to do on this beach other than throw stones, or launch a boat and go fishing and she could see herself baking on it in the summer, and had made herself an inventory of what she would have to bring, cushion, beach towel, water, food, before he answered. Over the last hour she had come to understand that he should not be hurried: he would hurry himself, his reactions were sharp, and he was far from being the village idiot. Translated into city terms, he would have been the computer geek who preferred screens to people; social graces were not his strong point.

'Jessica Hurly?' he shouted, throwing another stone that splashed into the water at exactly the same point as the first. 'Jessica Hurly? Don't be daft. Every lad else shagged Jessie, or she shagged him. Jessica was fucking nuts. Shaun Smith, Robert, Will, the whole lot from Primary, only girl I know who led a pack and shagged the lot of them, and that was only the kids, never mind the old men. Yeah, maybe she *did* have too much sex, I never got near, 'cos I was never part of any of them. It's not *that* makes Mrs Hurly so mad, not me shagging Jessica, it's her old man shagging my mother, that's what counts with her. Want to go down to the sea?'

They left the shelter of the boats and walked towards the sea. The land behind them and the village seemed irrelevant right at the water's edge and the wind became stronger. Looking down the deserted shoreline, Sarah could see the beginnings of the next town in the distance, and then another outcrop of boats and sheds where the real industry was, as opposed to this deserted encampment of damaged goods. She let the sea lap over the toes of her boots and then retreated, then advanced, wanting to dance with it, resisting the impulse to scream like a child. The sea was so calm that he could skim stones across the surface, making them bounce, once, twice, three times before sinking, a talent she had always envied, and told him so. He shrugged it off, the way she imagined he might shrug off all praise, even if he stored it away safely.

Throwing stones did not ward off the increasingly cold and darkening sky. By common accord they turned their backs to the water and half walked, half scrambled up the shingle bank to where the scrubland began, stopping at the boats.

'Tell me things,' Sarah said. 'Tell me about the Hurlys. Jessica's my friend, I need to know why she can't come back.'

Jeremy looked at her directly for the first time. He had blue eyes, like Jessica's, but then so did others. They might resemble one another in that way, as well as in the abundance of hair and their gangly height, if only he were not so lacking in lustre when he was not moving. He had Jessica's animation only when he was throwing stones and now, as he fumbled in his pockets for a ready-made reefer – the first of the day, perhaps, but certainly not the last. The smell of it hung on the air.

'Hurly was brought up here. Was a butcher's boy. Lived below stairs in that house you're going to be painting, only then it was a leaking wreck and them as poor as mice, my gran says. Laughed at, they were, she says. He certainly knew how to hunt for food. Pennyvale was stinking poor then, not like now. Anyway, they all went away and old Hurly got rich in the butchery business and came back, bought two or three houses, and a shop, always wanted the vicarage, but couldn't get it, see? Came back with a tart he'd married in London. King of the roost, he was, owned the abattoir. He wanted a fishing boat, too, but no one would sell him a boat, or let him moor it. Nobody liked him.'

Jeremy sucked smoke into his lungs greedily. Sarah nodded encouragement and stroked the fennel in her hands. She wondered if 'Gran' was still alive, how accurate the information was. She would like to meet Gran – or Mum, for that matter.

'Gran's dead,' he said, answering an unspoken question. 'And Mum never says nothing, never will, I don't think. She lives in Kingsley now, I don't know where. Anyway, she worked for the Hurlys, cleaning and that, and old man Hurly shagged her and she had me, and Dad left. Funny how she'd never been able to have kids until she worked for him. Gran worked it out. So did Mrs H, although nothing was ever said.'

'Gran might have worked it out wrong,' Sarah suggested.

'I don't think so. Why else was she sacked? Why else did she have a bit of money, all of a sudden? Why else would Mrs Hurly get so mad about Jessica and me kissing as kids?'

'Nits?'

'We all had nits in that school, so did the teachers. Lots of silly nits!'

They were back into the mysterious maze of plants: Sarah wanted it to be a forest. It was getting dark and she wanted to go home, but above all she wanted to know more.

'Did Jessica ever know about this?'

'No, not her. No one told her. She'd have come and found me if she did.'

'That's not why she left?'

'Everyone leaves,' Jeremy said, 'except me.'

It was almost dark by the time they were back in the main street, walking home. There were few enough street lamps to illuminate the road. She thought of inviting him in for a cup of tea or something, decided this was presuming too much. All very well to be at close quarters with Jeremy in the open air, perhaps not indoors, even at her age; but something had been established between them, so she asked him anyway and was relieved when he refused.

'Thanks a lot,' she said. 'That was wonderful. I was scared of the sea. Perhaps you'll show me the best place to swim when it's warmer?'

'Sure.' He shrugged. 'But you'd be better off learning to

fish, at least you can eat it. I'd teach you how to fish if I had a boat still.'

'What happened to your grandad's boat?'

'Don't know. Might have been one of those that Jessica burned. Look, I've got to go now.' He nodded towards the house. 'Nice house, this, I like this house.'

'Are you sure you won't come in?'

'No, thanks. It's Jack Dunn's house, really. Jessica shagged him, too. He was dead keen on her. Called his dog Jess. Perhaps because she was pretty.'

Once inside, feeling the warmth of home, Sarah paced up and down, thinking. There was an overpowering, interfering desire to acquaint Jessica with the fact that she might have a half-brother.

No, she would never do that: that would be gross interference on the basis of flimsy hearsay. Phone her anyway: she wanted to hear her, tease her about cleaning the block and be teased herself. Confess that she had met her mother and it had not gone well. Weekends excepted, it was a rare day not to hear from Jessica for a brief hello, how-are-you-doing, hurried chat at least and it suddenly seemed a long time. Three days: Sarah felt lazy and disloyal.

She tried all evening, but there was no reply. It did not worry her the first few times and then it began to nag like toothache. Jessica never ignored her phone unless she was ashamed of something: something was wrong; she had done something silly. It felt as if she might have known that Sarah was finding out about her, getting to know her from other sources and she had decided she did not want to be known. Withdrawing from contact. Jessica had the keys to Sarah's flat, to use as she wished: if her phone was lost, she could phone from there.

Maybe she was on her way here, wanting to surprise. But why not phone?

Sarah slept uneasily, waiting for sounds, hoping for a knock on the door or the phone to ring.

Ah well, another dawn.

CHAPTER SIX

Over breakfast in the morning, Sarah found the leaflet she had picked up in the church and stuffed into her handbag. Maybe best to have a little more knowledge before a morning with the vicar.

This church is named for Saint Bartholomew the Apostle, of whom little is known except that he was also known as Nathaniel, an Israelite in whom there was no guile. He preached the gospel successfully in Armenia, although finally suffering martyrdom, according to legend, by being flayed alive and beheaded. (Vicar's notes: what he did to deserve this isn't known, poor sod.) He was finally interred in Rome, on the site of an old pagan medical centre, which gave rise to other hospitals being established in his name. His emblem is a butcher's knife.

It is believed this church was once also an infirmary for men of the sea, and that is why it bears his name.

The day was dreary grey and bitterly cold, a great day for housework. Sarah was thinking what a forgotten word that was and was still astounded to find how she reacted to the weather. Here it dictated the course of every single day, instead of being the irritating irrelevance that it was in a city. Here and now it changed every minute, dictated moods and was the arbiter of events.

She checked the limited sea view, obscured by mist today, rain forecast. She checked Jessica's phone: *number not available*. All in all, a good day for distracting herself, because Jessica had swung back into her mind like a black cloud of mosquitoes that she wanted to swat away. She had forgotten her other agenda and now she had to remember it.

The vicarage was in the high street, at the downhill end, separated from the church by the graveyard. It was gloomily separate, with a small front garden boxed in by a privet hedge on three sides. There was no latch gate from the street, only an untidy gap in the hedge and a path, flanked by two patches of plain grass, leading to the front door. The frontage was Georgian in style if not vintage, with big ground-floor windows and pillars standing guard over the front-door porch. Someone had messed around with this house. The path was green with moss, the pillars were made of pock-marked concrete and the front door was painted in cheerless, blistered black. The walls on either side bore traces of recently removed ivy, leaving faint trails that crept away from the windows. Handsome but forbidding, the house seemed as if it was trying to repel visitors instead of offering them succour. The new electric bell played a hymn tune, possibly the same as the vicar's mobile-phone tone – a bit camp, maybe. He did slightly overdo the gay persona. Before the door opened she found herself thinking of Jessica's phone, which played 'Greensleeves'. Jessica's silent phone, nagging away, refusing to be forgotten.

'I can't believe this is happening,' the vicar said. 'I really can't believe you're doing this. Are you a mirage? Does God Almighty send you loaded with gifts? Come in, come in.'

Sarah was armed with a bucket of scrubbing brushes, cleaning cloths and dust sheets, a regular Mrs Mop. The first thing she noticed – for the second time – as she squeezed her way inside was the brown wallpaper in the dark hallway. The hall led on to stairs: two doors opened off it into reception rooms facing the front. Andrew led her into the first.

'I exaggerated,' he said. 'It's not really so bad. I'm not thinking of doing the whole house, it's really just this room. Oddly enough, Father Gavin and his wife, killjoys that they were, did all right with the upstairs and the kitchen, where they spent most of their time, but with *this* room, the receiving room, as it were, and the hall, well, it's as if they were trying to keep people out. You know, make it as dreary as possible so no one would be tempted to come back. No, that's being unkind, maybe they just couldn't afford it. The only person who can stand this room is Mrs Hurly, when she comes to tea, and even she doesn't take her coat off. It's a room for shouting in, and I sort of wish it was and wish it wasn't. It's got to have a better purpose than that, hasn't it?'

It was a beautiful room, begging for the light to be let in. High ceilings with plain cornices, two huge windows almost to floor level giving onto the front garden. On the wall opposite the windows there was a blocked-off fireplace with two armchairs either side, looking as if they were paying homage to non-existent flames. A meagre amount of heat circulated from the single radiator. A sofa stood between the windows, miles away from the fireplace. The ceiling was mercifully off-white, the walls a dull maroon, the carpet a drab olive green to match the darker green of the upholstery and the only other light apart from daylight came from an unpleasant triangle of bulbous spotlights in the centre of the ceiling. There was an additional optional standard lamp in stainless steel and with a bent stem, so crooked and discordant that it looked as if someone had hit it sideways. The ambience of the whole room reminded her of a spectacularly dull waiting room, deliberately designed to exaggerate the anxieties of anyone waiting in it. The central light in particular had a *we-have-ways-of-making-you-talk* feel, and the thought of Mrs Hurly taking tea in it cheered Sarah mightily. The most positive objects on view were six cans of white paint lined up against the wall, alongside a serviceable-looking ladder.

'If you can enliven this space I shan't know how to thank you, I really shan't. It needs more than magic, and if you really provide that I don't know how I'd ever repay you.'

She considered the view.

'It needs a bit of work, rather than magic. But as for thanks, you could leave that to God or you can take on my mortal soul for redemption – it could do with it. A cup of coffee would be nice to be going on with, and what the hell is this room *for?*'

The vicar paused for effect before announcing something ready-rehearsed. He found it difficult to articulate why it was that the room was slightly cursed.

'It's the padded cell of Pennyvale,' he said. 'My predecessor said it was the designated room for arguments. You know, like the bleak interview cell you see in TV thrillers, the anonymous room where you can lie on your back and squeal like a stuck pig, get your emotions out. It was where people came to take counsel and bad instant coffee. Married couples, people with children problems, people at screaming pitch one way or another, could come here and slug it out without anyone hearing a thing, because you can't, you know, you really can't. The last vicar fancied himself as a counsellor, which may have something to do with the diminishing congregation. I've got another view on that; I think he was lazy enough not to want it to look nice in case anyone would want to use it. I think a priest should encourage celebration, but this one needs help. Shall I make the coffee, I do good coffee, leave you to think about it?'

Surely a room for counselling should be small and cosy, or dark like the traditional confessional, which, when she came to think of it, also defied intimacy. This was a room for clearing the throat, saying *Hmm* and not knowing where to start. Did village people bring their errant children here for a rebuke from the vicar in lieu of a village policeman? It was a punitive room: it had sadness in its very walls, and yet she could see it full of people having a great party. No one had ever been allowed to relax in here, let alone smoke. Sarah was sorry for them all on that account, but pleased that the lack of any festive action had left the ceiling pristinely untouched by champagne corks or nicotine. She touched the dark walls – not bad, not too many cracks – but how many coats of paint would it take to make it pale but interesting? That central light would have to go. There were scuff marks round the skirting boards from enthusiastic hoovering of the sick, threadbare carpet, which should have crawled away before it met the moths.

Andrew came back with coffee on a tarnished silver tray, proper coffee in a cafetière, china mugs. The mobile phone in his pocket rang, loud in the space. He muttered 'Excuse me,' and left the room for a minute. She helped herself, sat in the uncomfortable armchair by the blocked-up fireplace, thought strategy, mobile phones and how to hire a steam cleaner. Sam the butcher would know. Either that or get Jeremy to scrub the carpet in the same way he scrubbed the block, just to see if there was anything to discover beneath the patina of genteel grime, otherwise haul it up and hope to discover wood. She strode to the far corner of the room where the carpet was fraying round the edges, grabbed it and pulled. Badly laid, cheap carpet, scarcely nailed down, it came away easily, revealing disintegrated yellow underlay and, beneath that, planks. The excitement was almost unbearable. By the time Andrew came back she had rolled away a whole noxious strip of the stuff and the air was full of dust.

'What on earth are you doing? You can't do that.'

'Why not?' she asked, panting.

'It isn't my house, it isn't my carpet . . . Oh bugger it, why not, indeed? I've wanted to vandalise this place so much it pains me. Oh look. A floor.'

Such a shared, wonderful joy, the finding of that floor. They stood and grinned at one another. Andrew wondered later if those who had discovered Australia felt the same unholy joy as he did on the discovery of a not-so-bad wooden floor. Not glorious, but OK. There's no money to sand it, he warned, it costs a bomb. OK, Sarah said, we scrub it and bleach it, that's what we do, just like you'd do with an imperfect soul you cannot make perfect, you do what you can. We could try sawdust and soap and water. First get rid of the crap.

It was one of the most refreshing and exhausting mornings he had had for ages, and the sun came out to cheer, briefly. He felt happy. Lord, he said, physical labour is good for the mind. By noon the carpet, which conveniently fell to pieces as they attacked it, was all sitting on the damp grass outside and the room felt relieved by its absence.

'The only problem,' Andrew said, as they sat and surveyed it through the window and ate the sandwiches he had made, 'will be when Mrs Hurly wants to come to tea. She won't like this at all, doesn't like change. It might have been her carpet in the first place, come to think of it, she was always donating things to the last incumbent; they were bosom buddies. I hope she doesn't notice as she goes up the street. I've made a point of going to tea with her today, rather than the other way round, so maybe it'll be all right.'

'So you have to be bosom buddies with my landlady too, do you? Why's that?'

He shrugged. 'Donations, donations, donations. We can't keep the organ going without Mrs Hurly and a couple of others, her most of all. And she claims huge affiliations with this house because her husband grew up here. He paid for a new roof here before he died and I've got every reason to be grateful for that. And the last vicar and his wife were so good to her daughter, blah, blah, blah. I'm being churlish. There's a good woman in there: she's just lost. She wants to open up, but she can't so she criticises.'

'You know what that sounds like?' Sarah said. 'It sounds like this bloody Mrs Hurly had the last vicar and his wife in her pocket and on her charity bankroll, and expects you to dance to order in the same way. Without the moolah, if you see what I mean. Just guessing.'

He sighed, looking at a callus growing on his hand with evident satisfaction. How fast things went when they were shared.

'It's not far off, for a guess. I don't seem to have much choice. What else do you know?'

Sarah took a deep breath. It was high time this man knew there was a quid pro quo for painting his front room and getting rid of his carpet. Nothing was for nothing, even if it was a pleasure. He clearly knew more than he thought he did, if only obliquely. She liked the man and did not want to deceive him. The thought of silent Jessica still nagged away, whatever the distraction. She was present in this room: Sarah could feel her presence.

'Look, vicar, sorry, Andrew, I may as well come clean. I'm a dual-purpose person, well, usually three at any given time. I'm here in Pennyvale, which I think is a wonderful place, apart from having such a twee name, because I wanted to be somewhere like this, not right here, necessarily, but somewhere with most of these ingredients: village, not town, roses round the door, all that stuff. I'm here in particular because Jessica Hurly, my young friend, introduced me to it and it turned out to be what I was looking for and her mother has places to rent . . . and, and, oh never mind the ands. And because Jessica told me things, alluded to things, and I know she's at odds with her mother and feels she can't come home, I just thought, while I was here, well, you know, I thought I might try and fix it, even though I don't know what's to fix. I'm worried about her, she's a bit messed up and everyone needs a mother, I should know and . . .'

Andrew was frowning at her from a distance, puzzled by all the 'ands' but listening intently. He would not judge her harshly. The mobile phone in his pocket went off.

'Excuse me,' he said again.

Sarah got up as he left the room and she opened the first can of paint. Ugh, dead white. She didn't like dead white; it always had to be white with an undertone of something else, cream or butter, or pink or blue. Dead white was the colour of dead skin and lard, but it would do for the first undercoat. She picked a brush from the equipment she had bought, dipped it in the paint and applied it to the purple wall in a tentative smear. Lovely, anything was better than that. She looked at her watch; at least a few hours of daylight for the task, they could do one whole coat if he helped. As long as he continued talking. She stripped off her sweater, revealing a sleeveless T-shirt, manhandled the ladder and stuck it up by the windows, start here by taking down the curtains. The room cried out for blinds, or no curtains at all. She was framed in the window stretching up, when Andrew came back. She might as well have been advertising herself to the street, a small, shapely body fully extended and with a straining bosom.

'Speak of the devil,' he said, 'and the devil arrives.' And then, as a spontaneous afterthought, 'What a jolly good figure you've got. You look perfectly lovely up there.'

'You're not so bad yourself, Andrew.'

He sat down heavily as if shocked at the sight of her, framed in the light with her red hair blazing, a revelation.

'Bugger. That was Mrs Hurly. She wants to come to tea after all. She has something very pertinent to discuss. Wants my advice.'

'Ah.'

He stood up and shook himself. Sarah got down off the ladder, entirely aware of the effect she had had, and came and stood beside him.

'You're using me, aren't you?' he said sadly.

'That's what friends do, even new friends,' she replied. 'I'll happily paint the walls for nothing, I'll even pay for the privilege, but I need to find out Jessica Hurly's history if I'm going to effect some sort of reconciliation. She didn't ask, I volunteered. It isn't much to ask, is it?'

'Are we friends?' he asked, his face breaking into the smile that transformed it.

'Yes, we are – at least, I am. You can speak for yourself.'

The smile widened into a laugh. He should do more of that, too.

'That's all right, then. That means I'm perfectly free to break the secrets of the confessional and all for a Christian purpose. Look, I really don't know the particulars of Jessica's disgrace, it was before my time, she left as I arrived, but it can't have been anything too terrible, youthful exuberance, oh, hell, yes, it was. Better come clean. She was the reason for the last vicar leaving, you see; she was how I got this job.'

He coughed: dust, embarrassment. She thought he was probably a compulsive divulger of secrets, given a chance. A perfect keeper of them too, just as she was. One day she might be able to tell him about her fear of fire, but not now; better to stick to the point.

'How come?'

'He couldn't go on, you see. Not after she accused him of raping her. She did it in church, just as he was starting evensong.'

Sarah dropped the paintbrush back into the can and watched it sink. Well, well. Anxiety for Jessica started all over again – as if it had ever gone away.

'Was it true?'

'I've no idea. In light of the fact that she also accused the doctor, the butcher and a couple of others of something similar, and withdrew the allegations, probably not.'

'I wish,' Sarah said after a long pause, 'that she'd told me that. Someone told you.'

'Not her mother, for sure. A helpful member of the

congregation took notes and passed them on, and the dreadful do-call-me-Gavin left me a letter saying I should be very careful in my dealings with one Jessica Hurly. I also gathered that my chief qualification for getting this job was being gay, so I've been camping it up ever since. How times change. I should also be kind to her mother, who had once been a generous Christian.'

Village life, the pursuit of perfection, attention to detail. Sarah felt utterly dismayed. She looked at the smear of virginal white paint on the walls for inspiration, remembering how she should never believe anything without checking, felt sick with pity. True or false, it was equally pitiable. Andrew was looking distinctly shifty. No, not shifty as in deceptive; shifty as in confused.

'Very interesting,' she said. 'So where did all this sexual mayhem take place? Here? In church, in this very room?'

Andrew walked towards the window, checking the street.

'I don't know. I'm not supposed to know as much as I do know and it hasn't seemed a good idea to find out the details. There weren't any charges or investigations, just an . . . outburst, so that was that, not discussed, everyone leaves and murmurs a bit, the Pennyvale way of doing things.'

He was looking at his watch, something he did involuntarily, as if it provided a solution.

'Anything else?'

He shook his head, trying to downgrade the information as soon as he gave it, possibly the approach he adopted towards sermons. Sarah could not see him describing the real temperature of hellfire. He would try to mitigate the burden of that for the children at least. She had watched him with the children, warmed to his indecision, even as there was more clearing of the throat.

'Not really. Only the *specific* thing Madam Hurly wishes to discuss and elicit advice on, which is . . .'

Cough, cough, cough.

'She says her daughter was seen in the village yesterday. Mrs Smith told her. She shouted at her that Jessica, or *Jez*, as she calls her, was back. *She* thought Jessica might have come straight here, although why anyone should think that, I don't know either. Apparently everyone in the hairdresser's thinks she's back, so it's definite.'

Sarah only heard that *Jessica was back*.

'So maybe now I'll get the whole story,' Andrew said. 'Like I haven't before. I thought I might put her in the kitchen, on account of redecorations, which are pretty obvious, what with all that carpet outside. God knows why she wouldn't let me go to her, but she insisted. And perhaps you can sit in the scullery and eavesdrop. She's due in fifteen minutes.'

They seemed to know one another very well; the instant recognition of strangers on a train, but the understanding was not yet entirely accurate. Sarah was cleaning the paint-brush against a wall, getting rid of the surplus, putting the lid on the tin of paint.

'No,' she said. 'I couldn't keep still, you see. I tell you what, you get the whole story, then you tell me tomorrow. I've got to go.'

Jessica's come home. She's safe. Glory be.

Sarah hurried uphill.

How did they pass news around here? Where was the conduit, the river running through it? Or was news confined to tiny cliques that did not impinge on one another, did they e-mail and text rather than speak out loud? How could you earn true disgrace around here, since no one seemed either to notice or care what anyone did? Was the church, with its diminutive congregation, the only place for making actual announcements? She was racing back up the street, thinking Jessica's come home, she might be at my house, she said she would come back after dark, and if she was here yesterday, where did she go? *Mummy owns lots of houses.* Is Mummy playing double bluff, and why didn't I stay and listen?

It was suddenly colder, the sun forgotten, the clouds gathering, rain imminent. Sarah hurried out into the street, pulling her hood over her head, giving out the don't-talk-to-me signal to the two single pedestrians she met going uphill before she was level with the butcher's. The school bus created a traffic jam by depositing a dozen children who ran away in the thin veins of roads and houses leading off, clutching mobile phones and screaming insulting goodbyes.

Jessica would be there, listening out for seagulls, or in the kitchen, chopping herbs, ready to tell the truth. Sarah had such a conviction of this that she wanted to call out her name. It was darkening, mid-afternoon on a spring day and it felt like the middle of the night. She hesitated outside the butcher's shop, but it was relatively full, three or four people in there, ordering, talking, delaying departure against the rain, Sam holding forth, gesturing, with a knife in his hand. Sam, a seducer of innocence, or merely a public figure it was fun to accuse? She waved as she went by: Sam was too busy to notice, but Jeremy did and waved back extravagantly, motioning her to come in, come in. She shook her head and carried on. That was the place, the only place, where the real business of talking was done. That would be the place for announcements and news, far more effective than church.

She checked her mobile phone. No word from Jessica, Jessie, Jezebel, *Jez.*

The rain was coming down by the time Sarah unlocked her door, giving way to the temptation to call out, 'Jess? Are you there?' The instinct to shout born of nothing but nights of bad dreams about her.

Silence in here. No messages, no response to the number she rang. *This person is unavailable*.

But all the same, someone had been here.

CHAPTER SEVEN

'My daughter wrecked my life,' Celia Hurly said to the vicar of Pennyvale. 'But that's what children do, don't they?'

'I don't know about that,' he said. 'Being gay, I'm not likely, etc.' He always mumbled around her; he did it a lot, especially when she was drinking the bottle of wine he had hoped to share with someone else and determined to resist himself, so that he could remember every detail in order to repeat it verbatim. How strange and oddly unchristian to be eavesdropping by proxy.

'Rubbish, Andrew Sullivan, you'll know all about having daughters and sons one day, probably, you're scarcely forty. I've seen how you really like the children. One day you'll know. I was over forty when *she* arrived.'

Celia Hurly was one of those women who believed that homosexuality was a curable aberration, which amused Andrew, although she was a little more accurate than she knew. He smiled the beatific smile he could always call up to order, reached forward and touched her knee, every inch the safe, solicitous parson. He disliked her for blaming her daughter for wrecking her life: that simply was not fair. As far as he was concerned, children were an enhancement to life, a piece of glorious good luck and a privilege, however they turned out. It made him disposed to pity the mysterious Jessica Hurly, whereas he certainly had not done so before now, even if he did have reason to thank her.

'So explain,' he said. 'I'm listening.'

He was trying to recall what on earth Celia usually talked about; something and nothing, never anything intimate. Parish affairs, flowers for the church, criticisms of the living and more of the dead, the agony of life with an errant husband and the loneliness of her own disgraceful widowhood. And then she would surprise him with something she had noticed, give him money for the children, to be used anonymously. She rarely mentioned Jessica, an awkward subject, best avoided. He had not lied when he had said there was goodness there.

'A sweet, spoiled child, untimely ripped from her mother's womb, like bloody Macduff. I still bear the scars. She took so long to arrive – God knows we tried hard enough, and then when she did arrive, she wasn't a boy and she left my body a wreck. He didn't want me after that, only her. All I was good for was cooking for them both. Christ, like mother, like daughter, hey? She grew up to be just like me.'

Celia handed him a crumpled photograph on paper. He smoothed it out on the kitchen table and saw a girl in a swimsuit, standing on a shingle beach, holding aloft a fish. A man hovered in the background. There was no resemblance to Celia Hurly that he could see in the vivid attraction of the girl, even allowing for the poor quality of the print. Puzzlement showed in his face.

'She still looks like that,' Celia said. 'And yes, I know I don't now, but I did. I meant she's just like me in other ways. A tart who learned to cook. I made her learn to cook, made her go to college for it, just to make her pay attention – oh, what's the use trying to explain it? She was just fixated by her own body, you know, and the power it gave her. Had sex standing up with any man or boy capable and some who weren't, ever since she was fourteen. She didn't even charge. I told her, if that's how you're going to make your living, you should at least charge.'

Andrew was not understanding any of this and did not want it to continue. Surely the past was the past and no one could advise this unhappy woman on how to rewrite it. Concentrate on the present: seek facts for Sarah.

'Anyway,' he said. 'She's come back, has she? Someone's seen her, you said. That's . . . nice.'

Celia nodded, vigorously.

'She may have been hanging round for a day or two, several sightings, I'm told. Even deaf old Mrs Smith said to me, on my way here, it must be lovely to have Jess back, and she's deaf, so it takes a long time for news to get through to her, then she repeats it like a parrot. I'd probably know more if I went to the butcher, but I couldn't face that today. He was very rude to me yesterday.'

Andrew realised with a sinking heart that she assumed he knew the whole background, so there was no way she was going to begin at the beginning. People like Celia Hurly often assumed that the tragedies of their lives were common knowledge; perhaps it was better than the realisation that they were neither famous or infamous, possibly the subject of indifference. And they might also fail to consider that the vicar, who was supposed to know everything, spent his life avoiding gossip for fear of causing it.

'Can you tell me why you thought she might have come here to the vicarage? Rather than to you, I mean.'

Celia Hurly looked at him incredulously, impatient with his unjustified ignorance.

'Because Father Gavin was her greatest friend, of course. He counselled her. This was her second home. She might have thought his successor would protect her.'

'Protect her from what?'

She leant forward intently and snatched back the photograph, crumpling it further in the process.

'From the several people of both sexes in this village who wish she'd never been born. From the ones who were ashamed of being seduced and would like to see her flayed alive, like our wretched patron saint, good old Bartholomew. She didn't just leave, you silly man, she was excommunicated. Well, you know what the church did with excommunicated heretics. They weren't welcomed back, whatever the degree of repentance, unless they happened to be willing to be burned at the stake.'

The vicar reminded himself of his role as teacher and pedantic pastor.

'I think you might be confusing heretics and martyrs,' he said. 'And it's an awfully long time since the Inquisition. Do you think you could help me by going right back to the start? Dates, facts, that kind of thing? Such as, for instance, could you tell me how she came to accuse my predecessor of indecent assault? Is there some explanation for her conduct? There usually is.'

He found that his voice was rising.

'Could she have been looking for love, Mrs Hurly? For attention? Was it drugs?'

Mrs Hurly glared at him, then stared down at her glass.

The rim was red with plum-coloured lipstick: her hand trembled with the effort to control it.

'She was ill. She saw enemies when they were friends. She had too much of everything,' Celia Hurly said. 'Too much of everything and never enough, once her father stopped loving her and left her by dying. She went on a crash course of promiscuity and destruction, messed on her own doorstep, big time. It was me who sent her away and told her not to come back. I thought it was for her own good, because the illness was *here*. I wish I hadn't done that. I locked the door on her. She set fire to the boats.'

Someone had been here. Sarah thought of the tale of Goldilocks and the Three Bears, living in a cottage like this and coming in from the day's labours to find traces of a visitor. Someone's been eating my porridge, says Daddy Bear. Someone's been sitting my MY chair, intones Mother Bear, and while the pantomime tension rises, they finally get the picture that someone is actually there, so they go upstairs to find a sweet little girl asleep in bed after all that porridge, and instead of tearing her limb from limb and eating her up, they adopt her, because she's so sickeningly sweet. Moral: virtue has its own reward; sweet little virgins will be left alone. For the moment, Sarah chose not to go upstairs. Her cottage was redolent with emptiness, nothing creaked or stirred; whatever presence had been there had eaten some of the food and gone. A bowl with traces of cereal was in the sink, the remnants of it set like cement. The drawer where cutlery was kept remained open, the kitchen chairs were in the wrong place as if the trespasser had been indecisive about where to sit. There were biscuit crumbs and milk spillage, a half-finished cup of coffee, nothing returned to its place, no subterfuge, as if he or she knew they were welcome and lived here already and would come back later to clear up or not, forgiven in advance for their own litter. The carelessness reminded her of a man, and also of Jessica. Jessica never finished a cup of anything. Hope stirred.

'Jessica?' she called out. 'Jessica? Where are you?'

Futile: there was no smell of her. A bunch of herbs had been left outside the front door as if to ward off the devil. Sarah was perturbed rather than alarmed by all these pieces of trace evidence because she felt safe here, could not allow herself to feel threatened in daylight. Perhaps it was a child off the school bus. Fear was for after dark. She went upstairs. *Someone's been sleeping in my bed.*

Apart from the casement windows, it was a featureless all-white room. The only colour was in the clothes strewn over a chair and the scarlet silk bedspread she had brought with her and straightened affectionately every morning because she liked the feel of it. A gift from Mike for his scarlet woman: she thought of him briefly and wished he were here. It was rumpled now, as if someone had lain down and got up again, thinking better of it. Her lovely bedspread had been rejected and there was something absurdly insulting about that. Sarah moved to the window and looked down into the garden. The rain came down solidly, bringing darkness with it, and there was a foreign shape down there, an alien thing sloped against the back wall and almost melding with the background brick. She ran back downstairs, opened the front door and propped it ajar in case she had to escape. Then she moved to the back and pushed open the door from the kitchen to the yard. It stuck in winter and spring, swollen with rain, burst open at the second shove, noisily.

The thing was a man sitting in the largest flowerpot with

his head on his knees and his arms encircling his legs, bent double over himself and looking asleep and very still, like an oversized garden gnome until the kitchen door burst open and Sarah stepped out hesitantly. Then he stood up and swayed towards her. He seemed either drunk or half asleep; there was nothing aggressive about him apart from his sheer size and his eyes were fixed on something beyond her – the light from the kitchen door, perhaps, a warmth that drew him back indoors.

'Door slammed,' he muttered to himself. 'Got stuck, couldn't get back in. Oh, shit.'

He stopped within inches of her. Because his presence was mesmerising, Sarah resisted the temptation to run back and out of the front door. The size of him was intimidating in the small space, but again, the little house seemed to give reassurance and the presence of a pair of spectacles hanging crookedly on his nose somehow took some of the threat out of him. The glasses were rain-streaked: he might have been as blind as a bat, with an alternative vision of the world he was in, but it did not say much for his ability to strike out. He focused on her for the first time, looking down at her, his shoulder level with the top of her head. He was soaking wet, looked up longingly towards the kitchen door and said, 'Oh, shit' again. A man of few words, wet and tired, was what she saw.

'Hello,' Sarah said, waving a hand in front of his eyes. He reached for his glasses, tore them off his nose, dropped them, swayed and reached out an arm to support himself on the door jamb, shaking his head to release a shower of rain from his hair.

'Would you like to come in?' she asked, formally, as if she was greeting a stranger at the front door rather than a burglar at the back. Then she stood aside. He lurched through the doorway and landed in one of the kitchen chairs, sat in it, hugging himself, beginning to shiver uncontrollably.

'Take your coat off,' she ordered, speaking loudly.

He shook his head.

'Take it OFF.'

He did. Sarah took the towels which had been drying on the kitchen radiator and handed him two. Yesterday had been washing day, they were bone dry and warm.

'For your hair,' she commanded.

He snuggled into the towels and ignored her, so she wrapped another towel round his head, sat back and watched the tableau they had created. Large man with luxuriant dark hair, wearing clean turban, beginning to get warm. The front door slammed, loudly. It did that routinely when both front and back doors were open wide enough to create a big enough draught, but it still did not feel right and she went to look. Mr Man at the table wasn't going anywhere fast.

Jeremy was standing in the hallway, holding in one hand the bunch of fennel she had found waiting on the doorstep and cradling a newspaper-wrapped parcel.

'Don't you want these?' he was asking belligerently. 'The door was open, I picked them specially, and I got you a rabbit, that's why I was waving at you, only you wouldn't come in. Should have been a fish, I reckon you might like a fish better, Jessica did. Someone said she was back. Only I couldn't get a fish.'

It was surreal in an oddly acceptable way and Sarah was pleased to see him. She smiled, motioned him to put his burdens down on the small table in the narrow entrance, and put her finger to her lips. Sam's words were in her ears. *Trust him to have a key? Help out in a crisis, yes.*

118

'Thanks,' she whispered. 'Can you come in a minute? Only this bloke's arrived and I don't know who he is.'

There was the sound of movement from the kitchen. Nowhere was far from anywhere in this house; all sounds audible.

'Like, he *broke* in?'

'No,' she hissed, wincing at the loudness of Jeremy's voice. 'He was just *here*.'

Jeremy squared his shoulders and marched through to the kitchen. She followed from behind, lingering at the door. There was a shuffling silence, then a laugh.

'Well, if it isn't Jack Dunn,' Jeremy said, punching him on the shoulder. 'Where the hell have you been? If you've come to find your dog, mate, you're too bloody late.'

Jack Dunn stirred. He banged his fist on the table twice and sat up, slowly. He was very thin, thinner even than Jeremy. They could almost have been brothers. Whatever place he was in, it seemed to be unbearable. He was shaking his head in disbelief, as if he had just awoken from a dream.

'Hello, Jerry,' he said. 'Where am I?'

'You're in someone else's house, you fool. You shouldn't be here.'

Jack Dunn, he of the letters and unpaid bills and unfinished business, younger than she thought, disgracefully young, took off his glasses and cleaned them with a towel. He looked completely defenceless and there was no longer any question of being afraid of him. Sarah reckoned she had put that fear behind her before Jeremy had arrived. Jack Dunn was harmless – pitiable, even. She had always had a soft spot for men in trouble.

'But this is my house,' he said. 'Isn't it? I put my key in the lock and it fitted.'

'*Was* your house, Jack. It's this lady's house now. You left the house and you left the dog. She got run over, Jack. Sam kept her for you to bury. You should have taken her with you.'

'I couldn't, could I?'

He was weeping now, big sentimental tears which made Sarah pity him less. Tears were an indulgence she rarely allowed herself: tears muddled things unless they cleared the head. She liked him better for excusing himself and stumbling back out through the door into the garden to cry in private. The rain had stopped.

'It was a black dog, wasn't it?' Sarah asked Jeremy. 'It left a lot of black hair all over the place.'

Jeremy smiled sadly.

'That'll be the one. A black dog, with a bit of white. Jess.'

He sat down at the other side of the table from where Jack Dunn had sat, showing no indication of wishing to leave for a long time. She had the feeling that this was a familiar seat to him and that he had sat there often.

Sarah tidied the towels, put the kettle on like a good housewife, thought better of making tea, found the plentiful supplies of beer and wine that were always ready for visitors, wherever she lived. Found wine for herself and hunted for the corkscrew. Jack Dunn was welcome to whatever he had eaten but at least he had had the grace to leave the wine alone.

'I think we could all do with a drink,' she said, wondering at the same time how often she had said those words.

'Good idea. Got any beer? Jack doesn't drink wine.'

She longed for a female friend, for the straightforwardness of female company, where there was always the chance that someone would tell the truth.

'Yes,' she said. 'I've got beer. Get him back indoors, he'll catch his death. Why was the dog called Jess?'

Jeremy looked at her in surprise, as if the answer was obvious, seeing her expression and realising it wasn't. There it was again, this assumption of knowledge that seemed to apply to everyone. It was becoming irritating.

'Why?' he said, patiently, as if stating the obvious to a slow learner. 'Because she reminded him of Jessie Hurly. He reckoned she was the one, silly devil, and he went a bit to pieces after that, but it didn't last and he's my mate, so can you be nice to him for a bit? Called her Jess because he just liked repeating the name. No harm in him really, only we both used to work at Hurly's abattoir as was and that's a bit of a bond, 'cos that stuff drives you nuts, really, unless you're born to it. He was the one Jessie might have settled down with, as if she was going to settle for anyone, but no one could love her enough and anyway the place was too small for her. Wonder why he's come back now? Silly arse. He's the best shot I know. Hope he's staying.'

'Bring him in and ask him.'

'OK. Don't worry, I won't let him stop long, I'll take him home with me. I'll take him somewhere. It's great to see him. We've had great fun and games, him and me.'

Jack Dunn ambled back into the kitchen, apparently recovered. Sarah assessed him as he sat down again and resumed rubbing his hair with the towel. He was either drunk or on something, or one brick short of a load, maybe just autistic. Perhaps a post-nervous-breakdown man, or a sensitive soul who had been dropped on his head sometime earlier in life. Good looks, good hair; stuffed with passive aggression.

'There's been quite a lot of post for you, Jack,' she said pleasantly.

'Has there? Sorry about that. Sorry for just coming in like that and eating your stuff, I was a bit off my head.'

'Why-have-you-come-back?' Jeremy yelled at him, loudly and slowly. 'It's been six bloody months.'

Jack Dunn sat up straight and reached for one of the cans that Sarah had placed on the table, cracked it open and took a long swallow – clearly not the first of the day.

'Got a job, didn't I? Couldn't pay the bills so I upped and went. Poxy job, but OK, because I do white-van deliveries, mostly up north. Then I got a delivery near here, put the wind up me, really, 'cos Jessie phoned me the other day, she does that sometimes. It seemed like fate meant I was sup-posed to call in, sorry about that.'

Sarah had the absurd notion of a black dog speaking into a mobile phone.

'You left the fucking dog, you bastard,' Jeremy said.

'No, I fucking didn't. I gave it to Jessica's mum and—'

'When did she phone you?' Sarah interrupted.

Jack shrugged. 'Don't know. Days ago. She always phones me when she's in the shit. She said she was in the shit, anyway. Said she was coming home.'

He sniggered nervously. 'She e-mails, too.'

'What, Jack? You doing e-mails and stuff, you clever bugger,' Jeremy said. 'Since when? You got one of them lap-tops?'

'Yeah, they lend me one with the job, so I can check in. Keep it in the van, only someone pinched it.'

Sarah slapped a hand to her forehead. Shit, bugger and damn. Jessica would have e-mailed, of course she would. If she couldn't phone, she would e-mail, the next resort if the phone was broken. She thought of her own laptop, currently residing under her bed, reserved for limited use. She had been determined to rely on the spoken word – she had actually forgotten about her machine and could have kicked herself.

'I want one of them,' Jeremy was saying, 'so's I can look at pictures of lovely girls I'll never meet. Better than the real thing, I reckon. Anyway, come on, Jack, drink up. Got to get up and get going. Things to do, people to see. You've scared this nice woman half out of her wits, time to get out of her hair. Shame about the laptop – I want to learn.'

'You're welcome to stay.'

Jeremy shook his head and grinned.

'No, we're not. You'd be mad to let us stay, you'd never get rid of us. Jack's behaved badly enough already, haven't you, Jack? It can only get worse, and besides you wouldn't like us smoking in here. Give her back her house keys, will you, Jack?'

Jack was looking round for his damp coat, looking foolish and furtive and more than ready to leave. He pointed towards the back door.

'I left them out there,' he said. 'Thanks for the beer and everything.'

Sarah glanced through the glass of the kitchen door and saw that the rain had begun again, and the wind was up. Where would they go in this? Back to sit in a van?

'No, don't go just yet,' she said. 'Wait until it stops. I don't care what you do in here unless you set the place on fire. I'm only a tenant and I'd have to pay. As long as you go eventually.'

Jack Dunn relaxed and laughed. It was an attractive laugh, made him look like a pirate, so that at once she could see the native good looks.

'Yup. Mrs Hurly would get her pound of flesh. Thank

you, missus. I'd like to stay a bit. Got things to talk about.'

It was early yet but deadly dark after the rain.

Jeremy was relieved and only slightly uncomfortable. They were both graceless louts, but sensitive about overstaying a welcome.

'There's plenty more beer in the fridge. The ashtray's somewhere around.'

There would always be more wine, more beer, more emergency food, like crisps and nuts and pasta and bread and cheese. No cook herself, but always sufficiently supplied with the wherewithal to stave off hunger, Sarah had not wanted or courted visitors but was always ready for them, consistently prepared for lovers, friends, and a rogue brother, the whole ersatz family she had in London, although as far as the lovers were concerned it was as often their place rather than hers. That was her eccentric living, after all, until she had fallen into need. Sarah produced her own version of rations.

'I'll leave you to it,' she said. 'You've got catching up to do.'

And a few joints to smoke. Her only fastidiousness was hating that particular smell, but this was not really her house any more. They had more claim to it than she did.

She went upstairs and straightened the rumpled bedspread. From the side of the bed she lifted the laptop she had forced herself to ignore at least most of the time since she had come here. *I want to rely on the spoken word*, that was what she had told Jessica, meaning that she wanted to rely only on what she saw with her own eyes and heard with her own ears in order to decide if she could live this way, without needing to read words, although now the existence of the laptop, which she had promised herself to access no more than once a week, was a terrible reproach. If Jessica had been parted from her mobile phone, she would have tried that. But surely not before she had gone to Sarah's flat, which she had permission to use in dire necessity: she would have gone there, used the phone.

Hell. There was an e-mail that had been resting there since the early hours of Sunday morning.

S,

Well, I know you don't like this any more than my mother, but you might just get it . . . I'll send it this time, not like last time, because I know what you said, only I like this thing late at night, it's the only chance to talk when everyone else has gone to bed. You know me, can't stop talking.

I did it, went back to his posh joint, confronted him again, only extra, extra quiet this time, no flowers, no touching, only talking.

Anyway, he saw the point. He saw that I can't stop loving him, and he can't stop loving me. I'm still coming home. But I wanted him to come with me, you see. I'm not strong enough to come back alone. I wanted to come back with someone who loves me. Make things right. Dream on.

We were supposed to be going out tonight, and I was going to be his girl. He told me to dress up, told me where to meet. JK Sheekey's for the fish. We love that place. Then he stood me up.

He left me sitting on my own where no one sits alone and me in my best dress. They stared at me. I tried not to cry. Don't cry in public.

He wanted to make a point. I waited and waited. Then this internet café on the way home, with a few lonely souls like me. What do I do, Sarah? Shall I come home? Shall I be angry or sad?

All I know is that I can't bear to feel as worthless as this.
Love, J.

Nothing else, except a message from Mike, saying ANY-TIME! ANYWHERE! The message from Jessica filled Sarah with dread. She wrote one back.

Where are you, dearest idiot?

You're here, you're everywhere here, like a ghost. Talk of you has filled my life. Last I heard from you, you might have been coming home to hear the seagulls, and for all I know, you did. There have been sightings, although I don't know if that was you or Jack's dog. The neglected beast that bit the so-called enemy? Was that you, too? Anyway, your Jack Dunn is back, he's gone off with Jeremy. Like everyone else, they'd just be pleased to see you.

Will you phone and tell me about the old vicar? The new one's great and rather tasty.

Don't ever think you'd be cast out here. You did what you did, and get this straight, nobody cares about anything for very long, especially sex.

There's something to explain. I know you want to be loved so badly it hurts, but you can't grab it, it doesn't work. It doesn't bring its own reward. You have to let it grow, or not. I know you wanted to copy me and get objective about it. You thought I had the perfect life as the kind-hearted hooker who could take them and leave them, but that would never have suited you. Get on with what you're good at, develop the other skills, and maybe one day someone will see what you are and love you for daftness and goodness, a touch of madness, and blue nails, as long as you don't spike his chariot wheels and stop him winning the race. The secret with men is to be undemanding. You can't make them need you.

If I don't hear from you tomorrow I'm coming to find you. I know you're reluctant to use my flat, but you're welcome.

Love, S

It took a while: it always took time to be careful with words, even words into the wilderness.

Jessica would have gone back. She might have waited a while, but she would have gone back. The anger would have won and she would have gone back because fury was easier to live with than sadness.

Sarah took off her shoes and wiggled her toes in their thick socks. She could hear the steady drone of indecipherable conversation below, interrupted with guffaws of laughter which drew her downstairs again and away from her own sense of dread. Again she lingered at the kitchen door, then sat down and joined them. They nodded towards her and continued as if she was not there. She felt like an indifferent but trusted relative, enjoyed it for what it was.

'Truth is,' Jack Dunn was saying, 'I got sacked. Pranged the white van and got laid off, the bastards. Didn't like it anyway. Always in strange territory. Don't like the fucking north and I miss the sea. I thought I'd come back, maybe get a job back at the abattoir.'

'Back to working in the Ab?' Jeremy asked incredulously. 'Never.'

'Best job I ever had,' Jack said, defensively. 'Professional, and treated like one, too, when Hurly owned it anyway, before it was sold and when we were kids. Remember the Ab, Jerry?'

He nodded at Sarah, including her, albeit remotely. There was a number of empty beer bottles. She stocked Belgian beer, eleven per cent proof, a little went far. The air was thick. She opened the back door and got herself white wine, sat quietly.

'Regular hours, afternoons off, good pay. Clean.'

Jeremy nodded. 'Yup, there was that. I liked the beef chain best.'

Jack turned back to Sarah, to share the enthusiasm.

'Beast gets stunned first, see ? Feels nothing, though it still moves. Has to. You get the thing hung up by the leg on the gurney, that's the hard-work bit. Gravity, you've got to have gravity. Then you put the knife in the neck, gotta be a sharp, sharp knife, you have to sharpen them all the time. Heart's still pumping, so the beast's still thrashing about which helps plenty, 'cos all that movement gets the blood out double quick, it's like a geyser. Gets most of it out, anyway, and that's the way it should be, because if it's still losing blood when you butcher it, it hasn't been killed as well as it should be. It's a real challenge, that.'

Jeremy shook his head, not really disagreeing.

'I like the piggies best. More polish to it, more to do.'

Again he turned to Sarah, vaguely including her in his happy reminiscence. Any audience would do.

'Same killing method as the cattle, really. Stun, chain up, still alive, but out of it, really. Only after the killing and the bleeding you have to move 'em on. They get dipped and tumbled in scalding water, that gets rid of most of the hair, see, you have to stand back a bit. And then there they are, back on the rack, and you shave them with a big broad knife. They're all soft and supple and clean, like babies. When we get them in the shop they're stiff and solid, but never as solid as beef, though.'

'Christ, it was hot in there, though,' Jack said.

'Would be, wouldn't it? All those warm bodies. All those steaming entrails. I'd never have had the vet's job, would you? Looking at the entrails for liver fluke and that. Silly sheep eat anything. Don't never eat anything not washed. Yes, it was hot. Fucking uniform didn't help. Nylon overalls down to the ground, like a shower curtain, with wellies and hairnets.'

'That John was the best at skinning sheep, put his whole weight into it, remember? Start at the feet and haul the whole thing off.'

'Barry was best at breaking necks and finding the joint at the knuckle. He could get a knuckle off in a second, skilled man.'

'Naaa, Mary was better at that, she really was.'

Sarah raised a hand. 'Enough,' she said. 'Enough. Time to go. If it was all so much fun, why did you leave?'

They squinted at one another, puzzled by the question. While she was imagining that work such as this might have scarred them for life, Jeremy shrugged and answered.

'Dunno. Got a bit boring. Got a bit boring, didn't it, Jack? Same thing every day, day in, day out. And girls don't want to go out with boys who work up there. They don't like you talking about guts. Don't believe the blood washes off.'

Jack nodded back. They were not half as drunk or as stoned as they were going to be.

'I think it was something to boast about, Jerry. At least it was an honest job. Better than being unemployed. Why did we stop? I think it was them bloody hairnets that did it.'

They collapsed into helpless giggles. Jack Dunn was not a man with a broken heart.

Jeremy was one of those who never wore enough clothes. He was ill-equipped for a night, grabbed Jack's damp coat and led him out, both of them laughing.

'We could go fishing. We could go shooting rabbits. Maybe go drinking. Man in the pub says we're welcome.'

Jack gave Sarah a thumbs-up sign, and then they were gone.

Later, she went back out into the yard and recovered her keys. No one needed keys for this house; you only had to push open the door. Alongside the keys was J. Dunn's mobile phone, dropped out of his pocket, ready to be returned. Such trust people had, such carelessness.

She came back into the kitchen, aware of the mess men made. It looked bombstruck.

Sarah would return the phone in the morning via the butcher's shop, first thing, and resist the urge to eavesdrop in the meantime because she did not want to hear. Instead, she charged the phone for him.

No call from the vicar. She would get up early, go the butcher soonest and find out where Jeremy lived so she could return Jack's phone. Jack would need his phone.

Then, maybe, she would paint walls, and listen, and after that she would go to London. She could not live with worry: she would have to go and find Jessica. The idyll was over. Jessica was not the only one who was homesick.

Sleep. Get up early.

One more call. Number unavailable.

No more e-mails, either.

Andrew Sullivan, vicar of the parish, continued painting undercoat onto the walls until three in the morning, arrived at the hour, dizzy and tired.

He looked forward to the morning, when he could make a difference, to his own life and to others.

Went to his laptop and composed a poem about female beauty.

CHAPTER EIGHT

The sky was fresh and the air was clean. The white van started OK, and there was nothing nasty along his route from the next town to here.

Sam whistled on his way to work. He was a happy man most of the time, one who loved his profession and could not really have done anything else. There were no hidden yearnings in Sam Brady to be a composer or a famous sportsman: he was already a philosopher and a celebrity in his own right. He drove to the shop from the next town where he lived with Mrs Brady who came from there and worked in the flower shop. Beauty and the beast, she called them; a formidable team. It had been easy for Sam to move from the place where he had been born to somewhere nearby. The Bradys were powerful people in their own quiet way, with a respectable core of knowledge between them as well as never-ending conversations. She knew when anyone had a birthday, anniversary or a death in the next town, since everything was celebrated and commemorated with an order of flowers.

Sam knew what everyone ate in this village and thus at least half of their habits. They joked about it.

It was still half-dark when Sam arrived at the shop. Plenty to do today, after early closing the day before. He could never have contemplated being anything other than a butcher/shopkeeper, it was in his bones, ha ha. He was honoured in his trade, a respected professional and it still struck him as odd that although he relished the dismemberment and presentation of dead meat he had never in his life killed a single thing bigger than a fly. That shamed him slightly, perhaps made him less of a man. He envied men who could shoot what they ate.

He put the key in the lock. The key would not turn, because the door was unlocked already. Silly me, or was it really silly him? For a minute, he could not remember who it was who had locked up yesterday, whether he had left Jeremy with that task or left it to himself because Jeremy had wanted to go somewhere. Or whether he had been distracted in any case because deaf Mrs Smith came into the shop saying she had seen Jess, and he did not know if she meant the dog or the woman, and he knew she could not have seen the dog, except in dreams. Not that it mattered, anyway.

All this fuss about security that people made these days, what with buzzers and alarms and coded buttons to press. No one had ever tried to burgle a butcher's shop with its empty overnight shelves, and besides, at least a dozen people had the key to the front door as well as knowledge of the key under the flowerpot for the back door. That included Jeremy, Mrs Hurly, since she was officially the owner of the premises, a couple of neighbours, Mrs Brady in case he forgot it and had to go back in the van, as well as others he could not remember. It really did not matter. The key under the pot was used by the delivery man from Smithfield, if he got there before opening time. There was nothing for this new bloke to steal; he came to deliver, not to take away. He would be wanting to offload and go home, because this was the end of the line. You had to know your way in the dark for that kind of job. Thank God he usually arrived so early on Mondays and Thursdays, so that nobody knew quite how much of Sam Brady's beef came from wholesale rather than the next field.

Folk were squeamish. When Sam came back from the abattoir with the pigs he backed the van right up to the door, cut off the heads while the carcasses were still inside, easy, since the necks were broken. Heads were optional, but there were a few old people around here who liked to make brawn. Best people did not know the raw appearance of what they were content to cook. Chickens were another matter, because they were so small. Even so, the customers preferred them without feathers.

The locks were so commonplace, both at the back and the front, that they would never have deterred anyone with an ounce of determination anyway. You could have got in with a wire. The door stuck, as it did at this time of year. He kicked it open, still whistling. There were footprints over the fresh sawdust put down on the floor after the old sawdust had been swept away and binned yesterday. He loved the sawdust; no had ever thought of anything better. Old butchers knew this and bemoaned the stupidity of Health and Safety regs that preferred plastic to wood, chemical cleaners over sawdust. No sawdust in modern wholesalers' markets, no wooden chopping blocks, either. Just sad plastic.

The sawdust was a clean and pale gold dusting on the tiled floor and he walked across it with pleasure, smelling the clean smell. He whistled because it was a whistling kind of day and the overnight rain had left everything fresh. Lovely night in with Mrs Brady and their visiting son, who was a good bloke, apart from his preference for Chinese takeaways instead of home-cooked meaty protein.

Sawdust out the back, too. He loved the feel of it beneath his boots, it seemed to ward off the cold of the floor. Then he noticed there was more of it than usual out the back; oh well, Jerry went mad with it sometimes, let him be.

Sam consulted the list of tasks he had stuck to the board: there was that three-week-old quarter to get out the chiller and leave out the front until later. The chiller was always a separate room, the cathedral or chapel of the place, an institution all of its own, with a satisfying humming sound as soon as he opened the door, ready to look at his stock with pride, ready to tut-tut-tut over it, sausages on one side, not enough, carcasses central, vacuum-packed stuff on the shelves to the left, contraband at the back.

And there she was, centre stage. A dead woman with her back to him, with an industrial-sized hook through her right shoulder holding her onto the central rail so that she hung level with the carcasses behind. Her head lolled forward, out of sight: he had a glimpse of dark hair. The body was not as well bled as any of the carcasses he collected from the abattoir, although she had begun to resemble one of them, with that waxy sheen to the skin. There was no blood seeping from her: she had bled out. Not well hung yet, not edible.

In other respects she was unlike the other beefy carcasses delivered or collected from the abattoir. She had all her toes and trotters. Her lifeless arms were slightly bent at the elbow and her hands were half contorted into fists with the palms facing out level with her thighs. Facing him. He could see traces of nail varnish on the fingernails, shockingly blue rather than red, all at odds with the dull yellow colour of her back. She had long feet, pointing downwards, as if she was used to treading on tippy-toes. They pointed like arrows towards the floor.

Sam's first thought was *wrong delivery*.

But there was no Smithfield delivery due.

The machinery of the chiller room thundered in his ears. He was noticing sounds he had never noticed before. He screamed once, shut the huge door and leant against it. He looked round the back, saw footprints in the sawdust leading towards the back door, nothing else disturbed. When the Smithfield man came in, he left his delivery on the block. Sam's imagination was playing tricks: there was no such thing as what he had just seen. It was the beer from last night, it was a reaction to noodles and all that rubbish, it was a sick joke, nothing real. He took a deep breath and opened the door again. The same rushing sound filled his ears, the blast of freezing air hitting him. Touch it, see if it's real. Touch it.

Sam pushed the corpse's buttocks with the palm of his hand, convinced he would encounter plastic, but it was cold, real flesh all right, as cold as any meat refrigerated for hours to just above freezing. She was rock solid, but the force of his pushing made her turn on the hook, lazily, so that for a second he saw her in profile, her downturned face covered by long hair, a stiff, solidified bosom. She swung back. He gazed, transfixed, and saw his whole life passing before him. There was a piece of paper tied to her wrist with the twine he used to dress hens. It read, in bold print, PLEASE BURY AT SEA.

Then he looked beyond her, to see if there was anything else. His brain began to function: he started the steady calculation of the day's tasks which he always did when he opened the door of the chiller first thing in the morning. He would stand there and work out what to get out for display, how many steaks to cut, how many orders to fulfil. It occurred to him that this thing, this *she*, might weigh less than a side of beef. The figure was both full and slight; she would be as easy to remove, if he could work out how to take the weight. He had hefted much heavier half-carcasses, but never a dead woman. The centre of gravity would be different. He had once carried Mrs Brady over the threshold and all the way upstairs, and she was much weightier than this. There was another factor to be considered, too. The last time he had carried a woman, the woman had cooperated. This one would not.

Sam shut the chiller door again and went into the front of the shop. It was still early, not quite daylight, not a soul in sight out there, although it would not be long before the dog walkers stirred. He paced over the clean sawdust, feeling that every step he made was incriminating, because after five endless minutes he knew what he wanted to do, what every fibre of his being was telling him to do. He simply wanted to get rid of her, and the urge to do it *now* was overpowering. He had even walked over to the phone on the wall to ask Jeremy to help, he could think of no one else, but of course he could not ask Jeremy to help.

He was ashamed of himself for thinking *get rid of her*, but it was all he *could* think. Anything else was ruin. The immediate and long-distance future stared at him. The shop would be shut, his valuable stock would be contaminated, Health and Safety would keep him shut for months of fumigation, new equipment, and would anyone, ever again, buy meat out of that chiller? As for his reputation, he might as well go and kill himself, quite apart from the fact that everyone would think it was him who'd done it. How else would the body of a woman have found its way into his fridge unless he himself had put it there? There was a fishmonger in the next town whose wife had disappeared. Everyone thought he had taken her out in his boat, weighted her down and pushed her over the side, no one would believe she had just gone. They would think him a murderer, too. Sam was not, at this stage, thinking of how this obscene spectacle had got there, that was a stretch too far: he was simply trying to go back to the moment when she had not been there and wanting desperately to retrieve it. Put her right to the back, then, pretend she wasn't there, cover her up with sawdust and sacking and vacuum-packed chicken breasts behind the curtain of sausages, and later, much later, she would simply disappear. Or stay where she was and await a decent burial, like Jack Dunn's dog. Until he could steel himself to cut her into unrecognisable pieces, to be disposed of with the other specialist waste. Sweeney Todd had done it. He wished there was a pie maker next door.

Sam found himself on the verge of hysterical laughter, which turned into tears. He sat where he was, paralysed, useless, unable to move towards the phone, to the dutiful, obvious thing that would ruin him. He was overwhelmed with sadness, anger: shame.

He registered the sound of a knock at the door. There was a figure framed in the glass of the window, a face peering in. His instinct was to move towards it and throw himself against it to stop anyone entering, and then he saw who it was. Sarah Fortune, out for an early walk. It had to be her, it had to be fate, that particular woman; a virtual stranger, but the only one he knew who had shown herself willing to tell a lie in a good cause. He had never been so grateful to see anyone in his life. Someone who would know what to do, just like she had with Mrs Hurly. He beckoned her in, gesturing that the door was open. She did not hesitate, slipped the bolt on the door behind as soon as she was inside. That small action made them conspirators.

Sam suddenly became his usual hearty customer-orientated self, slipping into another mould and amazed to hear the sound of his voice, which brought him down to whatever it was that passed for earth.

'Well, miss. What are you doing out so early? Fancy seeing you here, gracing my humble premises. Was it breakfast you wanted? Nice to see you, to see you nice.'

Then he burst into noisy sobs.

Sarah let him cry for a minute, then put a hand on his arm, lightly. The touch made him shudder, then made him feel better.

'What's the matter, Mr Brady? Shall we go out the back? Make a cup of tea?'

She was handing him a paper handkerchief to wipe his eyes. The gesture touched him with its sheer futility. She wasn't going to hug him better, she wasn't going to help. No one could help, but at least someone could share.

'Come out the back. I've gotta show you something.'

The door to the chiller swung open again. Sam could not remember which of them had depressed the handle. He remembered, later, the way she had stood next to him, looking in, standing there impassively like some kind of doctor, analysing what she was seeing rather than reacting. This time he noticed more details, such as the way the slender feet of the corpse were purple with congealed blood, while the clenched hands were pale, the fact that there was varnish on the toenails, as well as on the fingernails, things like that.

They both stared, like an old couple in front of a favourite programme on a TV screen. He heard her sniff, once, and realised that she had started an almost noiseless weeping, whereas his had stopped.

'Poor cow,' she said. 'Poor cow.' And then, 'Shut the door, will you? We don't want her getting warm.'

Her voice was hollow and neutral. Then they faced each other. Sarah smiled at him, tremulously.

'My word,' she said. 'She's let herself go a bit, hasn't she? I've seen her looking better.'

The bad joke, the graveyard remark, some sick bit of wit introduced them back to the everyday world. No wonder people laughed like hyenas at funerals: it was all part of grief.

'I hope she had a good enough life,' Sam said, responding in kind. 'And I wished she'd asked me before taking up residence here, otherwise I could have got her a room on her own. Either way, she's certainly going to be the death of me.'

'I expect she caught a bad cold,' Sarah said.

'What am I going to do?'

She stood there with crossed arms, as if considering. She seemed to have taken it all in, as if she had known everything that had gone through Sam's head in the last ten minutes, when his life and his business had flashed before him, and all he had wanted to do was hide that awful body. She shook her head, her face wet with tears.

'We dial nine nine nine, Sam. There is absolutely nothing else to do. Anything else will make everything worse. Then we wait.'

He nodded, humbly. She was right. He liked the 'we'.

'You do it. I can't. I want . . . I wanted to do something else. I wanted to hide her. Cut her up and bury her.'

'I know you did. I would have, too. Right. I'll do it.'

'I could have killed her,' he said, his voice rising in panic. 'They'll think I killed her.'

'But you didn't.'

'Do you know who she is?' he burst out. 'Do you know?'

'Yes. She's Jessica Hurly. Mrs Hurly's daughter. I'll call them now.'

Them. The forces of law and order. A mighty force of ineptitude, who would blame the nearest.

Jessica, you silly bitch.

They both conjoined in a minute of hating her.

Sam listened to Sarah on the phone. *A girl has been murdered and her body deposited in the fridge of the butcher's shop in Pennyvale. You'll need to send a whole team and someone to control the traffic. There's no need for sirens – she is definitely dead.*

It was the strangest of sensations, sitting there waiting. Sam pulled down the blinds at the windows. He only ever did that to keep the place cool on the sunniest of days. The blinds were stiff from winter disuse and he cursed them. Then they sat by the counter on the two chairs reserved for the less able customers.

'I can't work it out,' Sam said. 'Why would anyone do that to Jessica Hurly? She was the Pennyvale bicycle, but what was so bad about that? Why bring her back like this?'

'Perhaps there's another way of looking at it. Why would anyone do this to you? Were you one of her lovers?'

'How much do you know? No, I wasn't one of her lovers, far too old. But she did used to play here, when she was a kid. Maybe she brought them here later.'

'Here?'

Sarah was surprised.

'Not here, up there.' He pointed to the ceiling. 'There's a flat up there. You get to it round the back, up some steps outside. It's all Hurly property. Little wild Jessie had plenty of places to go. The rest of the kids had to make do with cars and the beach. Privilege not always a good thing, is it?'

He laughed, without any mirth, and then groaned aloud.

'I've just thought of something else. There are two Jessicas in that chiller. There's Jack Dunn's dog. They'll think I make a habit of it. Health and Safety'll kill me for that alone.'

'Jack Dunn's dog,' she echoed.

'Yes. I found it dead on the road, months ago. I picked it up, shrink-wrapped it, put it in the back of the chiller in the freezer section for him to collect whenever he came back. He'd want to bury it, I thought. Closure, innit? Besides, I couldn't report it. It was full of shot and with a cut throat. Jerry killed it. I should have buried it for him.'

He was talking to himself rather than to her. It made little sense. Sarah looked at her watch.

'How big is this dog?'

'Small.'

She was coldly decisive.

'I reckon it'll take them another ten minutes at least to get here. Go and get that dog out of the freezer. The dog's going to do for you as much as the body. The body's a bad accident that's just happened, but no one's going to understand the dog. The dog's really going to muddy the waters. Quick, get it.'

'Don't leave me.'

'I'm not leaving you. I'm going to take the dog home and fetch the vicar. Then I'm coming back. I'm your witness. You stand outside and wait.'

★

Seven-thirty a.m. A woman sauntering home after an early walk, bearing a white carrier bag with the butcher's distinctive logo. Sam Brady did good strong bags, everyone used them again and again. They were bags for life.

Sarah tried to walk nonchalantly, the way she did when she was walking home from a long stroll on the cliffs, genuinely tired. Tried and failed, so that by the time she turned the corner into her own road she was running, the big bag containing desiccated frozen dog banging against her legs. She felt more than a little mad, but it was often when she felt like this that she knew her instincts were right.

Jessica was dead. Someone she had loved was horribly dead, and there was nothing she could do about that except deal with it in her own time. Better get on and do what she could for the living. She had often mourned her own ice-cold objectivity, the fact that she was at her most clear-sighted when she was manic, the fact that she simply could not fall to pieces.

There had been enough grief in her life for her to know that, so she put the image of dead Jessica from her mind, knowing that it would return. For the moment, anger and energy was what she had to offer.

Sarah Fortune had always cared for dogs, but this one was stuffed unceremoniously into the old freezer in the cottage, such a big freezer that it must have come from someone else. A bargain buy, a giveaway, too big for the space. Then she ran back, because this time it did not matter if she was seen running back. She paused in sight of the butcher's and saw Sam Brady standing outside. No sign of a policeman yet. Traffic was beginning to flow. The great dustbin lorry was coming down the main road, cars building up behind it and a police car in no particular hurry at the rear. They made a small, impatient carnival procession.

She looked back to the street where she lived. Dream gone, long gone, a nightmare place. Then she looked downhill, saw in the distance, just turning the corner, Mrs Hurly, pushing her baby buggy uphill.

No.

Sarah grabbed the mobile phone in her pocket, looked at it. Wrong phone, Jack Dunn's phone, never mind. She had even charged it up for him, what a kind person she was. She dialled Andrew's number. He answered.

'Listen, Andrew, Mrs Hurly will be level with your house in about a minute. Get out there, distract her, do anything, but stop her. Just stop her. Just *stop* her.'

CHAPTER NINE

Mrs Hurly did not stop. She had been reading one of his old books last night. Mr Hurly had owned a library of books devoted to the history of butchery and The Worshipful Company of Butchers who had never let him become a member.

Before killing of any beast or bird; namely to make it tenderer if it be too old, and how to make the best relish, Petrocles affirmed that a lion being shewed to a strong bull three or four hours before he be killed causeth his flesh to be as tender as the flesh of a steer: fear dissolving his hardest parts and making his very heart to become pulpy . . . perhaps also for this cause, old cocks are forced to fight with their betters before they are killed.

Old cocks should fight, anyway; old women, too, but they should not pick on weaklings. She was not going to stop. The traffic was piling up behind her and the traffic coming the other way was stalled by the rubbish lorry. Refreshed and belligerent but also humble after a long talk to the priest the day before, her authority was restored and early in the morning, sick of the sight of the view through her window, she was going to Sam Brady's to have it out with him about the rudeness and violence inflicted on her and also to apologise for causing it. Then she was going to discuss the rumours and ask for help. She was feeling old and tough, tender as pulp beneath. She was going to change: she was full of hope. When Andrew Sullivan came out of the vicarage she waved him aside with a determined smile and ploughed on uphill until she was level with the hairdresser and the butcher's front next door. Sam saw her first and ran back indoors. She followed him in.

Sarah waved at Andrew, beckoning him on. Misunderstanding the gesture, he waved cheerfully and went back inside his own gate. The traffic began to unscramble and the sound of a police siren began to predominate above anything else. Sarah darted in front of the rubbish lorry and round the back of the shop. *Flat above shop. That's where she took them.*

So many secret places in this village. There was a small alley at the side, leading to the back door and the garden, a proper overgrown garden with beds for tangled herbs, half cultivated, half wild. Ingredients for sausages, perhaps. There was a growth of fennel and wild garlic here that might have blown in from the beach. There was a set of unsteady wooden steps attached to the side of the building, rising from the rubbish bins and the outside lavatory in the backyard next to the rear exit. Sarah trod carefully. The door at the top of the steps yielded to a shove, although it stuck a little, just like the back door at home. She pushed it open to reveal an attic space with good enough headroom for a six-foot man in the centre, sloping away to the sides where there would be space only for midgets. It could have served as a roomy bed-sitter, currently a wreck, with a plastered ceiling adorned with patches of damp around the dormer window in the roof. The window faced back towards the garden behind. The existence of this private space was invisible from the outside, like so much else in this village.

Daylight stole through the dormer window and another small window in the back wall. A shelf beneath held a kettle, a few dirty mugs in a tiny sink and a packet of Rizla papers. A tap dripped. She could see two mattresses on the floor, a miniature fridge suitable for a caravan, and not much else apart from a plethora of beer cans, ashtrays and other rubbish that filled in the corners of the view. There was a rucksack in one corner, visible beneath a yellow fluorescent jacket, signs of recent occupation, a certain warmth to the place which had nothing to do with spring, and a dank cannabis smell. That was all she noticed, with her feet sounding loud on the thin stained carpet of the floor – until she heard the screams from below.

Sarah guessed the source, although the sound was still shocking. The place where she stood was immediately above the back of the shop. The sound insulation was nil. The screams went on and on and on. She could decipher nothing but screams, descending and ascending into words; the words no more than word-sounds against the cacophony of screams. *I know who did this – where's Jeremy?* There were other sounds, too, such as footsteps below, echoing back up here, announcing the presence of other feet, other presences. Screams muffled into accusatory sobs. She could find it in her heart to feel pity for Celia Hurly, forcing her way in on the one day she should have stayed at home.

Sarah scuttled back down the steps, shutting the door

behind her, then out through the alley and back into the traffic jam.

A single police car had pulled onto the apron outside the shop. She joined the small crowd that had gathered around it. As they watched, the shop door opened and a man in uniform burst out clutching his throat and vomited onto the road.

Sarah went to fetch the vicar. Mrs Hurly would need him now.

PC Chapman was never going to eat meat again. He was remembering the sausages he had eaten from here, wondering what they were made of, what they had touched before he'd eaten them, greedily, with fried eggs and chips while telling his wife about a man and his dog. There had never been a corpse like this, because he felt he might have eaten part of her and because of the colours of her, blue nail varnish, black hair, bloodless, inhuman and still a woman who shamed him with her dead nakedness and left him standing in front of a crowd, wiping vomit from his chin, looking down at his shoes, remembering what he had said when he'd seen her hanging, what he had done. He had walked towards that vision, that corpse. 'Are you in?' he had said. 'Are you in?'

He ignored the growing crowd and sat in the car to radio in all services, to say no, it was not a practical joke. Doctor, ambulance, forensics, Health and Safety – it's a meat shop, right? He could feel bile in his throat. A face staring at him through the window made him angrier still. He slammed his way out of the car, got out the incident-scene tape and began to cordon off the area, ignoring everyone and refusing questions. 'What's going on?' 'Why don't you fuck off?', kicking a dog that came to sniff at his heels. The pool of vomit remained as a recrimination containing evidence only of breakfast. He went back into the shop for sawdust, remembered the training that never prepared anyone for reality. Bugger contaminating the crime scene, if that's what it was; it was contaminated already. The whole bloody place had the plague.

Once back inside, PC Chapman was aware of a greater dereliction of duty, because others had got inside to further disturb the sawdust on the floor. There was a red-haired woman, standing quietly next to Sam Brady, talking softly, and alongside a bloke in a dog collar, wringing his hands, for fuck's sake. The door of the chiller was closed. Sam Brady turned bloodshot eyes upon him, raised his hands in despair.

'I had to shut her in,' he said. 'She wouldn't stop.'

'For Christ's sake.'

PC Chapman tugged at the handle on the door and yanked it open.

Inside, the old woman stood, embracing the corpse by the waist, dragging it down with her own weight. That was as far as she could reach. He could swear the painted toes of the thing were now curled. The old lady was shivering and crying. He looked up to see if the hook still held.

It did.

This time he fainted.

A thoroughly contaminated crime scene. Everyone had laid hands on that body, even the red-headed woman who detached the old woman from it. Mrs Celia Hurly shrank from any contact with a man, but submitted to the embrace of a small, slender female half her size.

Celia Hurly was back in her white-painted room with the endless view of the sea and the sky. She was very cold, but snuggled in beneath an eiderdown in a white cotton night-dress. Her arms were free, and lay by her sides. The only colour in the room was the red hair of the person who sat on one side of the bed and the hideous shirt of the man on the other. Celia was responding to orders, dictating something, and the red-haired one was writing it down. She had the dim sensation that the people at her bedside were arguing, whilst she remained the centre of attention. One of them was cruel and one of them was kind: they had different agendas and that did not matter much. Celia felt as if she was swimming and talking at the same time. When she had come here first, still half a girl herself, she had loved paddling in the cold sea in summer. Outside, the sky was blacker than black.

Words came back. Write it all down in your own words, Celia, love. Write your own statement. Makes it easier in the long run, and I need to know.

What do you want to know?

Facts. If we write them down now, we can keep the police away from you. Let you tell things in your own words.

Statement.
My name is Celia Hurly.

I was born in 1943. I married Edwin Hurly in 1972, in London. We had one daughter, Jessica, born when I was forty.

My husband was a wholesale butcher by trade, a rich one by the time I married him. I was a cook. (No, all right, that isn't strictly true. I did a bit of cooking, and a lot of tarting around, looking for the right man. I wanted the sort you would meet in a boardroom.)

I did well marrying him, we were in love with one another. He was a magnificent man. I adored him.

We came here, I don't know when. He wanted to prove he was king of the village where he grew up as a poor butcher's boy. He told me he was raised on rabbits and pigeons and fish in the war years and the years of rationing afterwards. He bought half the village and the abattoir in Ripley, prices were nothing then. We became unhappy, he didn't do happy, he was only happy when he had a project and he went away a lot, but he got his own back, whatever that means, and I played Lady of the Manor, the way you could, and he wanted a son, he wanted a tribe, and it never happened. He had Jeremy. There might have been others: who could resist him? I couldn't. He had children that were not mine, but Jessica, she was mine, she really was mine, was ours, and we had a purpose, until she grew up. I was too old for a child.

A woman should work, you know. You have to have some power outside the home.

Odd, for a man whose fortune came from beef, that he should so prefer fish. Maybe he just loved catching things. He loved the sea.

That was how he died. He hated this place once he had conquered it. He could never conquer the sea. It would never let him.

'How did he die?'

Away from home. He died when he was deep-sea fishing in South Africa, he went every year. A storm, an accident, something. They sent back his ashes to be buried in the graveyard here. Jessica was fourteen.

'Enough,' another voice said. 'Enough.'

Celia felt sleepy.

The second voice asked another question. 'Is that when Jessica started to go wild?'

She was always wild. Wilful. She would never believe he was dead. She thought he had gone because of her. Then she blamed the boats, because he loved the boats. She was always trying to burn her boats. Can I have some water?

'Yes, whatever you want. When did she finally leave?'

She left to go to college, but she came back most weeks to make more mayhem. I got her counselling, she screwed that up, big time, everything. Then she got angry with everyone. She set fire to the boats. Three years ago. I haven't seen her since.

She kept her lovely hair, didn't she? Does your hair keep on growing after you're dead?

'There, there, you can sleep now.'

You're the one who kicked me. Why are you holding my hand? Don't go away. Don't go away. I sent her away, God help me.

Jeremy did it, you know. I told THEM that. Jeremy gave her nits. Jeremy always wanted what she had. Only Jeremy could do this. He knows I hate him. He reminds me of my failure.

'Don't you think this was very cruel?' Andrew Sullivan said, looking down at the sleeping figure in the all-white room.

'Necessary.'

He regarded Sarah with something like distaste.

'You're such a cold fish, and yet you seem so warm. You're cold and calculating and manipulative.'

'If you say so.'

'Why did you do this?' he asked angrily. 'Why did you volunteer to take her home and put her to bed, and hold her hand and then cross-examine her?'

Sarah ushered Andrew out of the room and downstairs. He spoke in stage whispers that sounded loud. It was a small and Spartan house, a strange place for the once lady of the manor to live. They moved into the book-lined living room flanking the front door. The wind was up again, disturbing the plush red velvet curtain, drawn half across the door, which moved slightly despite its own weight. An emphatically unmodernised house, low on comfort, albeit beautifully placed for a view of the sea, but a bolt-hole rather than a home and not a place to live alone.

'Why?' he asked, adoring Sarah and almost disliking her at the same time. She was so at home in here, so much at home everywhere; she knew no barriers. She was moving from the book-filled room to the kitchen at the back, then back again after making more of the endless tea they had drunk, as if it were her own house and she had been here before. It seemed grossly impertinent to him and he was wishing he had not been included. There was food in the fridge, mainly meat, which neither of them wanted.

'I didn't see anyone else volunteering to take Mrs Hurly home,' Sarah said. 'Or wait with her, or get her to take the tranquillisers the doctor gave her. Or sit with her, and stay with her. I merely wished to be useful. I'm happy to stay the night. I know you don't want to.'

Andrew shivered. She had nerves of steel.

'But to question her like that, when she's full of brandy and valium, wasn't that cruel?'

'Precisely the right moment to do it. I meant it when I said it would save time. She'll be questioned by the police tomorrow or the next day. If there's something to present to them in a statement form, however rudimentary, it'll make it easier. Besides, she can hardly suffer more at the moment. It'll be far worse tomorrow, or the next day, and all the other days to follow. She'll start lying again. I wanted to get her when she couldn't, when she was beyond it.'

'I'm told she was a kind woman, once.'

'She probably was. Bitterness is a disease. There could have been a breakdown.'

Andrew was looking round the cold room that was full of books and draughts, the distillation of a bigger house into a smaller one, cluttered with stuff. He noticed photos framed in tarnished silver and felt ashamed. They featured a younger Celia Hurly, with an uncanny resemblance to the beauty he had seen in the crumpled photo of yesterday. There were other photos of a man, holding aloft a large dead fish and looking happy in his achievement. A photo of Mr Successful Hurly outside a subfusc factory building, holding on to a SOLD sign, celebrating the sale of it. The abattoir, perhaps. There were also photos of young Jessica in fancy dress, young Jessica naked, and none whatever of all three of them together. There was a disused fireplace, and a desk with a brand new laptop still wrapped in polythene. Andrew shuddered like a dog shaking off water. At this point in time, he and Sarah did not understand one another. He wanted to go.

'Did you really mean you'll stay with her? Stay all night, I mean. I was just wondering, *why?*'

Sarah was angling one of the photographs, making it straight. Although she was so colourful, she melded in anywhere, like a shadow, taking in the colours of the walls, moving at her own pace, to her own tune, which was sometimes harsh, sometimes musical. She leant forward, examined another of the photographs.

'Because no one else wants to. You don't, no one else does, I don't either, but I shall. Your turn in the morning. She mustn't be left alone – she saw her own daughter dead, recognised her as instantly as I did, and no mother deserves that. So I'll sleep over. I've brought my stuff, so go home and don't worry. I shan't be murdering her. I'll just sit by her side in case she wakes up. Read some of these old books.'

Andrew hesitated. He was hesitation incarnate, somehow failing in duty, but above all he wanted to go away and pray. He rose to his feet, without grace.

'If you insist,' he said.

'I'll insist if it helps. Just for the night. Tomorrow her friends take over.'

'Such as they are,' he said.

So the pastor went with relief, leaving someone else to do pastoral care.

Later Sarah went upstairs and watched her sleeping charge. Wanting to wake her and ask more questions, such as why are there no Hurlys in the graveyard? Her own hands were as cold as ice. She warmed them on the ancient hot-water bottle she had unearthed in the kitchen, before placing it at Celia's feet and tucking the sheet round the woman's shoulders to ward off the draught from the window. What was a rich and not yet very old woman doing, living in a small house, sleeping in such a Spartan room with draughty windows? As if the bleak view was her punishment, or an antidote to grief.

Celia Hurly opened her eyes and looked into Sarah's face. She stretched her feet towards the new heat at the end of the bed. The look she gave was one of trust, confused by diazepam but still trust, carrying in its glazed glance the appalling responsibility conveyed by any reliance, even that imposed *in extremis*.

'She was here,' Celia Hurly said. 'She was here, and she never came to see me. I could have stopped him, I should have pitied her rather than envied her. No one will pity me now.'

'I do,' Sarah said. 'With all my heart. Sleep now.'

'Thank you,' Celia said, closing her eyes.

Sarah fetched a blanket, sat by the bed and waited.

She had no faith in police investigations. By now the witch-hunt for Jeremy would be on. Out of the corner of one eye she had seen him running away, like a shadow. Ducking and diving among the traffic, running for his life. Others would have seen him, too. Jeremy along with his friend Jack, the only logical suspect, the only one capable of carrying out such a sick joke. The only one brutal enough, skilled enough. The ones who ran away.

She could see the headlines in the local paper, even the nationals.

Tomorrow or the next day she would read those headlines and go to London. Plan the next move, find help, follow instincts.

Not running away. Running towards.

CHAPTER TEN

Body of local girl found dead in butcher's freezer. Two local men wanted for questioning.

This annoyed Sarah. It was not a freezer, it was a chiller. A freezer was another thing altogether.

The train was a cultural shock in itself after weeks of mostly walking, relying on her own two legs. Even an empty train, as far removed from the stuffed-up London Underground as a distant cousin with a faint family resemblance. Sarah had forgotten how much she could appreciate a train journey simply for itself; how much she had relished her first trip down here for this experiment in living, taking a shot in the dark, following Jessica's suggestions, feeling in control of her own independent destiny while all the time it was Jessica sealing her fate. But there had never been any real calculation in Jessica, as far as she knew. Jessica simply reacted to things. There had never been a master plan.

It was Friday afternoon; the journey was peaceful in the sort of train where a person could sit alone at a table for four without interruption until London loomed and the carriage filled with the smell of city pressures. Plenty of thinking time, the movement soothing, the constant stopping and starting nothing more than a light relief. Station names passed by like new acquaintances, passengers getting on and getting off: there was a flash of daffodils in a window box, reminding Sarah to regret that she had done nothing with Jeremy's fresh herbs which would wither and die in a jar in her kitchen. It crossed her mind that Jeremy and his friend might take advantage of her house in her absence. The lack of a key was no barrier to that and she found she did not particularly mind. It was no longer her house, if it ever had been, and the thought that she might unwittingly provide refuge to a couple of potentially homicidal throwbacks was faintly satisfactory, and far preferable to the idea that the pair of them would be hounded over the cliffs by vengeful vigilantes.

She did not care where they were hiding, only that she knew they would be hiding, probably successfully. They would be hiding because Mrs Hurly had shrieked Jeremy's name, blamed him, yelled at the police that he was the murderer, and the witch-hunt would be on for him. She was trying not to remember the callousness she had seen in his eyes, imagined the reactions of anyone reading his curriculum vitae. The natural killer, the man with a criminal record for possession of drugs, the man trained to slit a throat and bleed a large body, adept at the killing of small animals: a dispossessed bastard, half in love with someone he imagined was his half-sister, the perfect unbalanced candidate and yet, she was convinced, not the culprit, not the cold-blooded murderer, not even for a game.

He might have found her on the cliffs. He alone might have found her and treated the body with the same respect due to a stunned beast in a slaughterhouse. You bled it dry to preserve it from putrefaction and keep it at its best, then you kept it somewhere cold. That way it remained sweet-smelling.

Jessica had been dead for two or three days, Sam had said. He would know that better than a pathologist. 'There's a minimum of two days before we get them from the abattoir, takes them that long to cool down. If the beef comes from Smithfield, it could have been dead for weeks. But there was no Smithfield delivery due, never on that day of the week: there was nothing ordered the whole week.'

'But if there was, the delivery man would be able to get in, wouldn't he?'

'Yes, of course. He's done it before but there was nothing ordered. He didn't come.'

The notes Sarah wrote to herself on the train were only proof that she relied on the written word as much as the spoken. There were times when she regretted her own awful objectivity, but then, she had always had an ice chip resting in that large heart of hers. There was always a degree of resentment in herself that she could not cry instead of writing things down in quiet, cold anger.

Smithfield.

Notes to self.

There is no Hurly in the graveyard.

The man at the dinner party? Jessica being seen . . . get Andrew to check, who saw?

If Jessica came back she would have come to me, surely? Or is that vanity on my part? Where else would she have gone?

Jessica living rough? Feasible: she could live anywhere.

The only one with real motive to do this is The Lover.

Sarah had stayed long enough in the village to get the local knowledge, watched and listened during the day after the discovery, waited another night, made plans. For once the place was united in conversation and rumour and fear. They stood outside the closed butcher's shop rather than going in, digested not meat but information, writing the headlines for the local paper. *The body of a young woman was deposited overnight on the 8th March in Brady's butchers. Two local men wanted for questioning.*

A thrilling local murder, then. Definitely local. Revenge on local promiscuous girl who had never grown up, who had upset the smooth running of things and embarrassed so many. Plenty who did not want her back. Perhaps Jeremy had been paid to do it. No.

Sarah had talked and listened and looked at Mrs Hurly's library. She had listened to the messages that Jessica had left on Jack Dunn's phone. *Jack, I've pissed you off, sorry, I know you hate me, coming back to you like this, but please meet me. Tell me where and I'll be there. Please don't hate me.*

Wrong. Jack did not hate her, or mind when she phoned when she was in the shit.

Sarah had considered giving the mobile to a waiting policeman, saying she had found it in the street and that would have been her civic duty, but she'd used the phone, too. Civic duty went against her nature: anyway, the phone would incriminate Jack and implicate herself. So far, no one but the vicar knew how well she had known Jessica, or who had been in her house. Sarah was going to be away before they got round to her. She did not trust the police to listen to the theories forming in her own mind any more than she trusted them to depart from what seemed obvious. She and Andrew had agreed to keep one another informed, becoming conspirators. Ah, the blessings of e-mail.

London loomed. She dreaded it and embraced it.

It was not a local crime. It had begun here, in this city, she was sure of it. It had begun with an obsession. It was all about too much love, rather than about hate.

She continued to Charing Cross so that she could take the longish walk home through Covent Garden to reacquaint herself with the city she had abandoned. The walk confirmed her decision to attempt another life, and yet it made her nostalgic. The city was at its best on a spring evening, with everyone setting forth for shopping, eating, arguing and loving, fresh from work, winding down like springs uncoiled. Such clothes, such silly shoes, such chatter into mobile phones, sparrows gathering for a flight into unreality. Sarah wore the sort of boots better suited for walking on cliff paths and felt better equipped. The crowds were irritating; it was a novel experience having to sidestep all the time in order to get up any turn of speed. She could feel her love of human nature slipping away – but then, there had always been times when it was more precarious than others.

She was concentrating on what to do, and in which order. The priority was to find out who had murdered her friend, not out of any wish to avenge her but because it enraged her to see someone else accused. Jeremy would never have done that to Sam Brady. This was a London murder. No one in the village could hate Jessica Hurly enough to kill her. Jessica's promiscuity had been a social service.

Sarah's flat was cold and unwelcoming, relatively undisturbed. Jessica had been given free range to use it if she wanted, although she had expressed reluctance to take advantage. She had been and gone long since. The signs of her presence were minimal but typical, such as scrappy notes written on virulent pink Post-its, the aides-memoires of mobile-phone calls, a cup of long-dead coffee half-drunk and left. This was not home, either; already Sarah felt herself longing for the sound of the sea instead of the traffic noise reverberating outside. She turned on the lights and the heating and contemplated what she had never missed, namely a large and dusty place with marks on the walls where pictures had once hung, an apartment of many rooms, inhabited by the ghosts of many lovers, including the man who had left it to her. A slightly cursed place, but wonder of wonders, she could no longer smell the smoke of the fire which had haunted her. She remembered how Jessica had said *I want to be like you.*

'Tart' was a harsh description for Sarah's chosen profession during the most recent decade of her varied life. It was a word which applied equally to less generous, less dignified and far more self-centred pursuits. Sarah was an elegant and charming companion to a coterie of nice if socially dysfunctional men of whom she was fond for as long as it took. The offering of sexual and social confidence didn't seem such a bad thing to do. Most of the men remained friends. You had to like shy men to do what Sarah did. Jessica could not make friends of men: she needed them like a drug. She had needed one man with a destructive passion.

Sarah was sure that Jessica had not stayed overnight here: Jessica had drifted in and out a few times, leaving a small wake of mess, nothing more. No clothing, no kicked-off shoes. She had used it as a space to phone, to make black coffee or tea, and she had meant to come back. The spare bedroom was undisturbed; there had been no sleeping over, even though the location was so convenient. Jessica lived in a flat on the outskirts. The police would have combed it by now. To her shame, Sarah had never known where it was.

Whenever she had met Jessica and brought her home, Jessica had been en route to somewhere else.

Jessica's mess was easily tidied away, unlike her body. Sarah had been afraid she might find blood.

She consulted the wardrobe she had left behind, which included the better clothes, the smart stuff, the vintage, the nothing-off-the-peg stuff, the interestingly modest stuff, the how-to-pass-muster-and-never-look-like-a-tart stuff, and finally selected what she had worn to the first dinner party where she had gone with one of her paying paramours who had needed an affectionate escort to get him through an evening with his so-called terrifying peers. Dear Jonathan, such a sweet, insecure man who no longer needed her. Together they had witnessed Jessica Hurly pour soup over the head of the host, watching it, she had to confess, with great pleasure, and Jonathan had lost his fear. The host had been a prick and quite probably was bankrupt by now. He was one man who would have been happy to kill Jessica then and there, to avenge his own humiliation. In Jessica's case, there might well have been several such.

Thinking thus, Sarah went back into the kitchen, and only then smelt that smell of sharp decay. It penetrated beyond the fridge, leaking out all around it, so that Sarah had to marshal all her forces before opening the door. There was a terrible stink of dead fish, a sharp, accusing stench. Two once-fresh trout, two suppurating oily mackerel, wrapped in paper and bought fresh a long time ago. Perhaps Jessica had once intended to cook and eat here, a meal for the demon lover. Perhaps the fish had merely been forgotten.

Sarah wrapped it all in black bin liners, until the fish became a cumbersome parcel. She left the door to an otherwise empty fridge open and opened the window, too. In the dim recesses of an eclectic memory she remembered a revenge story, about someone who posted dead mackerel through the letter box of a rival who was away for a fortnight so that by the time the rival came back the house stank and the windows buzzed with feeding flies. I only left her a gift, the perpetrator said. A womanly kind of crime, it was said. Sarah herself had never felt rivalry with another woman: it was not her style, even though her intervention might have saved a marriage or two.

Once the fish parcel had been neutralised, Sarah completely revised her choice of clothes. She had left in winter, come back in early spring, which made the choices difficult. She was going out to dinner at the restaurant where Jessica had made trouble. DK. Das Kalb. She did not know what the name meant. One step at a time. She was hoping that she would meet the man who had obsessed Jessica most of all. The man she had wept about in the kitchen and shrieked about on the phone; the one she adored, the one who had dumped her, taken her back, dumped her again. The man in the restaurant where Jessica had become such a nuisance, the man who was always on her mind; the same man who had once taken her shopping in the middle of the night, and the man she had been trying to find when Sarah had met her that time, on her way back from Smithfield in the early morning, when she had not made much sense at all.

Sarah dusted and tidied automatically, as if she was really home and not in an alien, albeit harmless place. Showered and dressed, clean and with gleaming washed hair, she sat, completely transformed from country bumpkin to urbanite. An emerald-green cashmere sweater for luck, wide black trousers and tiny sparkly earrings, minimalist clothes that belonged to any age and any decade. She could have worn clothes like this when she was eighteen and might wear them still when she was sixty.

Her ally would approve – but then, Mike approved of almost everything she did.

Waiting, sipping a small whisky, she thought of sweet, hesitant Andrew the vicar, beset with secrets and sitting in his half-decorated room, wringing his hands and contemplating a dinner of beans on toast. Then she thought of Sam Brady, the butcher in this pack of cards, sitting in front of his fire, weeping at the enforced closure of his shop, wondering how soon he could open it again, and if he did, would anyone come back. Then she thought of the village that had lost its heart, and the sea which remained relentless. Let them eat fish.

Finally, she thought of Celia Hurly and the promises she had made at dawn.

Find him. Find out the truth.

Chapter Eleven

The sea was loud down at the bottom of the village, crashing against the shore as if angry with itself and the world around it. The sky was clear and full of stars. There were only two lights in the row of houses that led from the main village down to the pub at the end and the sea itself. One light came from Celia Hurly's bedroom window; the second was the light from the door of the pub at the end of the row. The publican was taking a last late walk across the beach with his Alsatian, leaving the door open behind him. The dog was excited and ran around in circles, barking, looking for a companion to play with. Her owner shushed it, even though there was no one to hear. Then he walked back and shooed her inside. She did not want to go; not enough exercise today.

Before closing and locking the door behind him, the publican took a carrier bag containing the day's leftover food – bread, cheese, pork pies, sausage rolls and anything else he could find – and left it tied to the smokers' bench. Plain snack food which was all the customers ever wanted, hardly haute cuisine, but someone would find it if they knew where to look. The food would be gone before morning. He added a bottle of water as an afterthought.

'Bit pretentious, innit?' Mike said. 'That's a word you told me, doll, love that word. It rolls round your tongue and says a lot. Blimey, look at it. I'm glad you're paying. At least you can hear yourself speak, and no one can hear you. That kind of place, innit? Confidential meetings 'r us. Discreet. I fucking loathe this kind of place. Credit crunch won't make an ounce of difference here. None of these is down to their last can of beans. Veal on the menu every day.'

Mike was a reinvention like herself, a self-styled butler/ housekeeper now, surprised to find that such factotums existed still in that other world where old and new money lived, and amazed to find himself in demand. A talent for diplomacy and impeccable domestic skills went a long way. He had been anything and everything – porter at Smithfield, conspirator, security man, confidence trickster and arsonist – until he lost his nerve. He was as much at ease in the gutter or sleeping rough on a park bench as he was in a place like this. It was all about copying the manners of others and wearing the right clothes, passing muster as long as you could mimic. Clothes were his weakness: he did wardrobe. They were in for a fine evening. A colourful redhead and a man with a handsome profile if you got his right side. The other was scarred. They were a striking couple.

It was ironic, to Sarah at least, that this restaurant should have a faintly seaside feel. She was trying to work out why that was, because it was not in the decor nor the furnishings. These were strictly modern classical: white tablecloths, brown chairs, lots of white napery and an imposing selection of fine glass. Perhaps it was the soothing blue-grey of the walls that reminded her of the colour of the English Channel most of the time, but no, it was the pictures on the walls. A meat man who liked the sea.

Sarah always looked at the pictures on the wall first, disappointed if there were none. She remembered the house of the man who had held the dinner party where Jessica had poured the soup. There had not been a single picture on any of the rag-rolled walls, which was rather a waste, as if the man had no taste to express. In this quiet, discreet, rich-feeling restaurant that felt more like a club and could supply pigs' trotters and offal delicacies, muslin-wrapped meat puddings for sentimental old schoolboys and those who imagined they had discovered such things, there were several gently lit oil paintings and watercolours. They all featured boats and the sea. The one behind her at their corner table was a colourful depiction of men dragging nets into a boat that rocked precariously under a stormy sky.

'You wouldn't come here if you were a vegetarian,' Mike said, looking at the menu. 'Fucking foie gras all over the place. Specialités de la maison, meat, meat and more meat.'

'Vegetarians wouldn't apply,' Sarah agreed. 'But there *is* a fish option.'

'Halibut steak in beurre blanc. Only the meatiest kind of fish.'

The restaurant was designed to reassure a certain almost exclusively male clientele. The sort of place where a man might bring a mistress rather than a wife. It was on the far side of Charterhouse Square, thus close to Smithfield and the City, equally convenient for lawyers, bankers, et al. A place for the kind of man who preferred to dine out and who could use it as somewhere to close a deal or discuss a project with another man in private, whilst eating the kind of luxurious protein that would be forbidden at home. Fat, sleek men, seeking the solace and reinforcement of chateaubriand, unlimited fine wines and the company of their own kind. The prices were astronomical and yet the place was full. They were served by a beautiful, almost monosyllabic waitress who knew the menu by heart but whose otherwise limited command of English would prevent her from overhearing much. There was a chatty sommelier who was delighted to talk to a man with Mike's cockney accent, which mirrored his own carefully disguised vowels. Mike would always find the weakest link; the one who was indiscreet, or bored or scared. It was a talent they shared.

It was definitely the sort of place where you were not allowed to pour your own wine. The sommelier hovered, filling the glasses half full only as necessary, while making it clear that they were the favoured customers for the night.

'No wonder,' Mike said to Sarah. 'There's only one decent woman in the house and that's you. The other two is floozies. We're the only ones who look as if we might be celebrities. I reckon that wine waiter fancies me.'

The place had an aura of success. The weak link in the wall of discretion was the bored wine waiter. The room, with its wide-spaced intimate tables and perfect acoustics for secrets, began to clear at about ten. The sommelier suggested a sweet wine to follow, and both of them agreed. Sarah had eaten fish and Mike had demolished steak tartare, something she loathed. Between mouthfuls, Sarah paused to wonder what terrible mayhem Jessica might have wrought in here. She could have ruined this business single-handedly – no, perhaps not – but she could certainly have done a lot of damage.

'Sit down and have a drink, why don't you?' Mike said to the sommelier. Such a diplomat. 'If you want us to have this fucking Sauternes, at least sit down and fucking drink it with us.'

The place was almost empty by now. Sarah gazed at the picture on the opposite wall. It was a seascape, with a battle scene. More storms, more ships at war with cannons firing and men jumping overboard, with a shredded Union Jack on the winning vessel and a lot of bodies in the sea. Maybe there was never a nautical theme here: maybe the artwork was simply about winners and losers. The sommelier sat willingly, a small bantam-like man with a flushed face and a wide smile.

'So who owns this joint, then?'

'Big man. Loves the place. Doesn't want to be famous. He's always here for lunch if you want to see him, not always around for the evening sittings, although he always comes back at the very end to sort out the takings and check the tidying-up, and then he hangs around until he goes out and buys the meat. Leaves us alone, pays well. He knows what works, only he likes to do the buying. He's always front of house at lunch because lunch is the most important thing here. He and the chef look after small private parties on Sunday evenings for regulars when I'm not here. Likes to charm the pants off the lunchtime punters because they're mostly as old as him. Leaves most evenings to me.' He preened. 'But he always comes back later.'

'The owner buys the meat?' Sarah said pleasantly.

'Big time. Buys for other people, too. Always goes around three in the morning, the best time he says, the prices start to come down. Likes to go in person, look at it, feel it, touch it, that's why it's so good. He loves the look of it. Only he's got the sense to leave veg to someone else, and wine to me.'

'Ever any trouble with the customers?

The sommelier sniggered. 'Not really, good as gold they are. He charms them, see? Money back if not satisfied and so it should be, these prices, but they *are* satisfied. Quiet. He did have a bit of trouble a while back with a female chef, who went and then kept coming back with a grievance, shouting and screaming and smashing glasses, saying you can't treat me like this. I'm new here, don't know the history, see what I mean? I reckon she was nutty. He got a bit cross about that. Pushed her out the back.'

'I used to work in Smithfield,' Mike said, leaning back in his comfortable chair as if he relaxed this way every evening. 'Paid well before the taxman got in there. I reckon your job's better. Does the boss have any particular supplier? Be nice to know where he gets his meat from. Could fancy buying some myself – not as much as I fancy your wine, though.'

The sommelier grinned and winked. 'Don't know where he gets the meat from. Smithfield, anyway, he won't let the chef choose, oh no. Has to do it himself. Walks over or calls a taxi, no room for a car here and he won't drive. Likes to walk at night.'

'Fascinating,' Sarah spoke breathily, disliking herself. 'Absolutely fascinating. So the owner doesn't do the cooking himself?'

'Good God, no. He's not Jamie Oliver. Chefs come and go.'

'Well, I hope this one stays. Could we possibly meet him and present our compliments? I'd like to book up for a party if he's here.'

She was paying the bill as they spoke, adding a generous tip in cash.

The sommelier, who doubled as cashier at this time of the evening, watched her hands and smiled into her wide-open eyes.

'You want to see the kitchen too? Proud of it – follow me.'

Sarah always wanted to go backstage, anywhere. Backstage at the theatre, the shop, the restaurant, the factory, anywhere where the real work was done and the real people dwelt. She had done many a messy job in her life, loved the kitchens which were the real heart of any building. She had admired Jessica's talent for making food. It was so much less ephemeral than her own talent for making damaged men happy.

The kitchen gleamed. It was in the process of being scrubbed down after the last orders had been delivered to the few remaining diners. She could see why there would be no hesitation in showing it off at this time of the evening rather than when it was in the manic stage of a fully booked house. The smell of food was masked by scents of detergent and steam, although the lingering smell of roasted beef was still detectable. That was the smell that always remained longest, along with an aftertaste of garlic: it would still be there in the morning, like the old smells of stale beer in a pub. A girl wearing an overall and with a paper hat covering her hair stood by a deep butler's sink, battling with a huge pan that she lugged out of soapy water and dumped on the draining board with a bang. A chef would need strong wrists to shake that pan. It would make a useful weapon for stunning an ox, but an industrial kitchen like this contained many other weapons far more lethal. Mallets for tenderising meat, an even greater variety of knives for slicing, chopping, filleting fish, dicing vegetables, metal skewers with pointed ends, more implements than she would have seen in a butcher's shop. The kitchen was full of sharp stainless steel edges and the floor was durable non-slip stone. Everything steam-cleaned every night, the wine man said.

The chef sat at a small table at the far end of the long narrow space, next to the exit door, which was open. Sarah could see a small chilly yard, with neatly stacked and sealed rubbish. He had his back to them and was writing in a grubby book. Above his bare head there was a cork board, festooned with the orders for the evening alongside numerous other bits of paper, invoices and notes stuck in there with pins. Sarah was trying to read the invoices as they approached, looking for the names of suppliers. The light in here was bright enough to read small print. There were no dark corners: no rat, no cockroach, no crawling beetle could survive the exposure of this bright light and the rigours of steam-cleaning.

'Someone to see you, chef.'

The man put his hands over his head as if to ward off a blow, groaned and turned round. There was a smouldering cigarette in an ashtray on his desk, alongside a tumbler of brown liquid. Close to, he had brandy breath. He was one of the ugliest young men Sarah had ever seen. His face was as pale as uncooked pastry, his hair was lank with sweat and his white hands trembled slightly.

'You can see why we don't put him front of house,' the sommelier whispered spitefully. There was another agenda here. The sommelier hated the current chef and was taking a delight in introducing him in what was clearly not his finest hour.

'Lovely meal,' Sarah said. 'Just wanted to congratulate you.'

'Thanks. 'S all right. Glad you liked it.'

'He's been like this all week,' the sommelier whispered.

The chef turned his face back to the wall and resumed writing. The illegal cigarette burned down slowly, more ash than stub, dripping off the edge of the ashtray. There did not seem much more to say. Sarah kept her eyes on the cork board, reading names of suppliers and companies with bright-eyed interest, wondering at the same time what the chef's finest hour was with the certainty that it would not be first thing the next morning. Nor would he be the most obvious person to employ if looks counted for anything, which they did. He would not have the greatest choices and would need this job more than most. The sommelier slapped him on the back. He flinched.

'You should go home, Jacques. You don't have to wait for the boss. Shake the lady's hand.'

The chef turned and extended his hand to Sarah. She took it in both of hers, shook it firmly, feeling it warm and damp like the mixture for a pudding, smiling at the same time and thinking, *This one was never Jessica's dream man. He doesn't buy the meat, he has no power or influence.*

'How long have you worked here?' she asked, sounding like the Queen with a duty to ask only the most banal questions. He seemed to respond to the coolness of her hand and brightened slightly.

'Not long. Few weeks. Not much longer. He won't let me cook what I want. All they want in here is meat. But you can't cross him. He knows best. I've got my lines.'

The chef's hand trembled as he turned back to the wall. The sommelier ushered them out the way they had come, into the more discreet gloaming of the restaurant room.

The last duty of the evening was to sit and have the obligatory drink with the sommelier, whom Sarah had come to see as a vicious little queen with a power complex and an undernourished taste for gossip. God alone knew what he creamed off the proprietor, but it was the proprietor who interested her most.

'Nice to work for, is he?' Mike was saying man to man. 'I mean life's too short to work for a shit. I've done way too much of that myself. I mean you've got to respect the bloke who pays the wages. Otherwise, what's the point?'

The vicious little queen preened again.

'I only work for the best,' he said. 'But,' lowering his voice a little, 'he might be getting a bit old for it. Pushing seventy or more. Some young Turk'll buy him out one of these days. He's getting on.'

'Happens to us all,' Mike said.

Outside, they stood in the dark for a while and then began to wander their way through the back roads that led far from the morass of alleys towards the church of St Bartholomew and then into Charterhouse Square. Sarah remembered what she had read in the night in Celia Hurly's library.

This was where the cur dogs gathered with the sheep and the pigs. The drovers and dealers bought and sold their wives, too. The word 'cur' came to mean 'scoundrel': the men regarded their dogs as scoundrels, abandoned them here and left them to find their own way home, as far as the far north, hundreds of miles, with food paid for in advance, because the dogs would go back the same route, to the same places and the same inns where they had stopped on the way south, back to the innkeepers they had known, who let the cur dogs eat the entrails of the animals that had died on the way. The men ate the rest.

The drovers were driven, cruel men, but if they did not get their livestock to market, they too would starve.

She had memorised it in the way she could, repeated it to herself now, the way she would sometimes repeat a poem to steady herself.

They sat on a bench in Charterhouse Square. Mike lit a cigarette, drew the smoke deep into his lungs and exhaled slowly.

'Gotta face it, doll, you might have hurt my feelings. You only asked me out tonight because you knew I worked Smithfield once. You want an entry there, right?'

'Right.'

He shook his head.

'You could have said so, doll. I thought you might have just wanted to see me. Buy me dinner and everything.'

Sarah plucked the cigarette from his hand and drew on it, then handed it back.

'I picked you for your looks, and the way you can talk to anyone. And because I'd rather it were you than anyone else, even though it was you who once set a fire in my house. I trust you and I don't and I do, and I must. You know the dark side of me and I you. I love you more than most. You can help or not. Up to you. Shall we go home?'

'For free?'

She looked towards the sky and saw the penumbra of light surrounding the Smithfield market building.

'Yes. It was usually free, if you remember. You smell so nice.'

He laughed and touched her cheek.

'Bet you say that to all the boys, but I believe you. Let's go home and get warm and you can tell me the rest. We've got the whole weekend to sort it. We can't do Smithfield until Monday.'

Sarah began to cry, clutching the lapels of Mike's coat.

He detached her gently in a gesture she recognised and appreciated. She would prefer to be treated with pragmatic detachment than with obsession. Practical kindness was better than anything.

'Up you go,' he said, hoisting her away from the bench. 'Told you the fucking countryside would do you no good. You'll be telling me you're shagging the vicar next. Let's go home.'

'I don't know where home is,' she said.

He kissed her gently.

'It's where the heart is,' he said. 'Even if it's only there some of the time.'

It was much later when she told him more.

'Daft bitch,' he said. 'Silly daft bitch. You've lost weight, you know.'

'And you've got fatter.'

'I never. Love that pendant you had on – what is it? Bit fierce, isn't it? Yes, I know what it is. Could catch on.'

Sarah had taken it off as she took off her clothes. A light ornament, capable of many uses, looking like an initial on the heavy silver chain she had found for it. An S-shaped hook, borrowed from Sam Brady, dipped and polished to a shine. A butcher's hook, a weapon. An icon, something to touch for luck. Or use to strike.

Exhausted by stumbling explanation, she found herself talking about a kitchen that gets a steam clean every night. Machinery to mop up pints of spillage and put it down the drain. There would never be any trace. That was where she was going, it has to be *there*. But Jessica's man was never that chef, she wouldn't have gone near him. I thought the Lover would be one of those powerful, emotional chefs who bought his own meat, but it's the owner who buys the meat in

Smithfield, but he's too old. He can't even drive. Way too old. Jessica liked prime specimens.

'You're never too old,' Mike said.

She dreamt of the sea.

Wait until Monday. It was always better to wait.

Wait and enjoy the waiting.

CHAPTER TWELVE

There was a fine mist over the sea. The line fanned out either side of the cliff path, looking half-heartedly for traces of murder. For where a body had been kept or dragged, or preserved. They had been slow to get going, checking the abattoir first.

Brady collected the small amounts of local beef he got from there as and when the orders were dressed, pigs on another day. Dressed, sanitised, hair singed away, cut into halves or quarters, never a whole carcass. They would help him load stuff into his van. He was fifty-six and could still move most of it all by himself. In the beef line, he sold neck, chuck, forerib, sirloin, rump, topside leg, leaving neck and breast for sausage. He had no use for heads, feet and tails, although he kept the odd pig's head for a customer. There was no time in this shop for making brawn out of brains or pet food out of beasts' cheeks. Everything that came from the abattoir was already beheaded. He kept a few bones for dogs.

There had been ice houses in the shallow reaches of the

cliffs, where people had stored meat in winter years ago. Celia Hurly knew about these because her husband had known of them: so had her daughter. There was no map: they were randomly placed, family-owned. Small outdoor larders, fashioned from the shallow caves that were formed out of the fissures in the clay, packed with perishable food to preserve it during the long days of Lent. The ice houses were found in the areas where the sun never reached, the coldest places. Apart from the local historian, the only other people who knew about the ice houses were the children who had played in them.

For Andrew Sullivan, it was the saddest of all things to see a few of the older village men leading a posse of policemen down into the lee of the cliff to find the places where they had once played hide-and-seek. They were looking for a place where a body might have been slaughtered, hung, bled dry and left undiscovered for two days. It had to be the older ones who led the hunt: it seemed that the younger ones no longer played in the same way and were not encouraged to explore on their own. They sat indoors in front of TV screens, or were taken to places in cars. Only a few volunteers had turned up for the delayed search. They consisted of the historian, and seven others who had once been Boy Scouts. The only upside of the murder had been a record church attendance on Sunday, where the police had used the occasion to plead for further information.

Andrew followed behind the search, feeling redundant. He was ashamed of his own ignorance of the place. He had never been interested enough in the details, took his mandatory exercise along favourite routes without much deviation or curiosity. Not only did he not know where to look, he had no faith in the search itself.

Sam Brady was also part of the ragged team. The ice houses had still existed, if only just, when he'd been a boy. He had no faith in this search either, but he had to join it because to refuse to do so would be suspicious and he was not beyond suspicion himself. He thanked his own God for the fact that there were other witnesses to the fact that the body could only have arrived overnight on the night when it did, otherwise, in the absence of Jeremy, there would only have been his word for it. Sam was also grateful for the fact that Sarah had taken away the dog. She was right: the dog would have damned him as a pervert.

They had searched for three days in what seemed like a desultory fashion. It had been a game at first, but all games must have winners and losers, and here there were only losers, so it became dull. The search went further afield in daylight hours only. After dark, everyone went home, locked their doors and drew their curtains close against the wind. Maybe they prayed.

They should have been searching at night, if they had either the sense or the courage, Andrew thought. At night-time the fugitives were as free as birds. The night was their ally. The night would allow them to sabotage whatever was found. They were safe at night. The night was their territory and they had allies.

Something was found. Namely, a shallow grave, recently dug, containing the half-frozen body of a dog, carefully wrapped in a sheet, buried with respect. Sam Brady kept his mouth firmly shut in public. Then there was disappointment, because this, after all, had nothing to do with anything. It was only a dog and people buried dogs.

'But it has everything to do with it, you see,' Sam said to Andrew. 'It proves they're still around. They're right in the frame because they were in the flat above the shop the night when Jessica was put in the chiller. They never drove off anywhere, the van was left, they've nowhere else to go. They've had plenty of time to bury the dog nicely. Look, vicar, let me tell you about the dog. I need to confess.'

'I don't think you've got anything on your conscience, Sam, I really don't.'

They had taken to sitting in the still half-painted drawing room of the vicarage in the evening. Sam had retreated there, weeping, after the police had removed every ounce of stock from his shop and sealed it. It was like another death. It all felt as if it was his own fault and his wife could not understand how he could have been so clumsy to let such a thing happen.

Grief, shock and anger combined into a kind of fog through which he struggled to find any kind of view at all. Surprisingly, the vicar helped; Sam had never been a person who'd thought he would consult a pansy vicar, but Andrew was all right, really. Wine and beer eased the passage. They had even laughed about Celia Hurly, confessing to each other that they were afraid of her. Sam did not want to go home and Andrew did not want to do his duty and go downhill and speak to Mrs Hurly again before tomorrow. He would have to do it then: he was under orders. Curtains were drawn. A summer's evening was a distant dream.

A reckless fire flickered in the fireplace. The chimney worked after all. Andrew had begun to use some of the hated furniture for kindling. One of the uglier rotting chairs that he had dismembered in a fury burned merrily in the hearth. Sam stretched his legs towards it.

'You never knew Jack Dunn, did you? Well, no, of course not. Feckless bugger, too much cannabis and no dad, adored

Jessica for a while, one of her regulars. He came and went and finally rented one of the Hurly cottages, the one Sarah has, and oh, I wish she'd come back. Anyway, Jack had this bitch mongrel and he called it Jess, out of sentiment, because he liked repeating the name. Loved it and neglected it, you know? The way blokes do with wives. A bloke can be crackers about his woman without having the faintest idea how to treat her. The bitch was demented. He left it alone when he went to work: he got drunk, she got out, didn't behave, how could she? A cur dog, really, too clever by half. Wrong temperament – I'm telling you, vicar, if you ever get a dog, and you should, by the way, don't get any kind of sheepdog like that. They need too much, they're too fucking bright. Pack animal needs a leader. It bit a couple of the kids, but it was a sweet thing really, if you knew what to do. If you let it lick your hand.'

He coughed in embarrassment. The comparisons between the canine Jess and the human Jessica Hurly were all too real.

'Jack left her with Mrs Hurly when he went away. In lieu of rent or something. Left her tied up on the doorstep, thinking she'd take care of her because of the name. I don't know if he asked first, but Mrs H. shut her out, and then she went a bit mental. She was roaming around for weeks and no one could catch her, not even Jeremy until he found her.'

Andrew shuddered and looked towards the closed curtains. Sam took a huge handful of nuts and shoved them down his throat.

'He was after rabbits with his air rifle when he found her. Someone else had shot her with a shotgun – she was full of holes, he told me. She was starving and wounded, dying in pain, so he killed her properly. Kindest thing to do. He finished her off and laid her out on the road in the warm. It's always warmer on the road in the morning. He wanted it to look as if someone had run her over, because he'd be blamed for the shooting, although he's not the only one out there hunting rabbits at night, and quite a few people wanted that bitch dead, but he'd be blamed anyway. Only it was me who found her next. I was coming back from the abattoir about five, saw her on the road, stopped in time. I always drive slow when I've got a load. I knew who she was, so I took her home, dressed her nicely, shrink-wrapped her and put her in the chiller. She was a lovely thing, really, and I reckoned that if Jack ever came right he'd want to bury her. Jeremy, too. Closure and all that. You got to give an animal respect, even when it's dead. Part of my code. We always bury animals. I've got two of my old dogs out in the garden.'

Andrew reached for the wine. Sam had a good taste for the stuff and Sam would need a taxi home.

'I don't get it. He'd be content for the poor bitch to be squished on the road, and then he'd want to bury it?'

Sam shrugged. He could see nothing inconsistent in that. Andrew shook his head, trying to clear it.

'But where did they get the dead dog from?'

'Sarah's freezer, I expect. They can do what they want after dark. No one's watching then.'

Andrew was still puzzled. He was angry with Sarah for defecting, as he saw it, both from them and from Mrs Hurly with whom she had formed a strange and unlikely liaison in the course of a day. But he appreciated what she was doing insofar as he understood it and he was answering everything she asked by e-mail in a spirit of trust. If she was convinced that Jessica had been killed in London, of course she had to do what she did, because no one else could, but he still had the disappointment of a man half in love and who has been left.

Celia Hurly, thank God, wanted little company other than that of the mad, deaf woman who fed the birds outside her house. He went every afternoon, often armed with Sarah's questions. Andrew wished he believed in God's ultimate deliverance rather than having to believe in the vagaries of human nature. He too found himself wanting to confess.

'I wish Sarah would come back. She reckons she needs a week. Why do I think she knows it all? Why do we listen to her and to no one else?'

'Because she phones us and e-mails us and we do whatever she says? Because no one else makes sense? Because she took away the dog? No, because no one else is making any sense. I don't believe Jeremy would kill Jessica. Why would he?'

'For fun? To finish off humanely what someone else had begun? For a game? Because she wanted to be killed and they obliged? At the very least, they were in the flat upstairs from the shop when the body arrived, so they must have known.'

Andrew was not convinced, but he was willing to be persuaded.

'Not if they went out shooting rabbits and not if they were drunk, stoned and dead to the world. They wouldn't notice a thing.'

'Have the police got on to Sarah yet?' Andrew said.

'No, but they will. They've only just cottoned on to the fact that she knew the dear deceased. And Jeremy. And lived in Jack Dunn's house. I had to tell them that.'

'What a bloody mess.'

Sam lumbered to his feet.

'Let's paint a fucking wall,' he said.

'You know how you think you know the truth about anything,' Sarah said, 'and then you work out that knowledge is never complete unless you apply imagination. It's imagination that squares the circle. That's why we need stories.'

'You mean no one knows the whole truth about anything, unless they fill in the gaps by making it up?'

'Yes. You imagine the bits of the jigsaw you can't see, and you're very often right. Never dismiss your own imagination.'

'You mean, like you don't know half the details of my sordid past, but you can imagine the bits I either don't tell you or tell you wrong. I'll go along with that. And this Jessica, she told you stuff assuming you'd imagine the rest? Relied on you to imagine the rest? Can't quite see where you're coming from, doll – start again.'

Sarah and Mike were outside Smithfield at two forty-five, inside by three a.m., the early hours of the morning. Mike looked as if he belonged and had been there for ever. He was wearing a hard hat that didn't fit and an undersized white coat that looked as if it belonged to someone else. Sarah was similarly dressed, only both her helmet and her overall were too big.

'We're looking for a man. We're looking for the man who Jessica was looking for when she came here one night about three months ago. A man she was in love with, was obsessed with. A man who owned or ran a restaurant, was a valued customer and who brought her here to Smithfield in the early hours of the morning, showed her off to other men in here. Perhaps he was trying to sell her? No, that's fanciful. A buyer of meat, anyway, probably rich and powerful, a man who commanded respect in here. A man who could either give orders to or blackmail someone here. The same man who brought her here with pride, once, and then dumped her. A man she came to haunt, stalked him, even. There was one night she did that. I met her afterwards. She went to Smithfield to look for him, because she knew he went there early in the morning. She came to find him and couldn't. Wrong time. I met her on the way home and she told me all about it, although not everything. I told her she was a fool and she should forget all about it. She said she'd been screaming in Smithfield and the men in white coats chucked her out. Like I said, I picked her up on the way home. She came back for breakfast.'

Sarah paused. Mike listened intently.

'I think this man hated her and he's the most likely candidate to have killed her. He's helped her once and then rejected her. She remained obsessed with him, full of revenge and something else. I believe her existence was a threat to him, or to his business. I know she went back to DK to make a scene.'

'Gettit. You thought the man was the owner of Das Kalb, the posh dump? Simply because you could kill and bleed a person in that spotless kitchen without leaving a trace, because your kitchen was steam-cleaned every night? And you could make your drunken chef help you get rid of a few pints of blood?'

'Sam reckons she was pretty well bled. And I think that's what might have happened because she kept going back there. She haunted a place where he might be, although at the wrong time of night, and she haunted DK. Very bad for business. She'd gone there again: they made it up, then he left her, stood her up and made her cry, that was the last e-mail. He'd rejected her *again*. I reckon she went back. She thought about it, maybe, nursed the anger and *then* went back, because she hurt too much to leave it alone. I think that's where she died and this could be where she was posted for redelivery.'

'Definitely bad for business. It'd be a bit like screaming in church and telling them they were all going to hell. But the owner's a bit old to be the demon lover, you said. Still plenty of gaps here.'

'Like you said, Mike, you're never too old. And he might not have been a *Lover*, just someone she loved obsessively and someone who was threatened by it; who comes shopping in here around three in the morning. That's why we're here. I wanted to see if this place was the way she described it. She called it a big unstoppable machine. A place where he was entirely at home.'

The entry was via some old Mike contact, with another friend in the wholesale end. Got them a pass, coats and hats and left them alone. The pretence was a fact-finding mission. Smithfield men were proud of their ancient market. They did not mind visitors as long as they had a pass, wore the uniform and were not amongst the legion of Health and Safety officials who plagued their lives with EU regulations. Benign visitors could come and go, especially customers. They were perfectly capable of keeping their own secrets. Sarah was remembering stall fifty-five, the number on the invoices she had read in the restaurant, one of the numbers on Sam's invoices, too. Stall fifty-five, suppliers to industrial concerns, large and small, butchers and restaurants, far, near and wide. No order too large or too small. Only the best.

'I want to start on the outside,' Sarah said. 'I want to see how it works.'

They began at the big gates that led into Grand Avenue. She admired these gates with their huge motifs of Tudor roses painted turquoise, pink and purple, strangely frivolous for such a businesslike place. Then they moved round the side. They watched a huge container lorry dock at an entrance, as if it was sealing itself to the building. The noise of engines was deafening: there were yelled instructions. Mike hoisted himself up onto the platform, held out his hand to hoist her up too. No one questioned their presence as long as they kept out of the way and wore their hard hats. They watched as two men unhooked beef carcasses from inside the lorry and then hooked them back onto a moving rail that transferred them down a wide corridor into the body of the building. The men wore gloves: the animal corpses were chilled to almost freezing: raw skin would otherwise stick to skin. Sarah followed the progress of the carcasses, Mike beside her, moving with them at a slow walking pace as they passed a weighing-in point that registered the weight and the number of each on a dial set in the wall. She was thinking that if there had been a human body offloaded and hidden amongst the rest, this would have been the first place it would have been seen. It would have weighed less than the others, but the system was automated and no one would have noticed yet. Walking along with the slightly swaying carcasses was like walking amongst a silent well-behaved crowd. Otherwise the noise was tremendous. The corridor was almost as dark as it was outside, full of echoing mechanical sounds, whirring and banging and shouting ahead. No one noticed them: there was no one to notice.

The back of the stall was a cavernous room, filling up with the serried ranks of carcasses which followed a prescribed route via the overhead rails and lined themselves up in rows. It was less dark here but still gloomy and cold. Light made heat: judgement of quality was as much by touch as by sight. Workers wore sweaters and fleeces under the white overalls and adjusted to it. Sarah shivered. They stood back and watched as the anteroom filled up, then they moved to the next room.

It seemed as if there was some kind of race going on. There were men in a hurry, chopping, dismembering, dividing carcasses with practised ease and no time to spare. It all had to be sold, and sold soon. Smithfield had limited hours. Most meat was pre-ordered, needed quick preparation to meet the orders before being sent back, labelled and packed, down the corridor to the waiting delivery vans outside. Whole carcasses would go that way, too, if it was a whole carcass that had been ordered. There were pre-orders and orders arriving via computer and phone from the offices high upstairs. The activity was frantic.

'Not all wholesalers work this way,' Mike said. 'They all do it different, but this one's big business. One thing they've got in common is limited time – they keep strict hours. Come and see downstairs.'

Sarah did not want to see, but she went downstairs with him anyway. Cold dungeons with freezer rooms and chilling rooms the size of garages. Notices announcing what was stored. Ox liver, oxtail, ox heart, lamb plucks, lamb tongues, lamb testicles. Chicken feet, sweetbreads, calf's liver – words that swam before her eyes. She put her hand inside the neck of her sweater and felt the hook she wore around her neck. For luck.

They went back upstairs and stood, unnoticed, in the cutting room. She was mesmerised by the skill of the butchers, the speed of work, the urgency, the shouted orders from the front. Meat came in and meat went out. She had an overpowering urge for a cigarette. She felt she had seen enough, but knew this was just the beginning. It was three-twenty in the morning.

They were back in the room where the untouched carcasses hung silently, like girls in a beauty parade awaiting selection. Delivery was complete. Now it was all process. As they stood there, she with a clipboard in her hand to provide some authenticity, Sarah watched a white-coated man lead two other men into the room. An overhead light came on, illuminating them.

'Customers,' Mike whispered. 'Someone who wants to choose his very own cow. And then say exactly what he wants done with it.'

The two men were distinguished by the fact that they did not wear white overalls. They wore winter coats and scarves. They were beyond regulations. Big customers or influential ones.

Each of them inspected the carcasses. One of the men gave an instruction to the helmeted butcher, who pasted a label on a carcass and listened to further instructions. Sarah could not hear what was said and besides, it could have been in a foreign or technical language. She heard the words 'nothing too good for Das Kalb.' Then the second man turned and noticed them. He was half hidden by a carcass. In the dim light, Sarah had an impression of size and authority.

'Hello,' he said. 'What are you doing here? Not often we see a woman in here.'

He turned his back to her, spoke to the butcher. 'You know it's no place for a woman. Not back here, anyway. Only in extreme circumstances.'

A deep voice, carrying a warning.

'Research for a magazine,' Mike said easily. 'Got a pass. I do the looking, she does the writing-down on account of me not being so good at that. Don't worry, we aren't here to criticise. Brilliant place.'

The London accent reassured the man, along with Mike's shirt collar and tie and the masculinity of him. The man moved away, his demeanour indifferent now. The helmeted man glared at them.

'No one told me,' he began, blustering.

Mike held up his hand, placating. ''S all right, mate, we're going now, but can you answer me one thing? How the heck do you tell one of these from another and why does it make any difference? They all look good to me.'

'You can tell a steer from a cow, can't you?'

'Not me, mate, not me. Story of my life,' Mike said, edging backwards with Sarah in tow, aiming for the dark corridor and with a nothing-to-hide air. His remark provoked a bark of laughter.

'Get her out of here,' the man said.

The trio did not watch them go.

They went back down the long corridor to the exit. The huge container lorries had disappeared into the night. Instead there was a proliferation of delivery vans, high-sided one-ton trucks, smaller vans, every variety of white van. Loading was in progress, porters running with joints of meat, packs of chickens, pre-jointed shrink-wrapped parcels and, destined for the high-sided trucks, half-carcasses of beef.

Sarah went towards a high-sided van where the driver was getting back behind the wheel.

'Excuse me,' she said. 'Research. Can you tell me where you deliver?'

He looked at his watch and back at her, amazed by the stupidity of a question he had no time to answer. He was looking at a woman full of manic anxiety.

'Where *don't* I deliver? Everywhere.'

'Do you deliver as far as Dover?'

'Not me, mate. I mean everywhere in London.'

He shut the door of the van and drove off.

'How do I find out which of these delivers to a particular butcher on the south coast?' Sarah asked Mike.

'Needle in a haystack,' Mike said. 'You don't start here, you ask the fucking butcher. What's the matter, doll? You're shaking like a leaf.'

'I saw him,' she said. 'I saw him. I recognised him, I'm not sure from where. I recognise him. I need to see him in the light. I might know who he is, why she loved him.'

Sarah wanted to tear out her own hair.

'Don't you see?' she said, almost yelling in frustration. 'What better place to hide a body and move it on? He can't drive, but he has the power to make it happen. They were afraid of him. He knew it would work. It was the only way to get her home.'

CHAPTER THIRTEEN

Mike said he was going shopping and left Sarah standing outside a caff in sight of the gates into Grand Avenue. She watched him plunge back into the vibrant light of the meat market.

Sarah imagined Jessica standing in the same place, summoning courage to go in there alone. She found herself looking towards the entrance and imagining Jessica being dragged out; remembered her saying *they threw me out quite gently; they make their own laws.*

She had said so much at the time. There had been a torrent of words, of explanation, a premonition of pain. Jessica had kept rubbing her shoulder, saying she could feel a hook. 'Did they hurt you?' Sarah had asked. No, they had not: she had hurt herself. *I went to find him. He was avoiding me and I knew I could find him there. I knew he would have to be nice to me in front of all those men. They revered each other, him and those men, but I got the time wrong. I got everything wrong.*

On the morning when she had met Jessica all those weeks

before, it had been much later in the morning than this. Now it was almost four a.m., peak trading time. There was a multitude of white vans, cars, white-clad smokers huddled by the entrances for a quick gossip with fellow addicts before going back in. She should be over there, talking to them, but what could she ask? In a minute, maybe. There was so much to ask.

When she had met Jessica, half a mile from here, it had been nearly six a.m., two hours later than it was now. Jessica had gone into the market at the wrong time to find and confront the Lover who went shopping around three in the morning. Sarah had taken Jessica back to her own flat, fed her something, listened to her rambling and ended up making her talk about home, about her childhood, her background, and the sea, simply to make her change the subject. She had been trying to distract the obsessive girl, talked about her own dreams of a different way of life instead and then Jessica had sprung into action. Jessica had been wildly excited in her own ability to fix it, to do something within her power to fulfil a dream. Jessica described Pennyvale as perfect for Sarah's needs, the perfect place: she was longing to be there by proxy. It had happened so fast and she was so delighted with herself that she was irresistible, no one could resist her, and then when it was done, and even in between, she returned to the old theme. *You want to live in a cottage by the sea? Really? You'd love it there, Sarah, you really would, I could tell you how to find a place, and my mother has places.* And then, *He loves me, Sarah, he really loves me . . . how can he not? How can he leave me? How can he not want to be with me?*

Sarah could hear herself saying, *Go on, and tell me all about home: tell me about the place where you grew up – am I going to love it as much?* Getting seriously excited herself, thinking,

Yes, here's an opportunity; I'll do it, I'll do it; I'll give the dream a try. Not listening to anything else as freedom beckoned. How thoughtless she had been not to listen to all the other things she could have been told.

She watched a duo of seagulls circling above the high glass ceiling of Grand Avenue. All roads lead to the sea and beyond: this place had the feeling of being the centre of the universe, the underbelly, the belly feeder of a nation, famous for meat. Smithfield, purveyors of food for the capital. All roads led to and from here, bringing the food in, taking it away. She remembered another passage she had read from one of Mr Hurly's books in Mrs Hurly's tiny house. The passage had made her angry.

There was a definite association between butchers, drovers and highway robbers, and butchers were known for their violent natures. A survey of those hanged in the eighteenth century showed that among the trades, the main ones to reach the scaffold were butchers first, then weavers and then shoemakers.

Sarah watched the seagulls and heard their voices. The words had made her angry because those who were hanged were the poorest, the desperate, as well as the most ambitious and the ones who refused to compromise. Reckless Jessica Hurly might have gone to the scaffold if she had lived then. She had gone to her own scaffold. Sarah sipped sugared tea and wished she could feel hungry, to displace the feeling of disgust. Mike had been gone for a long time in there, doing his artful man's work in an environment where only men could ask questions and in which she felt impotent and useless. She was working things out, slowly, if not necessarily surely, hoping that her imagination was not squaring too many circles, reminding herself of the disciplines of her former life and education which dictated that fact was the only good foundation for any well-built belief, and imagination was only the mortar. She was trying to resist believing what she imagined must be true; trying and failing, counting on her fingers.

Jessica had gone back to Das Kalb. *The owner does small private parties on Sunday nights.*

DK was within walking distance from here.

A meat market was the perfect place to recycle a body; that was what a meat market was for, and it would stop for no one.

He could have carried Jessica here. He could have donned a white coat and delivered her here. In dark deserted streets who would notice? He would be a butcher on his way to work with something bloodless in a sack.

Mike appeared, carrying two bulging carrier bags.

'You can get free-range eggs and bacon in there, too. Thought I'd pose as a customer. Got us breakfast. I need it.'

He looked quite different without the hard hat and overalls that they had abandoned, innocent and ordinary until he turned his left cheek and then he looked as if he had authority. No one could fail to recognise him; he had presence. He sat down next to her, shaking his head.

'I've fucked that up,' he said. 'I really have. Got enough meat for two weeks and nowhere to put it. I went back to our stall. And he saw me. He was at the front of the stall and he saw me. He clocked me. The old bloke sizing up the beef. He was putting it on the account for DK. Got to be the owner, like the wine waiter said. Look, he's coming out, over there. Get inside, quick.'

There was a narrow counter on the inside of the caff's window. He pulled her inside and they leant on the counter, looking out, shielded by the light. They watched the big, imposing man come out through the main gates, followed by a white-coated porter carrying bags, walking towards a taxi carelessly parked amongst the delivery vans. The bags were placed inside, the man followed and the taxi moved away slowly. From this distance, the facial features were blurred by light and dark.

'They're only going round the corner to DK,' Mike said. 'Das Kalb. I got that for definite. Our favourite place. They have veal on the menu every night. Know what it means, doll? Das Kalb. The Calf.'

She tipped the last of the tea into her mouth and hoisted her bag.

'Home,' she said.

A huge surge of hunger came roaring back. Sarah could not remember when she had last eaten.

'The way I see it,' Mike said, 'is like this. The Das Kalb man is important business. He's a buyer. Even without him, look at the way they work. If you looked after stall fifty-five, one of the biggest and the bestest, what would you do if someone got in the back in the dark and inserted the body of a woman on the delivery line and hung it up along with the rest so that it was delivered to you? You'd see it for sure, you'd see it as soon as it passed the weighing station, but *then* what would you do? Call the police? What would happen if you did? All hell would break loose, that's what would happen. You'd have to stop selling. The heavy-handed mob would come in and close you down. They'd close down the whole market. Your business would be bust; the people who ordered from you might never come back. The other wholesalers would hate you. Close the whole market and what would be the loss? A million or more? You're having a hard enough time as it is. What would you do, doll, what would you do?'

'I'm not a man. I don't have a business to run. What would *you* do?' Sarah was chewing a piece of toast that tasted of sawdust.

'What would I do if I were a hard-headed businessman butcher in hard times with people to pay and a living to make and a brotherhood behind me? I'd hide it away. I'd hide the body good and deep in one of those freezer rooms. I'd freeze it or disguise it until I could get someone to take it away. I might chop it into pieces. Business is business and the bitch is already dead. It's a body like so many other bodies – corpses don't faze them, they handle them all the time. It doesn't belong to you, you haven't ordered it, but it's going to ruin you. You haven't got a choice: there *is* no choice. Nothing gets in the way of business. You've got to sell and sell soon, so you get rid of it and get on with business. You get someone to take it away and pretend it hasn't happened. That's what I'd do. You'd get rid of it and you'd be safe. You'd be easily persuaded to do that.'

Sarah remembered Sam's impulse when he had found the body of Jessica. *I wanted to get rid of it. I wanted it to go away.* Even a decent man might be tempted.

'Especially if a favoured customer paid you or asked you,' she said.

Mike nodded.

'You wouldn't do favours like that on a regular basis, but you might do it just this once. You'd do it because you *could* and it would be the easiest way out. You might do it because it looked like the *only* way out. He's engineered things so that choice is the last thing on the menu. He's got you fixed.'

He had finished his poached eggs on toast. Sarah had averted her eyes from the yellow mess while being grateful for the existence of hard men with good digestions and clear-thinking minds.

The coffee also tasted of nothing.

'Any more of that? Yup, you'd store it out of the way, 'cos only one or two people would know. Better still if you could get someone to take it away immediately. Someone who really needed his job. A delivery man, maybe. Someone who would take it far, far away, dump it on someone else, either the last in the line or someone who deserves it, or who'd pass it on to someone else even further away to bury it for you or dump it in the sea.'

'Or someone who was going that way, anyway. Someone who was paid to take it home? That's what he did. He couldn't do it himself. He paid someone to take it home, someone who couldn't refuse.'

Mike sat back.

'Wherever, doll. Someone would take her, especially if he needed his job. Or was paid enough. It could be done, not easily, but it could be done. I might have done it myself twenty years ago, as long as I didn't know who it was. A corpse doesn't have a personality in a meat market. You can see what it's like around there. Frantic rush to load up, mostly in the dark. Who'd notice another small steer wrapped in a bit of sacking or any old wrapping being slung in the back of a van? Something less than the size of a calf.'

'Someone took her home,' Sarah said doggedly. 'Someone was forced – or paid – to take her all the way home. She was labelled for home.'

'So she was. Gottit. A freelance Smithfield delivery man dedicated to stall fifty-five, others too, maybe. Someone who leaves about four in the morning and does small orders, long-distance. Little deliveries to independent butchers. Last in the line is somewhere godforsaken like Pennyvale. Can get in any time and leave the orders, if he arrives early. Only he never, ever calls on Wednesdays and there were no outstanding orders, so no one looks for him or even dreams of him. Only maybe that Wednesday he did. Because he was paid. Because he *could*.'

Dear S,

I can scarcely believe you've been away for so many days. It feels like years and everything has stood still.

On demand, a bit of local history for you.

You've been asking a lot of questions, but I relish the chance to communicate, it brings you back into the house. The weekend was endless; selfishly, I hope it was for you too. I'd hate for you to be tempted back to Sodom and Gomorrah before you had a chance to start somewhere else.

Tea with Celia, sad. Both numb and raving at the same time, moments of crystal clarity when asked to recall.

Asks after you, saying where is she, will she come back? She's pathetically polite and grateful. I liked the other, ruder one better.

No Hurlys in the graveyard. He might have been there, except for the fact that the body was never recovered.

Next question. According to her mother, Jessica had always wanted to be buried at sea. A childish ambition: you know how children and teenagers can be wonderfully ghoulish and dramatic about death. Wanted to be buried at sea like a Viking in a burning boat.

YES, Sam is going to be allowed to open the shop again, soon! No blood contamination, apparently, so sooner than we thought. Date will be fixed tomorrow. He'll be placing orders and he's beginning to cheer up.

Him and me painted the walls grey. Looking good. I hope you like it.

No sign of J. and J., tho' no one else being suspected. Cops think they're long gone. Definitely not looking for anyone else. They found the dog, though, but no one helped them close that particular circle. They are very slow, these cops. They know Jessica was seen here, but they can't find anyone who actually did spot her.

Local paper full of the news. Copy in the post, as requested.

I do like you, Sarah. Very much. Please come back. Isn't it better not to know? Let it rest.

Love,

Andrew

PS. I'm not gay. It just seems to have been expected of me, but you knew that, didn't you?

Dear A,

Yes, I always knew that.

And I think I'm beginning to know how Jessica was killed, but I've got to stay until I can get something like proof. Let me know as soon as Sam has the all-clear, and has a date for Smithfield deliveries, will you? This is very important. Then I'll come back, maybe bring a friend.

City life OK, but confusing. At least we have seagulls.

Talk soon,

Love, S

Dear Sarah,

What friend?

Sleep on it. Too restless to sleep, even with Mike beside her. 'How do we find the delivery man, Mike?'

'You won't find him via Smithfield. Cover's blown and no one will say. What you do is you start the other end. You go to Pennyvale and wait for him to turn up. You really believe all this, don't you? And you want me to go with you? I hate the place.'

'You've got work to do first.'

Celia Hurly woke late and looked at the view through the window. A sky of brilliant blue with scudding clouds, bisected by the window frame. She closed her eyes to blot it out, disliking the invitation of a fine day. Good weather was demanding: it said get up and do something, clear the mind, use energy, you cannot sleep for ever.

But she wanted to sleep for ever. She had been sleeping for years in a fog of regret.

Soon everything would go back to normal. She would be a widow living in a village, sleeping as long as she liked, with enough income to live simply and enough mischief to entertain her, forgetting how her daughter had disgraced her and her husband had abandoned her long before he left to die that final time. No one wanted to go out in a boat with him: he had to go far away to fish from a boat. Tried to remember how she had loved it here. Perhaps when the summer came she would be able to love it again. Perhaps she would be able to walk on the cliffs without being mortally afraid of looking down. Perhaps she might be able to put her feet in the sea, because the worst, the very worst had happened, the event she had dreaded, and it might free her from her prison. Perhaps one day the image of her daughter's body swinging on a butcher's hook would begin to fade and allow itself to be replaced by the images in photographs and old videos of beautiful Jessica and her father holding a fish caught on a line from the shore. Images she had taken, lovingly, from which the taker was excluded. Perhaps God would help her now because she had been punished.

She could hear footsteps coming up the stairs, slowly enough for her to turn her head into the pillow, close her eyes and pretend to be asleep. The door opened softly and she heard the steps approach the side of her bed. A hand caressed her shoulder gently and briefly, with the right amount of contact to reassure without intruding. A touch that said it doesn't matter if you're asleep, or if you're pretending, I'm not offended either way. She could hear a cup of tea being placed on her bedside table and smelled the smell of it. Half deaf, only slightly demented Mrs Smith, friend of seagulls, knew how to make a cup of tea.

'There, there,' Mrs Smith said. 'Sleep on. I'll draw these curtains, shall I? Too bright out there. Oh and by the way, I've just remembered something. You know I told folk I'd seen Jessie? Well, they thought I meant your Jessica, but I didn't, and what I meant was that I'd seen that poor wild bitch – Jess, it was called, or was it Jessie – roaming around and playing with that Alsatian from the pub, and then I realised it can't have been. Ben Byrce shot her, weeks since, 'cos she bit his kid. Oh what a lovely day, just when we need a nasty one. Sometimes I hate fine days.'

Again, that small caress to the shoulder, which went with the soft voice.

'See you when you're ready, love. You've always been a grand lady to me. Always kind. You just sleep, now.'

Kind? Had she ever been kind? Yes. Celia waited for the slippered footsteps to go away and then opened her eyes. There was no view of the sea; only white curtains billowing round an open window. She tried to remember when she had last been kind. All she had ever done with old Maggie Smith was fail to yell at her for feeding seagulls, and yet the woman had stepped in with unfailing courtesy, stayed, made food and waited, a half-deaf ideal listener. She was so entirely without malice, as sensitive as a dove landing on a roof. The kindness was humbling. Celia wanted to copy it.

The information had come as relief. Jessica had never come home alive. She had not come home and failed to knock on the door. Celia had not been denied the last chance to take her in. It had tormented Celia, that her daughter had been so close and not come closer. Celia Hurly cried and cried and cried. She had been kind to no one, and yet kindness had been forthcoming. She had not deserved it, but it had been there. Brutal kindness from Sarah Fortune, kindness of an unquestioning kind from Mrs Smith; flowers from people she did not know she knew, tokens and cards from people she thought despised her. It meant that she was going to have to learn to live.

She stood on the window side of the bed and leant down to touch her own toes, just. Stretched her arms above her head, lifting her heavy bosom in the process. Lowered her hands and wept again.

She wept for the child and for the dog.

Maybe she might be able to be kind again. Maybe she had not lost the instinct. Accept. Forgive and pray to be forgiven. Find a child or a dog to rescue and, this time, honour it. Give up the anger that had sustained her. Let someone know her, if they were brave enough to try.

Celia Hurly fumbled for the tea and drank it down.

You have to be sure. You have to have confirmation, whatever kind. You have to eat lunch.

It was Thursday, towards the end of a long week, when Sarah sat at the table nearest to the door of Das Kalb. She had booked for two, arrived by herself, ordered a glass of wine and a bottle of water while waiting for her companion. She read her newspaper for ten minutes, studied the menu, checked her watch, spoke into her mobile phone like a natural.

The sommelier of that recent evening was not there: a waiter hovered. She explained that her friend was not turning up, could she order? She was not going to waste the opportunity of eating at DK, even if she had to pay for it herself. A salad to start, eaten slowly and precisely, to be followed by DK's famous veal.

Mostly the restaurant's customers dined in twos, with regular lone diners at lunch, although none of the other loners were female. Definitely worse to be dining alone as a female and far more conspicuous, which was what Sarah intended. The veal arrived: she regarded it with trepidation. Her appetite was robust, diminished by shame that the animal on her plate should not have had a chance to grow up. She had made herself hungry enough to eat anything. Devoted to her food, acting the connoisseur, she watched objectively.

The customers were decorous pigs at a trough, eating as if food were newly invented. Threading his way between them, elegantly for all his bulk, there was the gracious host, the big man stooping unobtrusively to request of the almost exclusively male diners 'Is everything to your satisfaction?' and receiving enthusiastic nods of affirmation. Sarah had the impression that none of them would have said no even if everything had not been to their satisfaction, because the man had such muscular charm. He did not pester his customers, simply offered reassurance. She was confident that he would not recognise her from his fleeting glimpse of a woman with her hair hidden beneath a white helmet in a dark room two nights before. The red-haired woman with the black polo neck and the dramatic piece of jewellery was a different kind of creature. A woman sitting alone in a place like this would always be thought of as pathetic, stood up, or on the make, so he was leaving her until last. She had already paid and was lingering over coffee before he stopped by her table. The restaurant was still full. He approached from the side, the way he did with all the customers, never facing them head on, never intrusive, saving the best for last.

'Has everything been all right for you, madam?'

Sarah turned to face him and gave him the full-wattage smile. The highly polished silver hook on its silver chain was clearly visible. An S-shaped butcher's hook, capable of supporting the twenty kilos of meat that he would be capable of lifting. Old, yes, seventy if he was a day, with the well-honed body of one accustomed to disciplined physical labour, a soldier not gone to seed, powerfully attractive. At close quarters it shocked her.

'Terrific, thank you,' she said. 'Apart from the fact that I hadn't planned to eat alone. I was waiting for my friend Jessica Hurly, only she was delayed. Apart from that, it was fine. Is she a regular here? Not exactly a woman's place, is it? Unless you don't care about your weight.'

The force field of the man's attraction and her sudden weakness in the wake of it made Sarah speak quickly, not as calmly as she had rehearsed. His skin was tanned and his eyes were piercingly blue. The smile was glacial and yet she would have loved to see him laughing. He pulled out the empty chair and sat down, his eyes fixed on the jewellery round her neck. For a moment, she thought he would touch the hook.

Instead, he removed his gaze from the pendant and stared at his own large hands, which looked starkly brown against the cloth.

'I'm glad you enjoyed it. We do our best. Jessica? No, I can't recall anyone called Jessica dining here. As you said, the place is designed for men. Shall I fetch your coat? Is the S for Sally or Sarah?'

She had left the local paper prominently displayed on the table and now she allowed him to help her into her coat. Felt his hand touching her neck, feeling the chain, making her shiver.

'Goodbye,' he said.

She did not want to say goodbye. She wanted to say, *Can I come back?*

No one would recover easily from a man like this. Jessica was right. There was a terrible warmth to his touch.

Sarah did not want to believe it was him. There was her weakness for an ageless, ruthless halfway-beautiful man like that. She did not want it to be him.

CHAPTER FOURTEEN

Sarah tried to put aside the treacherous attraction.

Thought instead that that had been a foolish lie of his. A revelation. A useful exercise. She was putting distance between herself and the kitchen of Das Kalb, sick with rich food, looking for a contrast.

The meeting had shown the man to be a liar, at the least, and had allowed her to look at him face to face again, to make sure. This man was certainly the love of Jessica Hurly's life. Her soulmate, her greatest loss.

Sarah needed to move, felt the same old, new irritation with people on pavements getting in the way, wanted to run away, fast, but you could not run in central London streets except at night so instead she walked demurely through the narrow City back roads, thinking out loud, massaging the ice chip in her heart.

It had been a silly lie of his to deny that Jessica had ever been to Das Kalb, because it denied a fact, not a supposition. Jessica Hurly had been there several times, might have worked there once; even the sommelier knew of her. They would all have been able to put a name to her, even if they had never known who she was, they would have known she was called Jessica and that Jessica was trouble. The powerfully urbane proprietor might have regretted his own lie by now, just as he would have regretted Sarah's presence in his restaurant. She had touched him with the blunt finger of suspicion; he would be a clever, cunning, systematic man, checking the bookings, just as he would check every day to see who his customers were, noting that S. Fortune had booked twice – once in the evening, once for lunch – in the space of a week. He would check what she had done on the first occasion, know that she had been backstage: he would work it out, and she would never be able to go back. She was betting with herself that if she phoned to make another reservation she would be told, politely, that they were fully booked. Or perhaps not; perhaps he would invite her back into the kitchen to see what she knew. Perhaps he would hand her Jessica's missing mobile phone.

She walked from DK through the narrow streets surrounding it and went into the church of St Bartholomew on the other side of Smithfield market. The very same St Bartholomew had been chosen for the church in Pennyvale; Bartholomew the Apostle, accredited with spreading the gospel in India and Armenia, finally martyred by being flayed alive and then beheaded. She remembered from Andrew Sullivan's pamphlet that St Bartholomew's emblem in art was a butcher's knife.

This ancient church was a plain building, warm and comforting, the interior an oasis of calm. It was all warm and yellowed stone, without any of the ornate Victorian additions and improvements of the far younger St Bartholomew's church of Pennyvale, which for all its fussy dark woodwork was still a cold place. This place had an ancient heart, which made it a humbling place to look for her own, to sit down and separate fact from imagination. She sat on a worn pew where hundreds of others might have sat over the centuries while paying as little attention to God as she did now, although wanting his protection without obligation, looking at the light coming through the windows. Built for warmth and protection, a great church once, a centre for the poor, a hospital. Sitting in silence, making scant reference to worship, but grateful to any belief that created such a sanctuary as this, Sarah tried to reconstruct her own version of a story.

Mr Edwin Hurly, a rich man who had once been a poor man, staged his own death. The details of the where and how did not really matter. He had staged his death carefully, because he could no longer bear to go home. He had had such expectations of home that the reality of his return and the unattainableness of an ideal life became unbearable. Those who had loved him loved him too much: others detested him. He had not proved himself to anyone, had impressed no one: no one admired his success, they only resented it, shunned him and his autocracy. He had reached the end of the line. He hated home.

The light inside the church was soft and forgiving. Music played, an ambient background sound which could have irritated but soothed instead, like the sound of the sea on a calm day. Sarah could not understand why the place was empty. Everyone needed such sanctuary. Did he come here, this haunted and haunting man? Who had still had power in Smithfield where he had earned his fortune.

She had the facts. Andrew Sullivan was seducing her with e-mailed facts, earning his spurs.

Dear S,

Hurly made habit of going deep-sea fishing. Liked to get away. Reported drowned. Affairs left in good order, always were shipshape. Will filed, no questions. No loose ends. Why do you ask?

A grown man with money could get away with staging his own disappearance in however clichéd a manner if he had a little help, if he belonged to a brotherhood, if he planned it. He could get away with death and reinvention as long as the death had a logic to it, was feasible and possible. Death by drowning was hardly original – the method made him a copycat of others who had failed in such a subterfuge – but distance added credibility, made it easier to fudge. People died in pursuit of challenging adventures every year and his was a responsible death, leaving provision for the nearest and dearest. Lies were only discovered when someone went in search of them; rigorous investigation would only follow if the death involved fraud or theft, but this man had died solvent, defrauding no one. Why would anyone question it, especially if it was, in its own way, a relief? It might have left Celia Hurly free to reclaim the love of her daughter. It would have driven the daughter mad with grief.

It would be the first great betrayal, therefore the worst, and no one would understand it. Jessica went on the rampage, just as she had when she found him again.

The music stopped, as if giving a signal to leave. A woman came in and walked briskly to the front of the church, carrying a bucket in one hand and a large feather duster in the other. Even a church could not clean itself. The sight of her broke the spell and made Sarah smile. Sanctity and practicality were always good companions, and she thought of practical things and tried to finish the story in her mind.

What happened next? This was for the imagination. Ten years pass. Then hysterical Jessica, who came to London in search of instant fame and fortune, driven hither, happened upon him by accident because they were in parallel lines of business. Perhaps they fell upon one another, the first love of her life resumed. At first, joy and embracing, tears and explanations. *Your mother was to blame.* He would take her up, help her, take her into his new world, take pride in her, take her places, be proud of her. They would agree it was their secret, rejoice in it. But Jessica was a hungry, demanding soul; she wanted more and more: she wanted the years she had missed, she wanted to be with him every day. She wanted, above all, to take him home. She wanted him to go back.

Soon he would not want to see her every day: she got in the way of business. And then she would blackmail him for his lack of attention because she was angry, stuck in childhood, recklessly needy, a girl without boundaries in search of the old exclusive love, ready to threaten his whole new identity. She would cajole, persuade, behave as she did when she was a child. Expose him, above all, make him go home to Mummy, make Mummy happy again, make up for what they both had done. An obsessive in pursuit of the perfect life she thought they'd had. A rejected, violent child, her father's daughter. Tantrums.

Jessica could ruin business. Jessica could never have enough. Jessica would never see how impossible her plans were.

The music began again, secular music rather than religious. This church embraced the non-believer. An old folk song, sung softly in the background.

Last night, she came to me,
She came softly in.
So softly she entered, her feet made no din.

She would not have come softly this time. Soft body, with eyes of steel, a woman scorned. *He stood me up.* Seeking him out in Das Kalb at night when she knew he would be there, when he was tidying up, when he was preparing, whenever. He was there on a Sunday night. They were closed on Mondays only: Sarah had checked. A fight, an accident. Ending with Jessica suspended by the ankles on a hook in that kitchen after everyone had gone home. A humane killing, a ritual cleansing as in an abattoir. Sanitised, slung over a shoulder when the blood was gone, maybe wrapped in muslin like a side of ham, taken to Smithfield that day or the next, inserted into the line. A brilliant method of disposal. Desperate men took desperate measures and had unreasonable expectations of their allies. When the man she was convinced was Edwin Hurly had set down next to her, Sarah could feel the power radiating from him. He was a disciplined bully with his daughter's wonderful charisma and, like her, he would never quite gauge the impact he had on others. He would probably overestimate it.

Sarah left the church, bowing to the simple altar, reverting to a long-forgotten instinct to genuflect and make the sign of the cross, which would either encourage the love of God or ward off the Devil. *I have nothing to be ashamed of,* she said to St Bartholomew, *but I shall have if I don't find out what happened. It is not about justice, because there is no justice. Truth would do. Truth helps the living far more than not knowing: there is no reconciliation without it. I would like it if I could guess what he might do next.* She had been trying to think like *him*, put herself in his shoes, but she did not want him to be a murderer. Part of her wanted to walk away and just let him live.

She walked back towards Smithfield, skirted round the building, reaching the crowded pavements again, slowing down. It was a walk of a mile to home, but where was home? It was nowhere: it was on top of a cloud: it was somewhere where you could make a nest and defend it. It was somewhere you taught yourself to love, even if it did not love you back. It was somewhere where you could be useful. In the meantime, there was this constant craving for the sound of seagulls squabbling.

Sarah considered going back to Das Kalb, feeling the same pull as Jessica and wanting to confront him, even just to see him again. No. Leave it alone now. She was not going to be flayed alive; nor did she want vicarious revenge, but her own God would damn her if she let someone else be blamed. Her duty, if it could be called so, was not to Jessica, it was to the living. Damn duty, but it was always there. She acquired it wherever she went, whatever she did, and with whomever she slept, although that involved the least duty of all. The love for a lover was a pale shadow of the child's love for a father.

She needed *proof.* She had found the bricks in the edifice of the story. The mortar was subject to decay. Proof was a long way off. The only fact of which she was certain was that the owner of Das Kalb was Jessica Hurly's father, first seen in a grainy photograph, holding a fish. It was time to go home. Begin at the other end.

The meal lay heavily on Sarah's stomach. She walked faster.

She wanted to pick up a bag and the chosen companion, go for the train and get home soonest, but it could not be today. Again, she would have to wait. Wait for the day when the delivery man would come to Pennyvale. The day would arrive soon enough. Another Sabbath would pass.

The mist over the sea was a glorious blanket. After his morning walk, Andrew Sullivan admired the pristine glory of the vicarage living room and then walked uphill to help Sam. Sarah was going to love the new room. The mist disappeared and the day turned grey.

'We made the national news,' Sam grumbled. 'For one day only. It's insulting when you think of it. Then we faded. Help me out here.'

Tidying, scouring, cleaning. Sam was back in his own premises, not quite as happy as a pig in shit but almost. Such a bonus to be allowed to open again tomorrow, within a fortnight of being shut. The day went quietly. The chiller was perfectly empty. *She* might never have been there.

'Smithfield delivery tomorrow. She says we have to wait. I spoke to the man, the same man, put in the order. He sounded fine, didn't seem to know anything. Just said he wondered why we hadn't ordered recently, not chatty. He couldn't say what time he'd be here, said it depended on other deliveries, traffic and stuff, could be very early, could be after opening time. Would let himself in, if need be, if the traffic was fine, etc. Any time, I said, the earlier the better, gives me time to display. I reckon the earliest he'll get here is five in the morning. I got the impression he wanted to be early.'

'So we wait for him,' Andrew said.

'Back to yours, vicar? She said she'd come and join us with some hard man she knows. Why do we listen?'

'Because we do. No choice about it. I don't like the idea of the hard man.'

'I'm glad she's coming home.'

'So am I. She'd better stay this time.'

'I'm not gay, you know.'

'Who did you think you were fooling? Wise man, you are. Otherwise you'd be target practice for all the widows in a place like this. Stay as you are, I would. Or confound them all by getting a wife. Are we ready?'

The darkest hours were before dawn.

Sarah Fortune was well used to the company of men, and wished with all her heart for the company of a woman on this occasion. She had never wanted to be the leader of the pack. Mike could take that role. It was he who had suggested the plan. *Find the delivery man? Needle in a haystack. Go and wait for him. Shake him until he rattles. Then you'll have proof, or not. Proof that Miss Hurly never came home alive.*

So they were waiting. The earliest time he could be here was five a.m., Sam said. OK – unless he really wants to avoid us, then he'll be sooner. They had foregathered at four in the morning in the tiny upstairs flat above the butcher's, with the window looking onto the dark street, a depressing place to be, although warmer than the back of the shop. There was a flask of tea, paper cups and grimy blankets on which to sit. Someone had provided sandwiches that no one wanted. The room was crowded with three men and one woman, the men feeling slightly ridiculous and manipulated. Andrew was gazing towards Sarah, looking for guidance, enjoying the sight of her, but wondering why he was there. Surely not as a priest; only as another male presence, a sort of makeweight who might curtail the excesses by his very presence, the soft man as opposed to the hard one. He had loathed Mike on sight and conceded to himself that there was jealousy in that.

They all knew the theory: they all knew why they were here, but the levels of belief varied, along with the anxieties. They were waiting for the delivery man who might have brought Jessica home. Sam had hardened his heart to anything except his chief priority, which was to make sure that the delivery was right so that he would open his doors for business and become himself again. Mike, the man with the frightening face, wanted to nail whatever bastard had killed a pretty woman, even if he did not care about the woman herself who sounded like a right spoiled bitch to him, but no one deserved to be hung. Sarah wanted to know if she was right. Mike and Sam were chatting man to man, Mike asking about business, always interested in someone else's business. You never knew when information would come in handy, all knowledge was useful. Andrew was losing the will to live. Conversation became desultory, fell into silence. Then they were tense and silent and waiting, waiting, waiting.

The main street of the village was in darkness. No door left unlocked, no curtains left open. A street of barriers. A mild night for the time of year: it had been a long mild spell since Jessica had come back.

Only two cars passed in the hour. They could hear the sudden acceleration up the hill, the whizz as they went by. Then as they sat stupid and quiet, there was the sound of footsteps and of someone wheeling a trolley. A knock at the front door of the shop. Then running footsteps, following whoever it was. A voice saying, *There, there, come away, they aren't open yet.*

Celia Hurly and her shopping trolley went back down the hill. Total silence fell again. It was six o'clock.

'Right,' Sam said. 'I'd better get on. Things to do. If that bastard doesn't come with that bastard delivery, I'll kill him. We can make better tea down there, anyway.'

He lumbered to his feet and went out of the attic, down the back steps and into the shop through the back door. They all got up and followed, crowding into the back of the premises. Mike put the kettle on and followed Sam into the still dark front of the shop, still curious, wanting to learn more. He would like to watch a skilled man sharpening his knives. 'That's one of the first things I do,' Sam said. Mike listened: he always wanted to learn; you never knew what you might have to do next. They began to relax. It would be dawn within the hour and everything would stop being so unreal.

Sam moved towards the front door to turn on the lights. Before he got there the whole shopfront was swept with fierce light from the headlamps of a white van pulling onto the forecourt, halting so close to the window that he thought it was aiming to drive straight through. The headlamps went off. A door slammed, then another. They scuttled away like cockroaches.

'Christ,' Mike said. 'There's two of them.'

CHAPTER FIFTEEN

'Better open the door,' someone said.

Sam turned on the lights and opened the door. Two men came in. The regular small scared-looking delivery man in a white coat, and a handsome white-haired man in a suit and overcoat.

Mike moved towards the knife rack, took one of the knives and held it behind his back.

Sarah came out from the back of the shop into the bright light at the front. The throbbing glare was strong enough to hurt her eyes, going right to the back of the eyeball after all the darkness, creating a sudden violence. Sarah put her hand on Mike's arm, let it rest there. She knew what he could do.

'Dear God,' Sam said. 'Mr Edwin Hurly as I live and breathe.'

The man in the coat blinked at the light and slumped into the chair by the counter reserved for the elderly customers. He looked old and tired. He shielded his eyes and looked towards Mike.

'You can put that down,' he said. 'I'm not dangerous. I'm nothing now, nothing at all. This light's too bright. Never was like that before.'

They moved automatically, mesmerised, to stand around him in a rough circle.

'You. You're everywhere. S for Sarah. Jessica told me about you. Said you were a high-class hooker. The woman with the hook.'

She spoke softly. 'Hooker, yes. High-class is overstating it a bit.'

He sighed and closed his eyes briefly, opened them again, pointing a finger at Andrew.

'Who's that streak of piss?'

'He's the vicar,' Sam said. 'And you just missed your wife.'

Edwin Hurly shuddered, sat up straight in the chair. He turned to Sarah.

'Would you sleep with me if I paid you enough? Are you that kind of tart? Jessica reckoned you would. She wanted to give me you as a present, said you would persuade me to do what's right. You did it anyway, didn't you? Never mind, don't answer. Thanks for leaving the paper. Thanks, but no thanks. The game's over . . . some bloody game. I thought someone would be waiting, but not you, and not so many. Nice to see you, Sam Brady. You were always a good man. I'm sorry if fetching her home was bad for business. I thought you'd deal with it like I would have done. Businesslike.'

'I don't know what you would have done, Mr Hurly.'

'Me? I'd have got her out in a boat and buried her at sea, just like I was asked. Best all round. Jeremy would have done that for you. That's what she would have wanted. And then I'd have got on with business. That's what it's all about. That was the decent, practical thing to do while she still looked nice. I left instructions, why didn't you follow them? I didn't want anyone blamed.'

He jerked his thumb in the direction of the delivery man, who stood by the door, quivering, looking for an escape.

'Blamed for what?' Sarah said.

'Bringing her home. He did it, all right, but only because I made him. It was the only way. I couldn't drive her myself – I don't drive. Besides, I liked the irony of it and I could make them do it. I always kept tabs on who delivered to Pennyvale, I knew the delivery men, made it my business, a sort of homesickness. You got it all worked out, didn't you, S for Sarah? Jessica died in my kitchen. I hung her up and bled her dry. Don't ask who helped. Me and chef, another poor bastard who needs his job, got her over to Smithfield and onto the line, day after. We, sorry, *I* carried her when she'd cooled down. Who notices men in white coats around there? Takes a long while for a hot body to cool, even when the blood's out. Especially Jessica, she was burning hot. Twenty-four hours, about. After that, they had no choice but to move her on or close up and they'd never do that. Not that lot. I knew they had no choice.'

Edwin Hurly reached into the pocket of his overcoat, took out a mobile phone on a leather thong and laid it on the floor next to his enormous feet. He was still a strong man.

'Want to know?'

They stood around him in a semicircle, nodding at him, protecting each other. Mike kept hold of the knife.

'She recorded it,' he said. 'Some of it, anyway. Didn't notice that she'd taken her phone off, put it down on the side. She was never without it, even ordered food on it. She turned up after about one in the morning when there was only me and chef, doing the business. I didn't see her come in, she was sly. She was high and drunk, whatever the order. I don't know what we do with this generation, expects too much, everything given. She expected too much.'

He coughed. It was a long, racking cough, sending his whole body into spasm. He gripped both sides of the chair, leant forward and spat onto Sam's clean sawdust.

'You can listen to it, if you like. She was never without that mobile.'

Sarah recognised it, a phone on a thong. Edwin Hurly saw her recognition.

'You with that hook around your neck. You. You could take a man's eyes out, any time. You go equipped.'

'Always,' she said.

He sat back and began to laugh. The laughter wrecked him as much as the coughing. Then he began to cry.

'I don't want anyone else blamed,' he repeated. 'For that poor little calf. Don't look for that chef, either – he's long gone.'

'You were never a bad man, Edwin Hurly. You were good to me,' Sam said, moving towards him, extending his hand.

The old man nodded and waved him back.

'I was good to everyone, always was, only it didn't always work. Always knew what was right for everyone, only no one else understood it. That's why I'm here. Tell it like it is, boy. Come on.'

The delivery man stepped forward. The light had not changed in its fierce brightness, except that with them surrounding him it felt more as if they were shielding him. He spoke awkwardly and nervously with a heavy accent.

'He's right. He got her hooked up inside a truck. It was dark. She went down the line, into the stall and back and I was called to collect her and put her in the van with all the other stuff. He wanted her brought here. He always knew us men. He always knew who delivered where. He knew I came to Pennyvale, he was in Smithfield most nights, always nice.'

The delivery man hesitated. 'I had to keep her in the van for a day, so's I could deliver on a day when I was never expected. She was cool about that: she was cool all the time.'

He stuffed his fist in his mouth, distressed. 'I'd seen her before, you see. Pretty lady. I *wanted* to bring her back. He said she was going home and he paid me and said I'd lose my job otherwise. He said I'd never work in Smithfield again if I didn't and no one would ever know because she'd just disappear. I'd never hear about it again.'

Edwin Hurly ignored the broken voice and waved him aside.

'Such confidence I had in you, Sam. You let me down.'

He had recovered from the tears, rolled his eyes, lifted a hand and wagged a finger at the delivery man.

'No, no, no. Look at him. Loco, you see, absolutely loco and foreign with it. They do good butchers in the Ukraine, but loco. That's his version, poor lad. Can't be doing with these unreliable versions, even if they have to be heard. Yes, she died in the kitchen, yes, I bled her. The chef didn't help at all. He did, poor sod, I made him. Yes, I took her to Smithfield to get rid of her, yes, he went too, or no, he didn't. She gets in down the line to stall fifty-five, where there's one man who owes me and wanted to keep his business open at all costs. He's the no-choice man. They all are. That's one version. Not a version I like.'

More coughing. Backstage, the kettle came to the boil.

There was the slightest tinge of daylight outside. Edwin Hurly continued.

'Deal with my version, OK? I want my version to be the only version, if you don't mind. Yes, she died in there, but it was me who brought her home, that's my version. Miss Oh-so-smart S for Sarah will know which version is best for everyone. It was me and me alone. I didn't kill her, although I might have done. My version goes like this, OK? It was me and me alone, because whatever else kind of a shit I might be, I was giving orders to no-choicers, they were thoroughly blackmailed and what I want now is *nobody* else to be blamed.'

He pointed his finger round the room, ending with the delivery man who stood back, shaking.

'Of course it was *him*, poor sod, who carried her here. But let's say it was me. Nobody need know I haven't driven a white van in twenty years, wouldn't be seen dead in one. I'm beyond all that, except for today. I couldn't bring her, but I knew who could.'

The stabbing finger was directed at Sarah. 'For the record, in front of witnesses, it wasn't *him*, it was me. There won't be a trace in his van, not the way he cleans it and besides, she wasn't bleeding, so don't go that way. Yes, the chef helped, but he was drunk and as far as anyone else is concerned he wasn't there. He's got his own lines and he's paid off. Yes, the Smithfield brothers could have known how I got her onto the truck that came from Scotland, got her off again and onto the line and out again, but I'm telling you now, they didn't. I'm old, but I can still heft a body. I could carry her for half a mile, it's easy when you learn young. You could have done that all by yourself, couldn't you, Sam? Especially if everyone else was busy.'

Sam nodded slowly.

'But you didn't,' Sarah said in a flat voice.

'Think what you like. Yes, I did. Better for all concerned if I did, isn't it? Stowed her in the back yard, somewhere, for a day, we were closed the next day. Then I carried her down here, hooked her up. I'm the one who best knows how to do it and I know how to get in. I worked here, once, didn't I, when I was twelve, long before I owned the property. I'm the one who knows how nothing changes here, nothing. I'm the one who would have checked with the delivery man that nothing *had* changed.'

Edwin Hurly glared at Sarah, leant forward, grasping the arms of the chair.

'Why exactly are you here?' Sarah said.

'Because you fucking told me to be. You left me the paper. You let me know I was busted, and you let me know that that bastard son of mine was going to be hung out to dry. Can't have that, either.'

'There's some goodness in you, then,' Andrew said earnestly. 'There's goodness in us all. We must concentrate on that goodness in ourselves, whatever our belief.'

He looked towards Sarah imploringly, as if he was begging for forgiveness for her, too.

'Oh, shut up, whoever you are. You look like a vicar and you'll be as bad as the old one, pious, pompous bastard, although he did have a way with the ladies. My wife used to think the sun shone out of his arse. You're a load of perverts and hypocrites. Spare me bloody platitudes.'

'I meant to say,' Andrew said, loudly and with considerably more dignity, 'that there really isn't much that can't be forgiven, ultimately. And there's nobody so bad that they can't redeem themselves with their own bit of goodness, however small. I say it because I believe it. Your daughter was in pain: so were you. And the fact that you want to exonerate others from blame for any part in it redeems you, it seems to me. Not completely – there's no such thing – but it goes a long way.'

To Sarah's surprise, this humble sermon was not met with contempt. Edwin Hurly listened as he let his head sink onto his chest. They waited in silence. Only Sarah came closer. Finally he looked up, and laughed.

'So that's why I'm here, then. My passport to heaven after a long spell in purgatory. Hell can't be any worse than living here. Look at the time. It'll be light soon. Any questions?'

Mike stepped closer, still ready to hit and still with the knife behind his back.

'How did she die? Why the fuck did you hang her up like that?'

'I wish you'd put that knife down. I've asked you already. Any more human blood in this shop and Sam Brady'll be ruined. You'll hear it all on her phone, she was recording it. There's your bloody evidence. A god-almighty row, right? Her coming at me with those nails of hers, threatening to tell Celia, telling me I had to come home with her. The floor was still wet from cleaning. She was out of her head, furious. I can't remember the sequence. Silly shoes. She was running, slipped and fell, she hit her head on the edge of the steel corner. You'll hear, I talk myself through it, too. I didn't kill her. I might just about have killed her mother by breaking her heart, but I didn't kill *her*. She killed herself.'

Such a cruel, handsome face, Sarah thought.

Mike put the knife back in the rack. The light inside the

room seemed to grow dimmer at the mere suggestion that another day was beginning outside.

'But slitting her throat, bleeding her . . . WHY?'

Edwin Hurly considered the question briefly, puzzled by it, as if the answer was perfectly obvious.

'I wanted her to look beautiful. It's the only humane way, right? I'd heard her neck crack, I know when a beast is killed, I know it. I trained in an abattoir. There's nothing as good-looking as a good well-bled carcass. Much more dignified than a body changing colour and stinking to high heaven within a day, I didn't want that. Was trying to keep her dignity, keep her clean and sweet so she'd get home looking good. Be at her best. Nothing nicer than a well-slaughtered carcass. It's a beautiful sight. Nothing more beautiful.'

Sam nodded agreement. It made sense to him.

'There'll only be ashes to put in the sea,' Sarah said.

There was silence in the circle.

'Look at the time,' Edwin Hurly said to the delivery man. 'Get that stuff out now. He'll be opening in an hour or two, got things to do. Got to get this show on the road. You should have sunk the daft bitch, Sam Brady, when she looked her beautiful best. Before somebody else gutted her.'

Strange, to hear and watch the workings of an alien mind. Master butcher Hurly had his own terrible logic and standards of beauty, so different and yet so real that Sarah almost appreciated them – for a minute. A bled carcass which looked fit for human consumption was a prettier sight than a dead body dressed by an undertaker. There was no comparison. At least he had stopped short of gutting her. She was watching the alternative but viable morality of a man so sure that someone else would do exactly what he expected them to do and so certain that others would behave and react as he would have done, with the same immaculate taste. Never doubting that Sam Brady, good butcher that he was, would feel the same admiration for a piece of work well done, take it out to sea in accordance with instructions, and get on with business. She did not want to listen to whatever was on that phone. Wanted to believe it was as he said. Wanted Edwin Hurly gone because, unlike Andrew, she could not muster a shred of compassion for this big old man who had slit the throat of his own daughter in order to get her home smelling sweet. He had done it for himself, not for her.

Edwin Hurly lumbered to his feet.

'Better I don't contaminate the place. I'll go now, before anyone sees me. I leave it to you lot what you say, but my version's better than the truth. The truth was the only way I could think of. For God's sake, Sam, get your order indoors and get to work. Let that boy get back to London – he's whacked. And you,' he addressed Sarah, 'you make sure it's my version, right? It's the one that gets everyone off the *hook*, if you see what I mean. That's your responsibility.'

'Where are you going?'

'About my own business, not yours.'

He seemed determined upon a course, ready to move, still confident of being obeyed. She noticed the heavy boots on his big feet, far removed from the smooth city shoes he had been wearing in his own restaurant where he had looked far more at home than he did here. There, he looked like a swarthier version of the bankers and stockbrokers he entertained: here, he looked like a fisherman in the wrong clothes.

'Going for a long walk. I need the exercise. I may call in

on my wife, only it is a little early. She's not often an early riser. Probably not. Tell her I loved her once. Wasn't her fault, it was this suffocating place.'

'What do you want us to do?'

'You know very well what I want you to do. Give my version, later in the day. Make it convincing, only give me a bit of time. Go home to your own beds. Keep the phone, it's all the evidence you need.'

The delivery man and Sam Brady unloaded from the white van, scurrying in and out like large ants. Vacuum-packed ham, ready-jointed joints, pork and sausages in packets, instant stock requiring the minimal preparation for attractive display, wholesale, ready-prepared meat not requiring a butcher's skill, except for one quarter of beef, a gift, the delivery man said. It was the only way to start again, for the time being. Organic local produce could wait, although in the meantime Sam knew it was the only way to go. Local produce was for later, because bugger the profit margins in the future; he wanted nothing else delivered in the dark from Smithfield. In the meantime, there was plenty for a display of meat within two hours. The future and the exorcism of ghosts depended upon it. The return of the village to a normal life, as a place with a centre, depended upon it.

Sarah and Andrew stood outside, standing back from work in progress, and watched the large figure of Edwin Hurly walking downhill towards the bend in the road, disappearing out of sight. He was veering left, towards the next town. Dawn was beginning in the sky, not yet touching the land.

'We should go after him,' Andrew said. 'Come on, let's go. I don't know what he's going to do, and he's a man of conscience, for all that.'

'No,' Sarah said. 'No.'

Ten minutes later, the delivery man, who'd never had a name, got into his white van and drove away, fast.

An hour later the Pennyvale traffic jam began.

Chapter Sixteen

How had she done this? What was it Edwin Hurly had said? *I didn't see her; she was there. She had taken the phone off and put it down.*

Sarah was on the cliff path alone, playing it back. The record of a Sunday night conversation.

(Calm voice, male.) What the hell are you doing here, girl? I told you, stay away. What are you on? What do you want to do, ruin me? Do you know what time it is? You should be in bed. Oh God. Dinner. I forgot. I got busy, I forgot.

(Female voice, hysterical.) Bastard, bastard, bastard, fucking bastard. You forgot. Like hell you forgot, you left me sitting alone. You were going to make it up to me for leaving me again and again. All you ever do is leave and get away with it. Every time, you leave and you lie. You say you love me, and you lie, you've lied to me all my life. You lied to my mother, you broke her into pieces. How could you let me think you were dead, how could you let me think it was ME who drove you away to die? How could you do that to me? You drive me mad.

You were mad before that, girl.

DON'T call me GIRL! MAD? What about you? You give out love like you've won some lottery, then it's all gone, gone, gone. Couldn't believe it when I found you again. You hugged me; you kissed me. You said I'd be the most important person in your life, for ever, just like it was. You were proud of me, just like you were once, wanted to take me everywhere, you said we'd do that again, only don't let Mummy know. We'll go to all the best places, you'd go with me, you'd get me work, get me started. You took me places, made me meet people, got me jobs, Daddy, you were proud of me. Why did you stop? What did I do?

You're a stupid little tart, Jess. You wanted me to go home. I got scared of you and I won't be scared of anyone. Grow up. You can't, Jess, you never could. You should go home. You're a home girl. You can't even cook. How could you think I could ever go back to hell?

Go home and keep quiet? Go without you? Not tell her? I can't go home ever again, because of you. I don't want to go anywhere without you. I love you, Daddy. I love you so much it hurts and you shut me out. I can't live without you. I want Mummy to be happy. I want to stop this pain and make us all happy.

(Him, wearily.) Get real, Jess. You're a loser. I can't make you a winner. You can't hold down a job. You're a fucking stalker. You'll ruin me . . . You've made a fool of me three times over. Look, what do you want? Money?

I want you to love me like you said you would, like you did. I want you to love both of us.

(Sobbing.)

Get real, Jessica. Can't love a stalker. Go away, please, I'm tired. If you show me up, if you come here again, I'll fucking kill you.

(Pause. Footsteps, metal clashing, fist on surface?)

(Female.) Where's that bloody chef? I'll tell him.

Go home, girl. Tell you what, if you're good, I'll take you . . . somewhere nice. PUT THAT KNIFE DOWN.

Again? Like a pet on a lead? And then stand me up? I'll kill you first, I'll kill you. It was better when you were dead. I was happy when you were dead.

Put it down, girl. Stoppit. It's sharp, put it down. STOPPIT.

(Shuffling, crashing, both voices screaming, indecipherable noise: duration thirty seconds. Silence one minute.)

(Male voice.) Shit. Where's your phone? Oh, no, no, no. Oh, you silly little calf. What have you done?

Convenient that the recording had ended there, the last messages curtailed by Edwin Hurly finding the phone. It was all oddly undramatic, sounding more like a Saturday-night screaming row between two drunks in the middle of a long-standing shouting match with threats, where nobody died and they all stood up again like characters in a cartoon film. It coincided with the prescribed version, leaving terrible ambiguities. Unclear throughout: there were intervals with nothing but white noise, mumbling, yelling, crashing; Jessica's phone could not record what went on in every corner of a room. The recording was unable simultaneously to show who had attacked whom while it worked to exonerate anyone else. Had Edwin Hurly really been sure that Jessica was dead when he'd used his own knife with such imperative speed? The cut would have had to be instant: otherwise she would not have bled.

Twenty-four hours for a bled body to cool; transfer to Smithfield on Smithfield's busiest day of the week. For the record, Jessica would rest in the cold dark backyard of a fashionable restaurant in the meantime. DK was closed on

Mondays: he could live with her corpse there for longer than that. After that, according to the record which would become official, Edwin Hurly had brought her home the long way, by himself.

Sarah knew that he had not done so. Edwin Hurly was a man who gave orders, did not deliver himself. Jessica had rested in the delivery man's cold van, waiting her chance to go home. Edwin Hurly was a man who forced others to do his will, just as he was doing now. He wanted them to know the truth of his ingenuity and his power and then act upon the untruths and Sarah, for one, was willing to comply. He wanted them to know all but the details and then wanted them not to know. Sarah wondered how long it had taken him to realise that this was the only way.

She was rationing compassion in the interests of compromise. Sarah had called the police and informed them that she would be arriving soon with new evidence and it was better that she came to them rather than them coming to her, because all it was was a phone. Mike and Andrew disappeared into the ether, following instructions. Let Sam Brady and herself be the only witnesses to Edwin Hurly's reappearance and confession: keep it simple. It was not good to make a man of the cloth tell lies: better that he had never been there. Andrew had shaken her hand on leaving, gazing into her eyes, his own full of questions and disappointment and hope. A hooker. A Mary Magdalene, ripe for redemption. Maybe she was.

The best part of the day had gone. Sarah had been accused, lectured and criticised for obstruction of the course of justice. She'd opened her eyes wide, and held her innocent ground. The light was going again before she walked past the bend in the road, turned left and followed the coastal path to the next town, deviating onto the shingle beach, following the pathways that Jeremy had shown her on the way back and because the beach was such a wilderness it was difficult to remember, until she gave way to instinct and let her own feet lead her. She had learned about instinct and finding her way in the dark and she was thinking as she walked that this hidden village was not as disjointed as she'd thought. There was a core to it: there was common opinion: there was secret knowledge of who was who and what was what, secretly shared. There had been a fine conspiracy to lead the police in the opposite direction from the obvious place where anyone who knew Jeremy would know where they might have gone. There was loyalty here; there was devotion to those who had not left; there was belief in innocent until proved guilty, whatever the evidence. Those two had not stayed free in the darkness alone. Someone had helped.

They had been in her house only once. They took a risk to bury a dog: they were savages with peculiar consciences. There was plenty of anarchic goodness in this place.

As Sarah approached the beach, she met a man returning from it, an old man who seemed to wink compulsively, accompanied by an even older (in canine time) dog that knew how to walk the paths on the beach without injuring its paws on the shingle.

Mike had come part of the way and then went back when he saw the emptiness of the landscape. He was afraid of nothing but nothingness like this. He hated wide empty spaces.

'Got to go home, doll, can't walk on this stuff. Can't stand this place, can't help anyone if I'm scared. When are you coming home?'

'Don't know. You've been brilliant. You are a star in my fir-mament.'

'Like those in this bloody great big sky? No, thanks. I need other kinds of lights. This scares me. Just don't tell me you're going to stay here and marry the vicar and raise kids.'

'At my age?'

'You're never too old. You can always hightail it to town. Don't leave it too long. I'm not waiting for you. You told me, don't.'

'No, don't wait. No one should ever wait for me.'

Sarah could hear his footsteps, going back, losing the path, afraid to go over the dip and be out of sight of the few lights on the side road and the twinkling lights beginning to emerge from the pub and the row behind. Mike could not bear this kind of darkness and whatever he did he always had to know the way back. He had to know his own territory to function, while she had never been afraid of the new. All she could hear was the sound of the sea and the distinctive sounds made by her own feet whenever they went left and right off the mean-dering path which led with such charming indirectness, somewhere and nowhere. The sound of boots on shingle was as loud as shouting, neutralising the sound of the water that seemed so distant and yet so close. They would hear her approaching long before they could see her. Better Mike had gone back: otherwise they might have run. A single set of footsteps was better than two.

The beach shelved as steeply as she remembered, levelled out and shelved again. She fell once or twice over the first slope, hazarded the next and followed her own feet. Beyond the amazing growth of fennel, garlic, thistles and soon-to-be vibrant flowers, there were only smooth hard-going stones. Sarah slithered and slipped, bore left, plodded on noisily, until she could sense as much as see the colony of damaged boats looming ahead, identifiable by shape alone, backlit by the reflection from the sea itself, still hidden beyond the last shelf. There was a single light illuminating the little colony; a light that was extinguished as soon as her steps became audible.

How clever that the search parties had always gone right of the village, towards the cliffs and the old ice houses, never to the left in the other direction, guided then by crafty local expertise. Sarah was carrying six cans which rattled in a bag. Her imagination, that mortar between facts, told her that even the sound of that burden was audible and welcome. She walked beyond the boat colony, with her all too noisy steps, as if she had not seen it, stepped into the beyond. This was vanity, she told herself as she slithered down the last shelf and sat facing a quiet, murmuring, talkative sea, so peaceful that she felt able to have a conversation with it.

She sat on her bottom, twenty feet from the mumbling waves, lit a cigarette, shook the carrier bag she had carried with her so that it made a tinny sound, waited. The bag had grown heavier with each step, given her ballast. She took one can from it, sipped from the rim and slung the rest to one side. Wine was her preference; lager would do. She wanted to swim out here when it was warmer. Home was where you could find your own way, backwards and forwards, a place where you had no fear.

Finally two figures slithered into shape beside her. Sarah ignored them and turned her face to the sea, sat with her bum on cold shingle, arms crossed over her knees, looking ahead. Greedy hands went towards the bag three feet away. Then they sat in a single line, facing the sea. Today the waves chose a time to mumble rather than roar: she was grateful for that.

The weather had been kind and calm all week.

'It's over now,' Sarah said. 'You can go back, you know. You can go back any time you want. Everybody knows you didn't kill her. Nobody here killed her. She died in London, where she lived, she was carried back here and everyone knows. Everyone knows it wasn't you. Everyone always did. You can go home now.'

'Who says so?'

'I do.'

Jack grabbed her and pushed her over. They set upon her like hungry wolves, scenting prey, tickling instead of biting. She lay spreadeagled on the concrete and let Jack sniff her like a dog while Jeremy touched her breasts and patted her body. They were like scavengers around a carcass. Darkness finally fell as she let them paw at her clothes. She lay as stiff as a dead starfish, felt afraid and then not afraid, until, ashamed, they fell back, giggling. They were giddy children. Only teasing and tickling. Different, maybe, if she had screamed or resisted. Only testing for response, testing toler-ance. In a brief moment she wondered if they were beyond hope: wondered what they were capable of becoming without kindness. If ever there were two young men in need of a fuck, it was these. She was too old for them and they were too young for her. She could find them friends, if she stayed.

'Sorry,' Jeremy said, and reached for another can out of the bag. They both smelt of salt and fish and unwashed clothes. They drank, moving away from being harmful to harmless.

Sarah sat up. Jeremy pressed his unfinished still-cold can into her hand. Greater love hath no boy. Her hands were colder than her body.

'I said everyone. I meant everyone who counts. Who's been feeding you and believing you? Get a life. You might not be exactly loved or loveable, either of you, but a lot of people know what you are.'

She got to her feet and walked uphill as noisily as ever, weaving slightly until Jeremy caught one arm and Jack the other. They linked their arms with hers, one each side and ran her up the steepest shelf of the beach, still giggling, paused for breath, walked on, stopped.

'We already knew,' Jeremy said. 'No, that's not right. We *thought* we knew.'

'How?'

He hesitated.

'Because he came here, this morning. We helped him shove one of the boats out. He wanted to go out in it.'

'They aren't seaworthy.'

'No, not exactly.'

They had reached the road and the glimmer of lights ahead. Sarah shook herself free of their arms and fished in her pocket for the key to her house.

'Here, go home. Wash, make yourselves human – you stink. Go and show yourselves in the pub. Sam Brady'll need you tomorrow, Jeremy, you too, Jack. You both owe him.'

She smelt the wild garlic that had brushed against her legs. It was a beautiful chilly night.

'She texted me,' Jack said suddenly. 'Sunday afternoon. Got the message on my phone. She wanted me to phone at one in the morning, Monday, that'd be. She wanted me to phone and listen where she was and record it. Only I didn't. I was asleep. Last thing she ever asked me to do.'

'Don't worry,' Sarah said.

'Mr Hurly gave me a wad of money,' Jeremy burst out. 'What do I with it?'

'Put it down on a boat? Give it to me for safe keeping. Get

on with you. You smell like shit. No girl's going to want you, smelling like that.'

'Aren't you coming with us?'

'No.'

She left them at the bend of the road, watched them canter uphill and then walked back along the row of cottages running parallel to the sea, divorced from the main village and ending in the pub. Few lights in these houses. She looked up at the stars on this clear night, then back towards where the road bent uphill, disappearing into an invisible street, a destination as hidden as if there was nothing there.

The church of St Bartholomew was just visible. Home? As good as; maybe there was no such thing. Home was a place where you might be able to make a difference. Make friends with your enemies, organise forgiveness, calm troubled waters, reconcile the elements, which was all she had ever done. Home was where you knew the way back.

Celia Hurly's house was well lit. Sarah knocked at the door, stood away from it and waited. The door needed paint.

If she was going to stay here it might involve becoming a Christian, and if that was the way she had better behave like one. It would not involve martyrdom and being flayed alive, or even asking forgiveness. She wanted to know the elusive Mrs Hurly; wanted to be a better friend than she had been to the woman's daughter. She wanted to know and be known.

She wanted to confirm that it was indeed Mrs Hurly who had sent the search parties in the wrong direction.

She looked uphill to the secret village. There was plenty of room for a Christian courtesan, for a while. God knew, the vicar needed one.

She noticed the smashed-up baby buggy in the garden,

along with a rubbish sack, and composed herself to tell a version of the truth.

Sarah was icy cold. If she was going to stay here she would need a woman friend. Someone at least as ambiguous as that woman's daughter.

She wanted to see the summer. She could live here for a long time and never know the half of it.

She would rely on the spoken word.

LOOKING DOWN

Frances Fyfield

Richard Beaumont hoped to see the elusive crow on the Dover cliffs.
Instead he sees a young woman falling to her death. No-one
recognises her, no-one has reported her missing and Richard returns,
shaken, to his wife. But instead of finding solace in Lilian's company,
he locks himself away and obsessively paints the scene
of the woman's broken body on the rocks.

His cool behaviour towards her takes Lilian to the flat below and the
worldly-wise company of Sarah Fortune. But Sarah, once Richard's
lover, is awkward with her and is also preoccupied with her brother's
unbreakable habit of cat-burglary and the suspicious traffic to the
penthouse at the top of the mansion block. Unable to forget what he
witnessed, Richard introduces Sarah to the recently widowed local
police surgeon. Together they trace where the dead girl came from
and in so doing reveal a trade which is both breathtakingly
lucrative and chillingly cruel.

'Her knowledge of the workings of the human mind – or more
correctly the soul – is second to none'
Ian Rankin

978-0-7515-3340-8

SAFER THAN HOUSES

Frances Fyfield

Sarah Fortune inherited her flat from one of her many lovers. Now a son has appeared claiming it is his, morally if not strictly legally, and he is using illegal means to persuade Sarah to give it up: abusive letters threatening her personal harm. As it becomes more difficult to ignore these missives, Sarah comes across Henry, a timid, lonely man whose upstairs neighbour is using every trick in the racketeer landlord's book to make him leave his home: litter in the shared hallway, continual noise, poison set out for his cat.

It seems that if they swap accommodation for a while they may be able to deal with each other's problems. But these two strangers have unknown connections in common: a well-meaning widow, a struggling therapist, and a man who sets fire to other people's property for a living . . .

'*Safer than Houses* is a deeply satisfying read . . . powerfully drawn characters and compelling tension'
Independent

978-0-7515-3621-8

THE ART OF DROWNING

Frances Fyfield

Rachel Doe is a shy accountant at a low ebb in life when she meets charismatic Ivy Schneider, nee Wiseman, at her evening class and her life changes for the better. Ivy is her polar opposite: strong, six years her senior and the romantic survivor of drug addiction, homelessness and the death of her child. Ivy does menial shift work, beholden to no one, and she inspires life; as do her farming parents, with their ramshackle house and its swan-filled lake, the lake where Ivy's daughter drowned.

As Rachel grows closer to them all she learns how Ivy came to be married to Carl, the son of a WWII prisoner, as well as the true nature of that marriage to a bullying and ambitious lawyer who has become a judge and who denies her access to her surviving child. Rachel wants justice for Ivy, but Ivy has another agenda and Rachel's naïve sense of fair play is no match for the manipulative qualities of the Wisemen women.

'*The Art of Drowning* shows Frances Fyfield at her best . . . a skillfully plotted story by one of our most elegant crime writers, piling on the suspense, right up to the unpredictable climax'
Sunday Telegraph

978-0-7515-3620-1

BLOOD FROM STONE

Frances Fyfield

Winner of the Duncan Lawrie/CWA Dagger

When the body of a successful criminal barrister is found outside
a chic Kensington hotel, it looks at first like a suicide. For colleagues
and friends, her death comes as a huge shock – Marianne Shearer
was at the pinnacle of her career, wealthy and stylish – but
for the police the case is open-and-shut.

There's something strange about the circumstances, though,
something that prompts fellow lawyers Thomas Nobel and Peter Friel
to dig deeper. Little by little, they discover that all is not as it seems.
Oddly enough, Marianne herself appears to have left a series of
small, almost imperceptible clues – clues that point to a far more
sinister truth. Retracing Marianne's steps, Nobel and Friel uncover
a carefully concealed darker side of her perfect life that leads them
back to her last, gruesome case – when she knowingly
sacrificed an innocent witness to let a criminal walk free.

'*Blood From Stone* has all the complexity you'd expect from this
award-winning grande dame of crime fiction – she's up there with
Rendell, James, McDermid and Walters . . . Simply terrific'
Observer

978-0-7515-3927-1

Other bestselling titles available by mail